THE
FIFTH
DAUGHTER

ELAINE COFFMAN

THE FIFTH DAUGHTER

WHEELER
PUBLISHING, INC.
ROCKLAND, MA

★ AN AMERICAN COMPANY ★

Published in large print by arrangement with Mira Books in the United States and Canada.

Wheeler Large Print Book Series.

Set in 16 pt Plantin.

Library of Congress Cataloging-in-Publication Data

Coffman, Elaine.
    The fifth daughter / Elaine Coffman.
        p. (large print) cm.(Wheeler large print book series)
    ISBN 1-58724-222-2 (hardcover)
    1. Yorkshire (England)—Fiction. 2. British—Italy—Fiction. 3. Tuscany (Italy)—Fiction. 4. Large type books. I. Title. II. Series.

[PS3553.O39 F54 2002]
813'.54—dc21   2002022617
                                                                        CIP

For Percival Livingston Reynolds
and his wonderful English name.

'Tis said of love that it sometimes goes, sometimes flies; runs with one, walks gravely with another; turns a third into ice, and sets a fourth in a flame: it wounds one, another it kills: like lightning it begins and ends in the same moment: it makes that fort yield at night which it besieged but in the morning; for there is no force able to resist it.

—Miguel de Cervantes (1547-1616), Spanish writer. Leonela, in *Don Quixote*, pt. 1, bk. 4, ch. 7 (1605; tr. by P. Motteux).

Prologue

Who can foretell for what high cause
This darling of the Gods was born?

Andrew Marvell
English poet and politician

In the spring of 1795, Mother Nature was especially benevolent and her obsession with everything green left England exploding with color.

Masses of flowers in every hue proliferated the countryside from sparsely populated woodlands to the orderly chaos of vicarage gardens. Soon, purple swathes of summer heather would cover the Northern Yorkshire moors. It would sweep around crosses and standing stones, to cover ancient ground, steeped in history.

The blush of May had arrived. Winter was finally over.

It was a time for jubilation, for long-awaited spring was here at last. But there was no rejoicing at Hampton Manor.

The Viscountess of Strathmore was dead.

Buffeted by the winds of an approaching

1

spring rain, shutters banged against the windows of the house, and almost drowned out the wails of Lady Strathmore's newborn babe.

It should have been a time of good cheer and celebration, but within the walls of the great stone house, sadness and grief closed in.

Inside Lady Strathmore's dim chamber melancholia gathered around, and the viscount stared down at his dead wife. The lines that etched his face were not those of agony or even grief, but of guilt.

Numb with disbelief, the viscount wondered how the morning could have started so happily, with his wife singing and laughing, and telling him to be patient, that his son would be joining them "any day now." How had so much promise turned to abject disappointment and gaping loss? It had all come to pass, faster than an indrawn breath. Over and over again, he asked himself the same question: What could he have done to prevent it, and where had it all gone wrong?

Only a few weeks ago, he encountered a gypsy woman in London, who looked at his expectant wife and said, "Buy a posy for the mother of yer son."

"Hold your tongue, you foolish old crone," he said. "I am a man cursed with nothing but four daughters."

" 'Tis a son ye will be having this time, milord," the old woman said.

He dared not hope, but he tossed the old hag a coin and presented his wife with a posy, symbolic of the hope he had that in a few weeks time, she would present him, not with a fifth daughter, but a son.

After four daughters, and no male to carry on the family name, Lord Strathmore was elated at the prospect of having an heir at last. Even his lady wife thought the child would be a boy, and up to the moment she had her first pains, she was in high spirits as she finished knitting a tiny blue sweater.

But something went wrong. Terrible. Irrevocable. And grievously wrong.

For eighteen hours his poor wife labored, unable to bring the child into the world. At last, when Dr. Downing came out of her room, and the viscount saw the disbelieving expression on his face, no words were necessary. The viscount already knew. He knew the news was not good, but he had no idea the next few words would shatter his world, no more than he could know the decision he would be forced to make would change his life so completely and cast him forever into the eternal pit of the damned and unforgivable.

A bolt of lightning ripped the sky apart to loosen a crack of thunder that vibrated throughout the house. The candles sputtered and grew dim. A long, low moan of wind blew down the chimney and caused the flames in the fireplace to reach new height.

The doctor wiped his hands on a bloodstained towel. "I am sorry. I have done the best I can, but there are complications, your lordship. I cannot save both your wife and the child. You must choose one of them."

Lord Strathmore held out his hand, as if to keep such a decision at bay, and turned his head away. "Nooo! I cannot! Do not ask this of me!"

"Your Lordship, please! I cannot make such a decision for you. Only you can make such a choice. You, or God, for should you refuse, you will surely lose them both."

"Choose? Good God, man! How can I choose between my wife and my son? How could any man?"

"I cannot answer that for you, your lordship. I can only say your wife has lost a great deal of blood. In my opinion, the child has the better chance of survival."

The viscount threw back his head with an agonized cry.

A moment later, he was composed, and he spoke with a low voice, wiped clean of all emotion.

"Save my son."

One

And now thou art a nameless thing:
So abject—yet alive!

Lord Byron (1788-1824)
English poet

Samuel Livingston Bronwell, Esquire, was happy for a lot of things, but he had never been happier than he was the moment he arrived with his family back in Yorkshire. One week in London was too much. One week in London, visiting his dear wife's relations, was torture.

Samuel and his wife had been talking quietly, when the coach suddenly slowed to a respectable pace. Both Samuel and his wife, Olympia glanced out the window and saw they were passing the cemetery. They looked quickly away as they passed the small group of people huddled around an open grave, where the Reverend Charles Constable presided over a funeral.

But the Bronwell's oldest son, Stephen, had his nose pressed flat against the glass. "A funeral!" he said. "Who died, Papa?"

"I don't know, son. Perhaps we will find out when we arrive home."

On the opposite side of the coach, Mrs. Bronwell tugged at Stephen's sleeve. "Come away from the window. You mustn't stare, out of respect for the dead."

Three-year-old Percy Bronwell, who had been sitting quietly beside his mother, decided to crawl over her to join his brother at the window.

"You see?" she reprimanded. "Now your brother wants to look."

Mrs. Bronwell put Percy on her lap and lowered the curtain over the window next to Stephen, and the carriage silently passed by the small gathering of grief, making its way on down the winding road.

Several hours after they arrived home, Mr. Bronwell was relaxed in his study, blissfully happy to be back home, when his wife rushed into the room. "I had a short visit with Mrs. Throckmorton. She was in the neighborhood and stopped by. You will never believe what she told me."

"To the contrary, my dear. I have learned never to disbelieve anything when women are involved, especially if one of them is Agnes Throckmorton."

"Well, you won't believe what I am about to tell you, Mr. Bronwell. It was the Viscountess of Strathmore, God rest her soul, and I must tell you that I have never been more shocked than I was the moment I heard it."

Samuel dropped the newspaper with a gesture that was both preoccupied and resigned, and gave his attention to his wife, because he knew she would not stop talking until he did so. "What did you say about the viscountess?"

"The funeral, my dear husband. It was hers!"

Equally shocked, he said, "You cannot mean Lady Strathmore is dead!"

Olympia took that as an invitation and took a seat on the horsehair sofa across from him. "Dead and buried," she said. "And to think we took tea together only a few days before we left for London." She paused, reflective a moment. "Mrs. Throckmorton laid the blame at Lord Strathmore's feet. Can you believe she is dead, and it was all her husband's fault?"

"Now, now, Olympia, careful what you say about the viscount. Although not too well liked, he is of an old and honorable family, and not the sort to murder his wife. To what purpose?"

"Don't go defending him until you know the whole of it, or don't you want to know what happened?"

Samuel was observing his wife with the look of a cornered dog. "It matters not. You will tell me regardless."

As her husband indicated, Olympia went on to rattle off the story of precisely how it was that Lady Strathmore came to die, and the events that led up to that most unfortunate occurrence.

She finished with a sigh and said, "When I think of how excited Teresa was about giving her husband a son at last, I want to cry. She was in perfect health when we left. A week later, she is dead. And the baby! Truly, I feel so sorry for that poor little, innocent waif...left with no mother, alone and helpless."

"Poor choice of words, my dear. The child

is hardly a waif. Her father is a viscount, so I doubt you could consider her to be abandoned."

Olympia ignored that. "She is motherless and that is heartbreaking. What a terrible burden to heap upon a child."

"What burden are you talking about?"

"Mr. Bronwell, really! How can you not see how it will be for a child to grow up with the knowledge that she exists only because her father made a choice to let her mother die?" Her voice broke and she pulled a kerchief out of her pocket and dabbed at her eyes, then gave a shiver. "It's all so cold and callous. How could any man decree his wife's death?"

"The child cannot be blamed for that."

"And who, pray tell, is going to inform the child of that?"

"You probably will, if she resides in the area long enough. However, I do agree that this is all quite tragic."

"Oh, my dear, you haven't heard the tragic part yet. It seems the viscount locked himself in his study with lord knows how many bottles of whiskey the day the viscountess died."

"That is understandable, and a long accepted manner for dealing with grief."

"Not when it reeks of abandonment! The coward! He hid himself away, and left the staff at Hampton Manor to cope and care for that poor baby. As if secreting himself away like that could make him blameless, or ease his regret."

"Some people choose to do so, because they cannot face the horror of the things they do."

"I find this whole affair abominable. His poor wife barely dead and her infant daughter in need of looking after, and what does Lord Strathmore do? Locks himself in his study with a bottle of spirits, as if that would do either of them any good."

"It's the guilt," Samuel said. " 'Tis said, the offender never pardons."

"Good. He deserves to suffer, if you ask me. What kind of man could choose to let his wife die?"

"A desperate one, it would seem. Do you not think part of the fault lies with that gypsy woman you mentioned? After all, if Mrs. Throckmorton is right, the gypsy is the one who told Lord Strathmore that the child the viscountess carried would be a son. I am sure that was in the back of his mind at the time he was faced with such a choice. And then there is the matter of Dr. Downing forcing Lord Strathmore to decide between his wife and child. I say the good doctor should have done all he could to save both of them. No one should be asked to play God. Surely you agree?"

"I will have to think upon it, Mr. Bronwell."

"The poor man is to be pitied, I suppose. He always wanted a son. He got daughters."

"Serves him right. His own selfish desires were put ahead of the well-being of his wife.

A son at all costs! Regardless the price his wife had to pay, poor woman."

"I am certain the viscount is most grieved."

"I don't believe that for a moment! Do you know he refuses to even see the baby? His own flesh and blood, and he has never even looked at the child. That goes beyond cruel."

"Well, what's done is done," Samuel said. "I am sure Lord Strathmore will come to his senses and embrace his child ere long."

Olympia harrumphed at that. "Mrs. Throckmorton said the viscount's housekeeper told her cook that Lord Strathmore would never accept the child. What need does he have for a fifth daughter?"

"I daresay the viscount's housekeeper isn't the final word."

"Perhaps not, but I also learned Reverend Constable was most concerned when he discovered the child was still unnamed. It's a sacrilege to allow such to happen. He said someone needed to see that the child was given a good, Christian name."

Mr. Bronwell picked up his paper. "I have a suspicion Reverend Constable said that knowing you and Mrs. Throckmorton would be the first two to come forward with a list of suitable names. Am I right?"

"Well," Olympia said. "Well, Agnes and I have given the matter some thought. And rightly so, considering we were both friends of Lady Strathmore's."

Gossip spread across the moors faster than a summer fire, and the news that Viscount Strathmore had departed for London with his four older daughters, leaving the new-born baby behind, literally flew, as if borne by the fierce Yorkshire wind.

It was on the following Sunday, that the dour, nonconformist minister of overly long prayers, avoided the subject of forgiveness in favor of the laxness of parents in seeing to the christening of their children.

After too many *beseech thees* and just as many *verilys* the sermon was over.

Afterward, Mrs. Throckmorton and Mrs. Bronwell approached the Reverend Constable and inquired about the status of the viscount's nameless daughter.

"I have not been informed of any action on the matter. If no name is forthcoming, I shall take the matter to hand, and name the child myself."

After Reverend Constable was called away, the two good ladies were appalled at the idea of the minister being involved in the naming, if for no other reason than the Reverend's own daughters were named Assurance, Loyalty and Devotion.

With the utmost discretion, they decided to pay a call at Hampton Manor, where they asked to speak to the housekeeper, Mrs. Brampton.

After a lengthy explanation of their purpose for being there, they asked if the minister had indicated he was considering naming the child himself.

Mrs. Brampton, a rather tall, spare and plain-looking woman, gave a sigh and said, "Yes, he said, 'even disappointments deserve a name,' and if Lord Strathmore was not up to the task, then someone else would have to do it, namely him."

"And have you decided upon a name?" Mrs. Bronwell asked.

"No, we discussed it of course, but we are reluctant to take the responsibility. We all fear the viscount's displeasure, were we to choose a name that he looked upon with disfavor."

"Well then, why not name her after her mother? How could he possibly find fault with that?"

"An excellent idea," agreed Mrs. Throckmorton.

"We thought of that," Mrs. Brampton said. "Except Lord Strathmore abhors the child already. To name her Maria Teresa after her mother would only serve to make him hate her more."

"Hmmm," said Mrs. Throckmorton. "I suppose you're right. Perhaps we could find another name that would be fitting for the child."

"Why not something Italian?" suggested Mrs. Bronwell.

"Italian? Why Italian?" asked Mrs. Throckmorton.

"The viscountess was Italian," Olympia

said. "Lord Strathmore met her in Florence, the summer he finished Cambridge, whilst he traveled abroad."

Mrs. Brampton nodded in agreement. "Yes, that is true. Born in Italy, she was, and never set a foot on English soil until his lordship married her and brought her to Hampton Manor. I came to work for them shortly thereafter. She was a beautiful little thing, but what an abominable temper. She ranted and raved in that foreign jabber, and broke nearly every piece of china in the house."

"I never noticed her temper," said Mrs. Bronwell.

"Oh, her ladyship mellowed considerably after her daughters were born. Made a right civilized English lady, she did."

"But what about her family?" Mrs. Throckmorton asked. "I didn't see any of them at her funeral."

"I suppose there would have been some difficulty getting word to them," Mrs. Bronwell said, "considering the war and all."

"Oh, yes, I almost forgot about Napoleon," Mrs. Throckmorton replied, "but surely he did send a letter, just in case it found its way over there eventually."

"No, he did not," answered Mrs. Brampton.

"Perhaps Lord Strathmore was so overcome with grief, he did not think about it," Olympia Bronwell said.

"Piffle," said Mrs. Brampton. "The only thing his lordship was overcome with were liquor fumes."

"Has someone been hired to care for the child...a nanny or a governess, perhaps?" Mrs. Bronwell asked.

"I inquired about that the day the viscount gathered Jane, Anne, Beatrice and Fanny together, just before they left for his lordship's town house in London."

"What did he say?" Mrs. Throckmorton asked.

"He said he sent word to a distant cousin of his—a young war widow, I believe he said, one without much hope of making an advantageous marriage. Seems she is one of the poor relations, and he considered it a charitable thing to offer her such a post as companion to his daughter."

"A young war widow?" asked Mrs. Throckmorton, looking somewhat suspicious. "How young?"

"Twenty-seven," I believe.

"Oh my," said Mrs. Throckmorton, "someone twenty and seven who has never had a child, is awfully young to take care of a baby."

"Well, it isn't our decision or our concern," Olympia said before turning her attention back to Mrs. Brampton. "You didn't by chance ask him about a name for the child, did you?"

"Yes, but all he said was, 'you take care of it Mrs. Brampton. Enlist the help of the staff if need be.' And then he departed, fast as can be, without another word."

Olympia had a vision of how George Marcus

14

Fairweather, the fourth Viscount Strathmore, must have looked, as he rapped on the ceiling of the coach and said, "To London, posthaste!"

Olympia was suddenly struck with a spark of ingenuity. "I've got it! I do believe I've got it. Maresa! We'll name her Maresa! A lovely way to combine her mother's two names, if you ask me."

"A splendid idea," said Mrs. Throckmorton.

"I like it," said Mrs. Brampton, "but is it Italian?"

"It is now," said Olympia.

Mrs. Brampton nodded. "That settles it, then."

A few weeks later, and to the eternal satisfaction of the Reverend Constable, the child was mercifully christened, Emily Maresa Fairweather, in hopes that by adding Emily, which was the name of the viscount's late mother, it would prompt his lordship to look more fondly upon her.

Sadly, that was not to be, for there was more optimism than truth to those hopes.

Two

I wandered lonely as a cloud
That floats on high o'er vales and hills,
When all at once I saw a crowd,
A host, of golden daffodils.

William Wordsworth (1770-1850)
British poet, 1804

For the first few years, Viscount Strathmore returned to Hampton Manor for Christmas and Maresa's birthday, but as the years began to pass, his visits became less and less frequent, until he stopped coming at all.

To anyone who knew the family, and that included the staff, the viscount's actions were understandable, for it was a well-known fact that the older Maresa became, the more she looked like her dear, dead mother.

Sadly, each time the viscount saw Maresa he was reminded of the fateful decision he had made the day she was born.

Her father's way of dealing with his terrible guilt was avoidance, and that meant he chose to keep her as far from his sight as possible. This unfortunate decision also kept her from knowing her four sisters or forming any kind of familial bond with them. To Maresa they were names she glimpsed in the family Bible, or heard on occasion, nothing more.

Her father's decision to save her life, instead of her mother's, meant she would never know a mother's love, or any of the things that entails. His decision to save her deprived her of a normal, happy life growing up in a loving family.

His all-consuming guilt placed beyond her reach forever the father she so desperately needed.

She was a lonely child, an outcast of her family, and although her distant cousin and companion, Mrs. Augusta Rightly did not spoil her, the staff at Hampton Manor did more than their share of doting when it came to Maresa.

As for Cousin Augusta, she was a woman small in stature and relatively quiet, but her eyes were warm, her manner pleasing and, at times, affectionate. When she spoke, her tone was cordial; her voice lively and animated. When she first came to Hampton Manor, everyone loved to say that only the rich had distant relatives, for they were certain money was behind Augusta's reason for coming to Yorkshire.

But in time, they ceased to be reminded of that, and began to see Augusta Rightly as a woman who gave in equal proportion to what she got.

As Maresa grew older, she learned that her cousin's heart, as well as her arms were open to receiving her with warmth—but only when Maresa's behavior deserved it. When Maresa was given to bouts of temper or spiteful disobedience, Augusta could be a very stern taskmaster.

Because the story of Maresa's birth and her mother's death continued to circulate and be bandied about, people in the village would stare and whisper whenever she came into sight. Frequently they would step out into the street, rather than pass too close by, for it was thought by many that Lady Fairweather was a witch—a witch who caused her own mother's death.

Whenever she was around the villagers, Maresa would hear their comments.

"She is cursed...."

"Caused her mother's death..."

"That's the fifth daughter...."

As if being the fifth of anything bore a special curse.

"Comments like that only hurt if you allow them to," Cousin Augusta told her. "Above all, you must not let them see their barbs have reached their mark. It only fuels a vicious fire."

Maresa understood what her cousin told her, but whenever she was around those who spoke cruelly, she forgot those words of advice.

It has long been established that children can be especially cruel to other children, and this was a fact Maresa learned early on. At church, she was teased and taunted with regularity by the other children, who told stories about how she put a curse on her father and caused him to make that fateful decision.

Sometimes they would make up rhymes and sing them to taunt her; "Roses are red, Violets are blue, I have a mother, Why don't you?"

"I don't care what you say," she would reply, but deep inside, Maresa did care, and the words and the taunts stayed with her long after the other children had put all thoughts of her out of sight.

In one particular incident that occurred on a fine Sunday morning after church, Maresa became so incensed when a young girl called her names and pulled her hair, that she spat on the child and called her a stupid twit.

Unfortunately, this earned Maresa a sound boxing of the ears from the girl's big brother, and a scolding from the mother.

Afterward, Maresa was too ashamed to mention it to her cousin, for she had forgotten again, to ignore cruel words and hateful barbs. Soon, she began to dread going to church at all.

The following Sunday, Maresa dressed for church and came downstairs for breakfast, but when it came time to leave, she was nowhere in sight. Everyone searched for her inside the house and out, and by the time she had been missing the better part of the day, everyone was in high distress.

After a trying day and near exhaustion, Cousin Augusta and Mrs. Brampton mounted the stairs that led up to the garret. They did not see Maresa inside, and were about to turn away, when they noticed the garret skylight was ajar.

"What do you make of that?" Mrs. Brampton asked.

"You don't suppose..."

"Perhaps we better have a closer look," said Mrs. Brampton, and they did.

Upon closer inspection, they found Maresa, huddled in a corner of the roof, near the chimney pot. It took the better part of an hour to persuade her to abandon her perch.

"I won't go back to church. I won't. I won't. I won't."

She was never certain who was more surprised—herself or her cousin—when Augusta got her by the ear. "Then I shall be forced to write your father that you refuse to go to church. Do you want to grow up a heathen?"

"Yes! And I don't care!" Maresa shouted. "And if he comes here, I shall run away!"

"And live on the moors like a wild urchin, or shall you go to the dales and run wild with the sheep? Have a care, Missy, that you do not chop off your nose to spite your face. I can see now, that we must include some lessons on kindness, and what it means to be a friend, in your studies."

"Everyone here hates me, so why shouldn't I run away?"

"Then perhaps it is time for you to try changing yourself. You are far too mischievous and wayward. You frighten away anyone who would come close to you."

"I'm not always mean!"

Her cousin agreed. "No, thankfully you have to sleep, and when you do, you are as gentle as a lamb."

"But with the coming of the sun, a lion awakens," her cousin said later, while admitting later to Mrs. Brampton that it wasn't that Maresa was insolent, it was simply that she was wholly insensible, and thought everyone at Hampton Manor existed for the sole purpose of bending her every whim and running to oblige each wish.

Because Maresa never knew her mother, she was enraptured by anything connected with her. She cherished the books in the library that contained her mother's name, and every painting that bore her likeness.

During her early years, she would spend a great deal of time in her mother's bedroom, looking at the beautiful clothes in the trunk at the foot of her bed. Other times, she would sit at the bottom of the great stairs and look at the painting of her mother, surrounded by Maresa's four sisters.

It was her favorite painting of her mother, and she would sit and stare for long periods of time, at the vivid-green gown and the magnificent emerald-and-diamond necklace around her neck. Maresa thought her mother was more beautiful than the roses in the garden.

Yet, there was always something about the painting that made Maresa sad, and it wasn't until she was older that she realized it was because she was not, nor would she ever be, a part of the family, just as she could never be a part of that painting. She would look at her mother, and her sisters, realizing she was an outcast, something different.

She was the fifth daughter, and that carried its own special curse.

Maresa would never forget the first time she saw the necklace that her mother had worn in the painting. It was the night of her eighth birthday, and one of the rare occasions her father had remembered—if indeed that was why he came to Hampton Manor.

On her way to her room, Maresa passed by her father's study, when a flash of something brilliant caught her eye. Curious as to what her father was holding that burned like fire, she paused at the doorway and saw her father clutching the emerald necklace.

"My mother wore that in the painting," she said.

Without looking up, her father said, "It's time you were in bed."

"May I see it, Father?"

"No."

"Please. Just once? I promise I won't hurt it."

"Look to your heart's content," he said, and tossed it on the desk before he turned away to pour another glass of Scotch.

Maresa picked up the necklace and the moment she touched it, her heart began to pound. This was the closest she had ever felt to her mother, and for a moment she closed her eyes and imagined her mother standing in this very room, wearing the necklace.

It was so real; she could even smell the lovely fragrance of her perfume.

Maresa's lip began to tremble and she was afraid she might cry—something she knew her father would find displeasing. "My mother wore this," she whispered, unaware she said it aloud until the viscount swore and threw the glass into the fireplace.

"Take it," he said. "Take it and get out!"

Maresa clasped the necklace against her chest and ran from the room. As she rushed up the stairs, she could hear the sound of her father's violent outburst of destruction, as he took a poker and tried to break everything in sight.

He left the next morning, but not before Maresa saw him at the door, and begged to go with him. "Please take me with you. I'll be good and quiet."

"You must stay here with Cousin Augusta."

"I don't think Cousin Augusta likes having to take care of me."

"Nonsense. She has been your teacher and your companion these many years, and your place is here with her. You're too young to live in London," he said.

Maresa knew that was not the real reason.

She stood on the steps of Hampton Manor and watched her father leave for London in a coach and four. After he was gone, she went upstairs and looked at her mother's necklace again, and then she locked it in a small jewelled casket, hiding it in a drafty passageway behind the fireplace in her room.

Well she knew what would happen to it if Cousin Augusta discovered it, for she would declare it far too valuable for a child to play with, and she would insist upon locking it away. And if Maresa put up a fuss, there would be another one of those boring lessons about kindness and turning the other cheek, which always sounded positively horrid to her.

She would have to admit though, that her world would have been a much smaller place had it not been for her cousin's love of books, and her gift for arousing Maresa's curiosity about mankind and the places they inhabited.

Although her cousin always had a ready answer for everything, there were some things Maresa could not talk to her about. She had never known Lady Strathmore, so she could not answer all the questions Maresa had about her mother.

Consequently, whenever Maresa wanted to know something about her mother, she would ask a member of the staff. One afternoon, she asked Mrs. Brampton about the necklace her mother wore in the painting.

"Such a lovely piece it was, and so beautiful on her. I was told your grandfather gave it to your mother on the day she married your father. It had belonged to one of her ancestors who received it as a gift from someone named Cosimo de Medici."

"Who was de Medici?"

Mrs. Brampton thought about that for a moment. "I think he was a king of Italy, but I'm not certain. Why don't you ask your cousin? She knows much more about such than I do."

Later that evening, Maresa was working

on her embroidery when Cousin Augusta poked her head through the door without knocking.

"Maresa Fairweather! Whatever are you doing? It looks like a spider's nest in here."

"I'm embroidering."

When her cousin walked over to see what Maresa was working on, her expression softened and a smile curved over her mouth, for she saw that Maresa had embroidered her name upon it.

"I am making this for you," Maresa said.

Her cousin displayed a certain amount of discomfort, which Maresa had never seen her do. "Well, if you must make a mess, clean it up when you are finished." She paused and looked down at the embroidery. "You should be very proud of yourself. I have never seen finer stitches."

Cousin Augusta was about to close the door when Maresa said, "Mrs. Brampton said you knew a lot about history."

Her face brightened. "It's a fact. I do love history. It's just so...so old."

"Do you know about Cosimo de Medici?"

"Cosimo de Medici?" she repeated. "Upon my word, where did you hear that name?"

"Mrs. Brampton told me. He's the one who gave my mother's grandfather the emerald necklace she is wearing in the painting downstairs. Mrs. Brampton thought he was the king of Italy."

"He was more powerful and more wealthy than any king. Do you know he bought the town of Siena from the king of Spain, when the king was bankrupt?"

"Where is Siena?"

"It's a town in Italy."

"What is bankrupt?"

"Perhaps it is time for a history lesson."

"Are we going to study Italy?"

Cousin Augusta smiled. "Would you pay attention if we studied anything else?"

Maresa laughed and shook her head.

When Cousin Augusta left, Maresa followed her down the stairs.

"Siena," her cousin said to herself as she descended the stairs. "Now, where shall I look to find something about Siena?"

Maresa hopped down the stairs behind her. "Italy," she said.

"My thoughts exactly," Augusta said as she made a hasty departure in the opposite direction.

Things seemed to grow even closer between the two of them after that.

For the next several days, Augusta devoted a great deal of time to teaching Maresa about her mother's country.

After Maresa learned all she could about the de Medicis, she asked her cousin, "I wonder why I never get a letter from my aunt?"

"There is a war going on."

"Napoleon," Maresa said. "Is that all he likes to do?"

"Apparently, yes. And he has crowned himself king of Italy, so it would be very difficult for anyone to leave Italy and come to England.

There are privateers to rob you, and blockades to run. Not to mention the Barbary pirates. It is not safe to cross the channel or to sail the Mediterranean."

"I thought my father didn't want them to come to Hampton Manor."

"Perhaps he doesn't."

"Do you suppose it would be all right if I wrote Aunt Gisella a letter?"

"I don't see what it would hurt, but I doubt it will reach Italy, or in the event it did, that their reply would make it back to England."

"Then I will pray that it does," Maresa said, firmly believing prayer made it so.

Maresa wrote her letter and her cousin had the upstairs maid post it in the village.

It was almost a year later when Maresa received a reply from Aunt Gisella, who made profuse apologies for her poor English—which was not so poor she couldn't fill five pages.

She wrote about their home and life in Italy, and their desire for the war to be over so they could see her. In the letter, Maresa was also happy to hear more about her Uncle Tito Bartolini and cousins, Serena and Angelo, who were not much older than Maresa.

Maresa saved the letter as well as three others that managed to make it to England over the next few years. They were letters she kept hidden away with her mother's necklace, to read and read again, until they were so fragile, she dared not read them any more, not that it mattered.

As the years passed, she had read them so many times, she knew each word, every curve of her aunt's handwriting by heart.

The letters contained many things that were dear to Maresa, such as the time Aunt Gisella wrote, "Your *onamastico* is *19 maggio*," which she said meant Maresa's saints day was the nineteenth of May, but the greatest gift that came was the knowledge that she did, in fact, have a family.

Someday, she would tell herself.

Someday I will go to Italy.

After that, Italy became a magical place, a paradise that was forbidden: At least for the time being.

Not long after she received her aunt's letter, Maresa announced during her studies one afternoon that she wanted to study Italian.

"We will have to call in a tutor for that, I fear. Latin I can teach you. But Italian? Who could teach you Italian? Hmmm."

After giving it some thought, Augusta announced, "I have it! I have heard Miss Millwood lived in Italy for many years, and only returned to England because of the war. And even better, she lives only a short distance away."

"Miss Millwood is as old as Hadrian's Wall."

"Then she has had a long time to learn Italian, so she should be very good at it. I shall speak with her after church."

The following Sunday, Maresa was informed that Miss Millwood was simply thrilled to have the opportunity to tutor Maresa in Italian.

But not even the learning of her mother's native language could ease the loneliness and the pain of having no mother. Frequently at night, after her cousin had doused the candle, Maresa would slip out of bed, so she could hold her mother's necklace. It was when she felt the closest to her mother—close enough that she began to tell her about her day.

Sometimes she would even ask her opinion, as if her mother were there, in the room, with her.

She was glad for the close feeling she had toward her mother, especially after the day a group of workmen appeared at Hampton Manor, to close the door to her mother's room forever.

Maresa was never to know why her father decided to have the door to her mother's room sealed. She only knew that one day it was open and she was free to enter in, and the next day, a team of workers came and closed off the door and closed the shutters over the windows, nailing them firmly in place.

She was never allowed to see the inside of her mother's room again.

But she had the lovely Italian necklace that once belonged to Cosimo de Medici, and for her, that was enough.

Although Maresa was well provided for, it was a lonely existence—a solitary child growing to adulthood in an enormous country house on the windswept moors, with no one but the servants and a distant cousin to guide her.

Three

All who joy would win
Must share it,—Happiness was born a
    twin.

            Lord Byron (1788-1824)
                English poet
        Don Juan (1819-1824)

This year, as he did every year, the viscount sent word that he was unable to come to Hampton Manor for his daughter's birthday. It was something she expected; something she thought herself prepared for, but when Maresa read her father's note, she slipped away from the manor and went for a walk on the moors. She did not want anyone to see how the news saddened her.

As it happened, on that particular day, a group of boys from the village happened to see her and decided to have a little sport.

They chased her far out onto the moors, shouting and calling her names as they threw rocks.

Hurt by the pelting of rocks, she ran, faster and farther than she had ever been.

It was only when dark and threatening storm clouds began to roll overhead that the boys tossed their last rock, and with a taunting laugh, turned away.

Great drops of rain began to fall, driven by a cold spring wind that drenched her clothes.

Jagged bolts of lightning ripped across the sky and for the first time in her life, Maresa knew what it was to be truly frightened.

Lost, terrified and shivering wet, she sought refuge beneath a gnarled old tree. As she hugged her knees, she felt a thousand miles away from Hampton Manor and the comforting solace of the beautiful Italian necklace.

Before long, the storm blew itself out and the sun began to shine weakly through the remnant of clouds and the clusters of yellow daffodils lifted their soggy heads in an effort to chase away the gloom.

There were other plants beaten down by the wind and rain—plants that did not recover with a flourish when the inclement weather passed. Instead, they lay flattened in muddy puddles, and in danger of being trampled beneath the feet of any who passed.

Maresa found inspiration in the hardy little daffodils, for she remembered when buffeted by the strong winds, they lay among the stones, almost parallel to the ground. And then came a fierce pounding by the rain that caused their saturated blooms to droop beneath the weight, as if resting their heads on the stones like a pillow. But all was forgotten when the storm passed and they lifted trumpet-shaped faces to the sun.

She saw a parallel between herself and those daffodils, and decided that although her life was subject to its own particular storms, she would not give up. No matter how beaten down, she would survive. She would overcome. She would! She would!

And she would be as beautiful and invincible as those flowers, who lifted sunlit faces in triumph, to laugh at disaster's mocking face.

But not today, for she was still sitting beneath the tree, thinking about what she should do, when a young man happened by.

Three years older than Maresa, Percival Livingston Bronwell had been hunting on the moors when the storm came up.

"Ho!" he said, when he saw her. "Are you some kind of tree elf?"

"You know that I am not!" She had learned long ago to be hostile to strangers, before they had a chance to start calling her names.

"I suppose you're right. I've never seen a tree elf in such a muddy dress."

Maresa looked down at her yellow dress, unable to find even one tiny patch of yellow, so covered with mud, it was. With a slow movement, she tilted her head to one side and studied him. He seemed nice enough, she thought, as she looked at the gun slung over one arm, but she knew it was an arm that could just as easily throw rocks.

Still, he did not look as if he were about to taunt her, or throw rocks, like the other boys had done, but if she had learned anything about life it was that one could be too trusting, but never too careful.

"What's your name?" he asked.

"I don't know. What's yours?"

"Percy," he said. "Do you live nearby?"

"Maybe. Do you?"

He grinned. "Yes, I live at Danegeld Hall, not far from here. How about you?"

She did not say anything.

"Are you lost?"

"No, I'm not. Are you?"

"No, but I'm not sitting under a tree in the mud looking as lost as last week."

"I'm not lost. I'm thinking."

"Is that a special outfit you wear for thinking and do you always do it under this particular tree?"

She did not answer.

"Would you like me to walk you home? Which way do you live?"

"That's what I was thinking about."

He laughed. "You are lost!"

"No, I'm just not sure which way my house is. I live at Hampton Manor. Have you heard of it?"

"No, but I am certain my father has."

She frowned crossly. "It has been here for a very long time. You are very strange if you have not heard of it."

He shrugged. "I've been away at school"

"Then they must not be teaching you very much."

He laughed again and Maresa thought she had never heard anything as beautiful as Percy's laugh. It was a laugh that seemed to part the clouds and send a shaft of sun straight down to warm her.

Percy stepped closer and held out his hand. "If you take my hand, I'll help you up."

"You'll let go and laugh when I fall!"

He truly seemed shocked by her comment. "My father would have my hide if I treated a lady in such a way," he said.

Again, she did not say anything.

"You are a very peculiar girl."

"I like being peculiar."

"You must. Otherwise you wouldn't go to so much trouble to be that way, would you?"

"It isn't any trouble."

"Ahh, such honesty."

He reached forward and clasped her hand. "Come on, up with you. I'll take you home with me to Danegeld Hall. I'm sure my father will know where Hampton Manor is, and he will have the coach take you there."

Maresa thought about her options—which at this point were precious few.

"Well? What shall it be? Do you go home with me, or do I go off and leave you sitting here?"

Still, she did not say anything.

He surveyed the sky. "I better go. It will be getting dark soon."

She gave Percy her hand, and for the first time in her life, trusted a stranger.

The Bronwells were a remarkably fine family, wealthy landowners who opened their hearts and their home to Maresa.

Percy had two older brothers, Stephen and Max, whom she did not meet, but saw from their portraits that they were decidedly handsome, although strikingly different in coloring from Percy.

Even his mother's pug, Pugnacious, was

friendly, especially when licking the remnants of a gooseberry tart from her hands. At first, Maresa was very timid and shy, and terribly ashamed of her muddy appearance, but Biddy the maid had worked wonders with Maresa's hair and dress, and although not as good as new, she did look as good as could be expected.

It did not take long for Maresa to feel at home around these kindly people who put themselves out of their way to see to her comfort and entertainment.

Mrs. Bronwell, who had been making artificial flowers when Maresa and Percy arrived, tried with the patience of the most dedicated saint, to show Maresa how it was done.

She patted the seat next to her. "Come and sit beside me, and I will show you how it is done."

Maresa took a seat on the outer edge of the chair.

"Now, you cut the paper like so, and then you roll it around the pen like this, and when you finish, you push it off, and voilà! You have a flower. Now, you try."

Maresa cut the paper like so. She rolled it around the pen. And when she finished, she pushed it off, and had what Percy called, "A red, airborne projectile that Napoleon would covet for his cannons."

After three more tries, all Maresa succeeded in doing was wasting a good amount of red paper.

For someone who was always alone and

found something to fear in every place she went, it was unsettling to be around so much gaiety and laughter, and in the company of those who truly enjoyed the presence of those around them. She was touched by Mrs. Bronwell's kindness and soft voice, and awed by Mr. Bronwell's height and gruff voice—which seemed in direct contradiction to the soft regard in his eyes.

Here, she was accepted. No one laughed at her clothes, or poked fun at her lack of a more formal education. And not once did anyone mention the unfortunate circumstances of her birth, or accuse her of being anything, save a girl.

The grandeur of Danegeld Hall was a bit overpowering at first. The rooms were not any larger than those at Hampton Manor, but they were far lovelier, and so lushly furnished.

Maresa's favorite was the formal salon—carpeted in blue, with a settee and chairs covered in cream and trimmed in gold. Overhead the ceiling was ornately plastered and trimmed in gold. In the center was a painting of clouds and angels, with a shimmering fall of glass lights as beautiful as raindrops, suspended over a round table.

Percy's home was everything Maresa's was not—happy, full of life and bursting with family reminders. She saw how easy it was for Percy and his family to love each other, to enjoy the presence and the blessing of being together, in a huge old manor house that went back to the time of the Danish invasion.

After tea and dainty tarts, Mrs. Bronwell declared Mr. Bronwell must make arrangements to take Maresa home. "They will be worried about her, I am sure."

Maresa neither denied nor validated that statement, but she did become suddenly quiet.

Percy and Mr. Bronwell accompanied Maresa in the coach back to Hampton Manor. On the way, Percy promised to meet her the next day near the old Priory ruins.

It was the beginning of a long and lasting friendship.

Four

So we grew together,
Like to a double cherry, seeming parted,
But yet a union in partition,
Two lovely berries moulded on one stem;
So, with two seeming bodies, but one
    heart.

William Shakespeare (1564-1616)
English poet and playwright

One can get lost in the wild and varied scenery of the Yorkshire moors. If the wind is right, one can smell the sea.

Often, while wandering the undulating paths of the moors with her dogs, Maresa would close her eyes and imagine the sound of the waves as they crashed against the massive cliffs, or the call of kittiwakes as they flew overhead.

Other times, the picturesque villages that clung to the cliffs called out to her, and she would ride across the heathery moors to the edge of the precipice that hugged the coastline, sometimes stopping to sit and watch the rocking motion of fishing boats harbored below.

Like people, the sea was not to be trusted, and she never allowed the tranquillity to lull her into thinking all was peaceful and right with the world. Maresa knew when the wind came up, the serene harmony would be gone, for then the sea would swell and throw itself against the craggy rocks, as an angry reminder that man would never tame its wildness.

The moors were a part of her, wild, lonely and isolated.

Rejected by the family who should love and accept her, Maresa searched for love and acceptance elsewhere. When she was a child, the protective doting of the staff at Hampton Manor was enough, although the sympathy they felt toward her and their tendency to spoil her, helped produce a young girl who was independent, headstrong, determined and a bit selfish when it came to having her own way.

Percy was one of the first who began to notice the shift toward selfishness, and scolded her one afternoon as they hunted with the dogs. He had returned from school only that morning, and was eager to see her, but not even his eagerness could hide her self-centered ways.

"You are truly a selfish child," he said, "wild and knotty as a gooseberry bush," and he quoted an old Yorkshire proverb, in the vernacular. " 'If tha does owt for nowt, do it for thysen.' "

Maresa turned her face toward his and wrinkled her nose. "What does that mean?"

"If you do anything for nothing, do it for yourself."

"Hmm," she said, and turned toward the house.

It wasn't that Maresa set out to be selfish, it was simply that all her thoughts were preoccupied with fresh plans to make life as comfortable as possible, because in her mind, she had been dealt with most unfairly, and felt she deserved to be compensated in return. Now that Percy had entered her life, she did not wait long before trying to bend him to do her bidding as well.

One cold, blustery day, Percy came by with his dogs and invited her to go hawking.

"I did not know you were coming home. Why did you not write me?"

"It was an unexpected break. Over half the school has come down with the measles. They sent everyone home."

"Measles? Dear me, I hope I don't catch it."

"Imps don't catch the measles," he said. "Come on, let's go work the hawks."

"It's too cold and damp," Maresa said.

"That's an old wive's tale, that says you must only go when the weather is dry, not too cold, with only a slight wind. This is Yorkshire! If we followed that advice, we'd never go hawking."

She was persuaded.

Percy brought two hawks, and he let Maresa have her pick.

She chose the darker, larger male and left the smaller female for Percy. He did not seem to care which hawk he had, and set about releasing the female.

Maresa did the same.

When it was time for a break, Percy sat down beside one of the dogs, and the birds seemed to know it was time for something to eat, for they turned and began to glide back toward land.

His birds were well trained, and responded when he called. He called in Maresa's male first, and then the female, which landed on his glove.

Maresa glanced over to the day's catch—a brown hare, a pheasant and one rabbit. The brown hare and pheasant caught by Percy's falcon far outshone Maresa's lone rabbit.

"Your hawk is better than mine."

"Although the male is larger, he is three years younger than the female."

Caught up into the rush of emotion that came from hawking, Percy said, "Did you see the way the female caught that pheasant cock in midair?"

"You ought to trade with me."

"Why, because my catch is bigger?"

"Let me fly the female."

"No, you chose the male. Next time, you can have the female."

"If you don't trade with me, I shan't go with you again."

"If you persist in such petulance, we will go home now."

"I don't want to go home. I want to fly the female."

Percy said nothing, but he did take the falcons and tie their jesses to secure them.

"What are you doing?"

"We are through hunting for today."

"Keep your old falcon, then," she said. "I hope it gets killed by some hunter's arrow."

Cool of head, Percy said nothing until they reached Hampton Manor, where he left Maresa with a word of caution to her to "manage your black temper," and a formal goodbye.

Because she had observed the cold exchange between the two of them when he brought her home, her cousin questioned Maresa as soon as she came inside. When Augusta learned the truth of what happened, she said, "I fear you will have a long time to think about your prideful behavior, for I doubt young Mr. Bronwell will be anxious to spend much time with the likes of someone as mean-spirited as you."

Later, when Mrs. Brampton commented on Maresa's loss of appetite and disheartened mood, her cousin said, "I fear we have been guilty of giving Maresa too much freedom. It is time to rein her in a bit, I think. She is becoming quite self-centered—a disagreeable trait in anyone, especially someone so young."

Mrs. Brampton thought about that for a moment. "It does seem her selfishness is packed in a big box with a loose lid. What are you going to do about it?"

Augusta sighed. "At this point, I am not certain how I should handle it. It is quite difficult to deal with, for on the one hand, I understand why she is the way she is, but on the other hand, I know this will not serve her later in life."

"Why she is the way she is? Are you saying you think it's all Lord Strathmore's fault?"

"I thought as much in the beginning, yes, but now I believe we have all contributed to it, each in our own way. I think Maresa has a hard little acorn where her heart should be, and without love to occupy her attention, she is preoccupied with herself. It's already apparent that she is going to be a great beauty, with her Italian black hair and English blue eyes. However, I cannot help but worry over what will happen when she begins to realize it. Dear me, that may be the real beginning of our troubles."

"Well, maybe our little nursling of the moors will find something worthwhile to devote herself to," Mrs. Brampton said. "Perhaps young Mr. Bronwell..."

"Yes," Augusta said with a nod. "I have

thought about that as well, and I must say that is what I dread most of all. The problem with having a lovely young woman about is that they attract young men." She began looking around. "Now, where did I leave my scissors?"

"Would that be them hanging around your neck?"

Augusta looked down. "Oh my, yes. I put them there so I wouldn't forget where I left them."

"You might try hanging them in a more prominent place," said Mrs. Brampton with a laugh.

As far as companions went, Maresa's cousin had a few shortcomings. Although she was compassionate, sympathetic, forthright and more than capable, there were occasions when she was hard to penetrate intellectually. Sometimes this came across as being the last word in incompetence.

Over the years, she and Maresa had not come to love each other as a mother and daughter would, but a strong bond of friendship and verisimilitude had formed between the two of them.

After all, they were related, and in spite of their differences, Maresa always knew that deep down, Cousin Augusta always had Maresa's best interest at heart. As the person responsible for Maresa's well-being, she was devoted to her charge, and often served as a mother figure and a mentor to her, usually by default.

There were, after all, some things Maresa could not ask Percy about.

Cousin Augusta was Maresa's tutor and advisor when it came to womanly things, although there were those in the Fairweather household who did wonder on occasion, just where it was that Augusta Rightly got her facts.

When Maresa wanted to know where babies came from, it was perfectly natural that she would ask her cousin.

Apparently aware that one could give too much information, her cousin looked at her blankly and responded by simply saying, "They come from the mother's stomach."

By the time Maresa was thirteen and Percy sixteen, Maresa knew that in the person of Percy Bronwell, she had the affection, devotion and acceptance she had been searching for, and as their friendship deepened, she began to outgrow many of her spiteful ways. As she did, she began to turn to Percy for the support, guidance and nurturing her father should have provided.

"Lud!" the new maid Lucy, said one afternoon as she watched Percy and Maresa ride off together across the moors. "Those two are stuck together like mortar and brick. Whatever did she do before he came along?"

"Drove the rest of us mad," Mrs. Brampton said. "Stretched my tolerance till it threatened to snap a thousand times a day. Her mind was always working with mischief, from the moment she opened her eyes in the morning, until she closed them at night. It was a rare day, indeed, that one of us went about our daily

44

chores without a worry as to what she might do next."

Cousin Augusta nodded in agreement. "And if she wasn't into mischief, she was singing at the top of her voice and banging on the piano, or letting the dogs inside, so they would chase her through the house." She paused, reflective. "I fear I have grown completely out of touch with my own youth. I suppose one has to experience life in order to grow, gain strength, confidence and reach maturity."

"If she doesn't put us all in an early grave before she reaches it," Mrs. Brampton added. "It was always so difficult to discipline her, you know."

Augusta nodded. "Oh yes, I know all too well how she will withdraw into that private little world of hers whenever any of us try. We have Mr. Bronwell to thank for a lot of things, especially providing us with the greatest punishment we could invent, for I have discovered the most devastating thing anyone can do to her is to keep her away from him. Breaks her heart, it does, to miss seeing him even for one day. She idolizes him so."

That much was true, for Percy Bronwell was Maresa's best friend, her mentor and her idol. It was Percy who defended her against all gossip and ridicule. He was the one she always turned to in time of trouble, and for a barely supervised child running wild on the moors, it sometimes looked to Percy like a full-time job.

When she was younger, he pulled her out

of mud holes and fights, and stood up for her when others teased her. As the young men about began to replace their teasing with attention, the girls Maresa's age became more harshly critical.

By the time Maresa was fifteen, Percy was still coming to her defense, but it was usually to rescue her from the overzealous attention of a suitor or two.

"I fear I shall never marry," she told Percy one afternoon as they rode toward Danegeld Hall.

Percy laughed. "You aren't old enough to worry about marriage."

"I'm almost sixteen."

"You're barely fifteen and you've got a few hearts to break before you'll be ready for marriage."

"I have yet to meet a heart I'd care to break."

"Just you wait. You'll find one soon enough, I'll wager."

Percy's words held more truth than even he realized.

The following Christmas, Percy took the dogs out for exercise, and rode across the moors for half an hour, in spite of it being a damp day, cold and windy.

On his way back, he remembered his brother was coming home today, so he stopped by Hampton Manor to invite Maresa to join the family for dinner.

"Stephen is coming home for the holidays and will arrive late this afternoon," he said. "There will be much singing and dancing tonight."

Percy had a cup of tea while Maresa changed into something she called "festive." When she came back downstairs, she was wearing what she identified as "My new Christmas clothes."

Percy was surprised. "You have opened your Christmas gift already?"

"Of course! How else would I see what it was?"

"And ruin the surprise? What shall you open on Christmas day?"

"I still have two other gifts—one of them yours, that I am saving for then."

Wrapped in a fine blue cloak with the hood pulled low over her forehead, Maresa rode to Danegeld Hall with Percy.

As they neared the front of the house, they saw a carriage stopped in front of the door, and the members of Percy's family gathered about, along with most of the servants at Danegeld.

Suddenly Percy let out a whoop and spurred his horse forward. "Stephen is here!" he shouted.

By the time they reached the house, Maresa was in a pout, more than put out that Percy had ridden ahead of her.

"And who is this?" Stephen asked when Maresa rode up.

Before Percy could help her dismount, Stephen moved to her side. "Allow me."

"This is Lady Fairweather," Olympia said, and then to Percy, "Where are your manners, Percy?"

"Stephen Bronwell, at your service," Stephen said before Percy had a chance to offer his hand at introducing his brother.

Stephen helped Maresa dismount.

The moment her boots touched the gravel drive, she looked at him squarely and said, "I've heard a great deal about you, but no one told me you were such a gentleman."

Stephen glanced at Percy. "Not all of the Bronwells are as rustic as Percival."

"I can be civilized when I need to be," Percy said while giving his brother a glower.

At the sound of low rumbling thunder in the distance, Olympia said, "Dear me, it looks like rain. Let us go inside before we're struck by lightning."

"I think I already am," Stephen said, and offered Maresa his arm.

Percy lagged behind, until the first fat drops of rain began to fall, and then he too went into the house.

Once inside, Maresa threw back the hood of her cape, and beneath a feathering of clipped beaver, a glossy fall of inky black curls cascaded down her back. She untied the strings of her hat and handed them to the butler, who also took her blue cape.

Beneath the cape, Maresa wore a green plaid silk frock that fit her rather splendidly, and it seemed that everyone about had noticed, especially Stephen.

"Percy, you did not tell me your friend was so ravishing."

"I fear I have only made that discovery myself," Percy said, while sounding rather bewildered over the transformation of Maresa from the wild child of the moors, to a beauty of great and gentle breeding.

"Come, come," Mr. Bronwell said, "Let us go into the grand salon, where there is a great fire that will be burning the Yule log a few days hence."

"Yes, do come in," Mrs. Bronwell said. "There is much to eat and hot spiced drinks to make the day merry and the weather less dreary."

Stephen took Maresa's arm and walked her into the grand salon and found her a seat near the cheerful fire.

"Shall I fetch you something hot to drink?"

"Oh, yes, please do. I did become rather chilled during the ride over here."

Stephen glanced at Percy who was sitting a few feet away. "Why didn't you take the carriage over to bring her here? The idea of expecting one so lovely and dressed so fine to go traipsing across the moors in this damp weather...you better pray, brother, that she does not take a chill."

"Maresa is too bad-tempered to take sick."

"Percival!" Olympia chided, "what a terrible, un-Christian thing to say."

"Sorry, Maresa," he said, and excused himself to get a cup of tea.

Nestled in the comfortable house, where the

49

air bore the rich scent of heating spices and almond cakes, Maresa took in the sight of the room, so full of Christmas changes. It was decked out with ropes of holly and bright-red bows...and the splendid sight of Stephen strolling toward her with two silver mugs filled with mulled ale.

Soon there was laughing and the singing of Christmas carols, and then a lovely dinner of roasted goose, and afterward more singing, drinking and dancing, until Maresa thought she had never spent a more lovely, enchanting day in her entire life.

Stephen was a splendid dancer, much more so than Percy, as Maresa commented.

Stephen was charitable enough to say, "Percy has not yet had the opportunity to spend much time in London, dancing with the offerings of the season, not that I blame him. If I had known what was keeping him here in Yorkshire, I would have returned ere now."

"Do you think Percy really wants to go sample life in London?" she asked.

"No. Of late, he has been talking of a life as a naval officer. I am surprised he did not mention it to you."

"Probably because he knows how I would feel about him going off to serve in the war."

"Exactly the way Mother feels, I would think. She is his biggest deterrent, and feels our family has given enough to the cause, with Max having joined the light cavalry to fight Napoleon. Of course, I cannot fault her for that. It is normal for a woman to want to discourage those they love from taking action that might be harmful. Mother keeps insisting that Percy should study to be a barrister."

"Youngest sons usually become ministers," Maresa said, unable to fathom why she said it any more than she could picture Percy a minister.

Stephen stopped dancing long enough to give a shout of laughter at that. "A minister!" He gave a glance in Percy's direction, and apparently humored by Percy's silent glower, said, "Can you honestly see that standing in the pulpit on Sunday morning?"

Maresa refrained from looking at Percy as Stephen had done, but the corners of her mouth did curve a bit.

"Has anyone told you that you have the sweetest smile, the fairest skin and the lightest foot in the parish?"

"No, but I am delighted to be hearing it now, and that it is you telling me that."

"And I might add you also have the bonniest blue eyes I have ever had the pleasure to gaze into."

"Keep talking like that and you shall spoil me."

"That is my fondest wish," Stephen said, as the music ended and he walked her back to sit beside the fire.

Maresa took a drink and gazed in Percy's direction over the rim of the silver cup. She was surprised to see he was no longer there. She glanced around the room, and saw he was nowhere to be found.

"Excuse me for a moment, Stephen," she said as she put the mug down and went to search for him.

Unable to find him anywhere, she inquired of Mrs. Bronwell, "Have you see Percy?"

"Why no, dear, not since he was sitting over there, near you and Stephen."

At that moment, Stephen joined them. "I believe I saw him go outside."

"In this weather?" Olympia asked, her smile turning to a frown of concern. "The weather has turned abominably bad...wet and freezing. I would not be surprised to see sleet or snow. Whatever was he thinking?"

"He was thinking to spare us all by carrying his ill humor out to the moors," Stephen said.

"Why would you say that he is in an ill humor, Stephen? I fear you do your brother an injustice. Whatever could be the cause?"

"I daresay he is jealous of the attention I pay Maresa."

"Oh, poppycock! Maresa and Percy are not romantically linked! They are the dearest of friends."

"So say you," Stephen said, "but I have my own observations that say something quite to the contrary."

Olympia seemed surprised by what Stephen said, and then her face took on a thoughtful expression. "Hmmm."

Maresa did not see Percy again for quite some time, and when he did put in an appearance, he kept well away from her and Stephen.

This was not the Percy she knew, and she truly wanted to speak to him, but Stephen kept getting in the way, and then it was time for her to return home and the opportunity slipped away.

"I don't think you should return tonight," Mr. Bronwell said upon returning from the out of doors. "The weather has turned to ice. The roads will be slick."

By the time they had decided the weather was far too atrocious for Maresa to return to Hampton Manor, and that she should stay the night, Percy had already retired.

Five

Love is like the wild rose-briar;
Friendship like the holly-tree.
The holly is dark when the rose-briar
    blooms,
But which will bloom most constantly?

Emily Bronte
English novelist

Morning came, and brought with it a change in the weather, which was greatly improved. The stubborn cold lingered on, but the sun was out and the wind had virtually disappeared.

Olympia, delighted with the weather, announced they would all go to church.

Bundled against the bite of the cold, Maresa joined the Bronwells in the family coach for the ride to church, with Stephen at her side—a place he seemed to favor, Olympia noticed.

From time to time, Olympia would glance out the window, concern for her youngest son marring her usual happy expression. It was not like Percy to decline the invitation to ride with the other members of the family in favor of riding his horse, any more than it was usual for him to separate himself from Maresa.

He looked rather splendid on a horse, and was by far the best horseman in the Bronwell family. She could not understand why such a horseman would want a life walking the decks of a ship any more than she understood his determination to avoid riding in the carriage.

Stubborn man! No amount of persuasion could ever change his mind once it was made up, not that it should surprise her. Percy was born stubborn.

Olympia tried to keep her mind off Percy by observing Maresa, for she was chatting gaily with Stephen, looking quite composed with an air of indifference. It was a shock to see her like this, for Olympia had never thought of Maresa as uncaring or heartless, but to see the way she obviously gave little or no thought or concern for Percy—his feelings or his whereabouts—left her wondering if she had misjudged her all these years.

Later that night, as they prepared for bed, Olympia mentioned her feelings and observations concerning Maresa to her husband. "I fear I was wrong in thinking her quite the most selfish, indifferent human I had ever observed, and now I feel so guilty."

"Why would you feel guilty, love, if you observed these most undesirable traits in her behavior? From what you said, it sounds as though you judged her correctly, although it surprises me as much as you."

"That's what I find so upsetting, because I was too hasty to form an opinion and to judge her—incorrectly, I might add, and it has left me feeling wretched."

"What happened to change your mind?"

"I happened to glance over to where she sat beside Stephen during church and was shocked to see her staring down at her muff, her cheeks red and damp with tears. Once, she feigned a fit of coughing so as to bury her face in her muff, but I saw the way she wiped away the tears and stole a sideways glance in Percy's direction. I daresay I realized I had been wrong to judge her so unfeelingly, for it was obvious to me that she suffered greatly because of the breach in their friendship. Faith, did you not notice how she seemed to go through the day, looking every bit as miserable as Percy? If I did not know better, I would swear she was suffering the purgatory of lost love."

"Do not overly upset yourself, my love."

"Oh, I cannot help it. If you could only have seen her face when she placed that shilling in the Christmas box!"

"Whatever do you mean?"

"She dropped in her coin and our eyes met.

At that moment, I truly would not have been surprised to see her burst into tears and run from the church, so wretched she looked."

"Well, it is over now, and she is safely ensconced in her own bed at Hampton Manor and I am sure before she went there, that she and Percy made up."

"No, they did not, for that scoundrel Stephen was always in the way."

"Stop your motherly fretting. Percy and Stephen are grown men, and quite fond of one another. They will settle this thing in their own way, and at a time of their own choosing. All will end well between them. You will see."

"How can you be so certain?"

"Maresa is only a temporary diversion for Stephen...a passing fancy to interest him during his holiday stay, and when he leaves after Christmas, I daresay he will not give her another thought."

"Hmmm," Olympia said, but she was not convinced of that.

Not in the least.

"I was only being nice," Maresa said in her defense the next afternoon, after Percy confronted her about being in a swoon over his brother.

She took a chestnut from a bowl and began to eat it. "I do not know why you are so angry with me and yet you have not said one word about Stephen's behavior. After all, it was Stephen who pursued the matter, not I! I

56

think you are being most unfair to single me out in this way."

"You are not being singled out. I gave Stephen his due before I came over here."

"I do not understand what this is all about, or why you persist in being angry with either one of us. You know I would never do anything to hurt you, Percy. You are my dearest friend."

"I know that, but I also understand Stephen's appeal."

She continued to look at him with the mien of skepticism.

"I am not saying this insincerely. I really do understand my brother's appeal. He has always had a way with females. Mother says that he wasn't much more than a babe, when he learned that maidens, like moths, were enticed by a bright flame. He has always been a favorite of women, and love is a constant necessity in his life." He paused a moment, thinking that last bit could be said of Maresa, as well. He decided against telling her that, however. "I would not be honest with you if I did not say that there have been times that I thought he handled matters of the heart with unparalleled stupidity, blundering from one affair to another, usually with maximum indifference to the feelings of those he abandoned."

"My, you make him sound like a perfect rake."

"That is not my purpose. I am here to enlighten you. My brother is a gentleman through and through. Father has prepared him well to inherit all and take over the management of his estates."

"I never thought it bothered you...being the youngest and inheritor of nothing."

"It doesn't. I would never suit being a landowner and country gentleman."

"I know, but you do have a fine head for mathematics. I remember how you excelled in spherical trigonometry."

"Which will serve me well in the Royal Navy."

"Don't you think one son in the war is enough for your family?"

"Then perhaps Max should come home. My knowledge of French and Italian is better than his."

"Can you never be serious? War is a grave situation, you know. You could be killed."

"I could be killed right here, thrown jumping a fence, or struck by lightning."

She ignored that and continued with her own line of thinking. "I thought your father preferred a career for you with the East India Company."

"He does, but he will help me obtain a commission as a lieutenant in the Royal Navy, if it is truly what I want."

"I will worry if you choose the Royal Navy," she said, and picked up another chestnut.

"You will be too busy with my brother, to worry overmuch."

"That isn't true!" she said, and refusing to discuss it any further, tossed the chestnut back into the basket and left Percy standing alone.

On Christmas Eve, Maresa again joined the Bronwell family at Danegeld Hall, only this time, it was not Percy who went to fetch her from Hampton Manor, but Stephen.

Upstairs in his room, Percy was writing a letter. Gusts of wind kept driving a limb of the fir tree against the casement until the scratching and scraping sound was such an annoyance that he threw down his quill and made an inward vow to break the offending bough if he had to chop down the tree to do it.

He rose and took himself to the window, where he flipped the lock and threw back the window. He had no more than leaned out to grab the noisy branch, when he saw the carriage in the courtyard below, and Stephen, as he helped Maresa alight from the carriage.

With all thought of breaking the offending limb forgotten, Percy watched Stephen touch her elbow. He saw the way she gave a start at his touch, and turned her head to look up at him.

Stephen leaned closer, and for a moment Percy thought he was going to kiss her, but she ducked her head and he whispered something in her ear. The sound of her laughter danced across the courtyard and pierced his heart.

Stephen kissed her cheek and smiled down at her, with a possessive air that was obvious even from such a distance, and Percy had the impression of a pirate about to add a rare jewel to his cache of treasures.

Percy never had the opportunity to study Maresa from a distance like this, and it surprised him to see from this vantage point, what he had never noticed up close. She was delicately made and slender, hardly past her childhood, and not yet comfortable with her new role as a woman.

That his brother might be, in all likelihood, the one to usher her on into the bloom of womanhood made him more aware of his feelings for her, the feelings he had felt toward her for some time now, but never seemed to find the right time to share with her.

Now, it seemed, he never would.

He was not angry with Stephen, or even Maresa, for that matter. His feelings floated in the air, somewhere above hopelessness and disdain.

Percy forgot about the fir bough and closed the casement. He left his writing on the table and went downstairs to the kitchen, to make himself a cup of tea.

The kitchen was warm. The smell of cinnamon and bread still lingered, a leftover from breakfast. Someone had raked the burning coals together in the fireplace, and added new ones. A kettle hung over the low flame and rocked back and forth, as if someone had stirred it only moments ago.

Percy looked around. No one was present, except an orange cat asleep on the settle, who showed not the slightest interest in waking to see what he was about.

He made his tea, and took a seat beside the cat, unable to understand why he felt as empty as the room inside.

It wasn't until the dinner hour that Percy ended his time alone and rejoined the family gathering. By the time the evening meal was nothing more than a vague memory and a full stomach, it was decided that Maresa should spend the night at Danegeld, so she could share Christmas morning with the family.

Shortly afterwards, Percy became the first to bid everyone good-night, and soon made his way upstairs, where he lit a candle in his room and placed it on the table, next to the letter he had been writing earlier—a letter to the Admiralty office of the Royal Navy.

He was tired, but determined to finish the letter tonight. He had not mentioned his correspondence to anyone, but he knew the time was fast approaching when he would be forced to divulge his plan of taking the first step toward a life on the sea, and away from Maresa.

He unbuttoned his shirt and ran his fingers through his hair, still not fully comprehending why it upset him so to see Maresa and Stephen together. He knew his friendship with her did not offer special privileges, and that he should have spoken of what he felt in his heart long before Stephen returned. But he had not, and now it was too late, for he could never declare himself to her any more than he could ever come between his brother and the woman he loved.

He was about to remove his shirt, when someone tapped on his door. His first thought was that it was Stephen, but he quickly realized that his brother would not knock, for it had always been Stephen's way to walk boldly into his room, unannounced.

Percy picked up the candle from the table and walked to the door. When he opened it, he was not prepared for the shock of surprise he felt at the sight of Maresa standing there. He knew his face must be as white as the candle that was now dripping down over his fingers, yet he said not a word.

"Let me come in, before someone sees me standing here," Maresa said, and stepped into the room.

"Maresa...what are you doing here?"

"Shush! Not so loud! Do you want everyone in the entire household to know I am here?"

"Maresa, you cannot stay here. You must leave, now. Don't you realize what would happen if anyone saw you here?"

"Yes, we would be forced to marry, but not even that will deter me. I cannot sleep, nor can return home until I speak to you."

"What is so important that it cannot wait until morning?"

"I saw you watching me from the window today."

"It's possible. I was not trying to hide it."

"Our friendship does not entitle you to spy on me. I have every right to be with Stephen, if that is what I desire to do. You and I are not sweethearts...we have never come close. You have no hold and no claim on me. Why are you behaving like this? Where has all this jealousy come from?"

"I am not jealous any more than I was spying. I went to the window to rid myself of a nuisance—a fir-bough scraping against the casement. Of course I stared down for a moment when I first saw you, but then I turned away. It was nothing you, yourself, would not have done, had you been in my place."

"I am glad to hear that, because your being angry or spying on me won't change anything, you know. If I decide I want to marry Stephen, it is none of your concern."

Percy's heart iced over. "Marry him, then, or anyone else you like. Do you truly fancy yourself in love with him, or is it the idea of being in love that pleasures you?"

"You are spitefully mean to say such to me."

"Then I apologize."

"I am merely enjoying Stephen's company. I have no designs upon him, and most certainly do not intend to marry him."

"Then there is nothing to worry over, for time will prove everything, even the truth."

Six

But love is such a mystery,
I cannot find it out:
For when I think I'm best resolv'd,
I then am in most doubt.

John Suckling (1564-1616)
English poet and playwright

Apparently Percy knew Maresa better than she knew herself, for three months after they met, Maresa accepted an offer of marriage from Stephen Bronwell.

"Tell me you are happy for me," she said to Percy, as they walked along the jagged cliffs overlooking the sea.

Percy said nothing as he turned away from her to stare out across the water.

"Well, I can see you are angry, when I would have thought you of all people would be happy for me."

"Is my opinion that important to you, or do you want my blessing?"

"Both. Of course I want your blessing, and you know your opinion has always been important to me. How can you not understand that? You are my dearest friend."

"Sometimes I wonder if it is friendship, or someone to agree with you, that you truly seek."

"I care deeply about what you think."

"Only if I agree with you."

"I didn't ask you to agree. I asked if you were happy for me."

"It's the same thing, but if it's an answer to that, then, no, I am not happy for you, because I don't believe you love Stephen, although I do think he has fallen quite hopelessly in love with you. I regret that his heart will be broken in the end."

"You are wrong, Percy. I have no intention of breaking Stephen's heart. Why would I accept his proposal if I didn't love him?"

"Call it immaturity. Call it youthful folly. Call it anything you like. The point being, you are too young to know any more about conscience than you know about love."

"The three-year lead you have over me gives you a tremendous advantage when it comes to wisdom—is that what you are saying?"

"I have lived a bit more than you, Maresa, in spite of only being three years older. I am a man. I have not spent my entire life running wild on the moors, doted on by an indulgent cousin and a sympathetic staff."

She fought back tears.

He was not moved.

"Have it your way, then!" she said in waspish tones. "You know I cannot marry Stephen if it means losing your friendship."

"I daresay it will not come to that. Someone else will catch your fancy, ere long, and Stephen will be as forgotten as yesterday's dinner."

"Oh, you're so cruel! How can you say that?"

He turned toward her and took her in his arms. "Because I know you better than you know yourself. You uncork your imagination and fancy yourself in love, while clamping a lid on common sense. You and Stephen... forging an eternal bond? I don't think so. It is more than a brief, forlorn wish. It is impossible."

"I shall prove you wrong."

"I hope you do."

"I know I love him."

"For the time being."

"I do love him. I knew it the moment he kissed me."

"How did you know?"

"Because I have never felt like that before."

"How many times have you been kissed?"

"Well you know that was my first."

Percy drew her close against him, close enough that he could feel the warmth of her breath against his skin. He bent his head.

"What...what are you going to do?"

"An experiment, nothing more," he said, and to what had to be her complete and utter astonishment, he did something they were both unprepared for.

He kissed her.

"Oh, my," she said when he released her.

"Did you enjoy that?"

"Why do you have to ask when you know the answer already?"

"Are you certain it's my brother you love, or is it a temporary infatuation?"

"That wasn't very kind of you."

"No, not kind, but necessary."

He did not give her any more time to think upon it, when he took her hand. "Come, we need to go back. It will be dark soon and your diligent cousin will be after my hide if I keep you out overlong."

It was only a few weeks later when Maresa sent Harold, her father's groom, to Danegeld with an urgent message for Percy to meet her at the crossroads.

She was waiting for him, with her black Highland pony tied to the road marker, when he rode up.

"What's amiss?" he asked, and dismounted.

Maresa was sitting on a rock, resting her chin in the upturned palms of her hands. She released a dejected sigh. "Everything! Oh, Percy, I am so miserable, I don't know what to do. I need your help."

"Trouble brewing, and all my brother's doing. Is that it?"

"You were right," she said with utmost despondency.

"A rare admission. We are speaking of Stephen, I gather?"

"Yes. I cannot marry him."

Percy shook his head, tied his horse and sat down next to her. "Have you told him?"

"No, I was hoping you would do that for me."

"You know I would do almost anything for you, Maresa, but breaking your engagement to my brother is not one of them. You accepted his proposal. You must explain to him why you must cry off."

"How can I do that?" She began to wring her hands. "Truly, I don't think I shall be able to tell him such. I don't want to hurt his feelings."

"Strange that his feelings never entered it until now."

She ignored that, preferring to concentrate on her own feelings. "It's so humiliating. How can I ever face your parents?"

"I'm sure the humiliation will pass. As for my parents, they will not hold a broken engagement against you, for that is preferable to a lifetime of misery with their son."

"I was so certain," she said. "I don't know how I could fall out of love so quickly."

"Unless you were never in love in the first place."

"But, I was so certain." She turned her face toward his. "Percy, couldn't you simply say—"

"No, Maresa. This is something you must do yourself and the sooner the better."

"Will you at least come to Danegeld with me?"

"No, I think this is one journey you should make alone."

She jumped to her feet and walked to her horse. "You are spitefully mean, Percival Livingston Bronwell, and I shall never forgive you for this for as long as I live."

Stephen's was the first heart Maresa broke, but it wasn't the last.

Seven

Friendship is Love without his wings!

Lord Byron (1788-1824)
English poet
L'Amiti est L'Amour Sans Ailes

After Maresa broke her engagement with Stephen, she told Cousin Augusta that people were talking about her, and calling her an idiot.

Always the comforter, her cousin replied, "Well, let them talk. We both know you're not the average run-of-the-mill idiot."

When Maresa wanted to write a letter to her aunt and uncle in Italy to invite them to Hampton Hall for a visit, she asked her cousin what she thought her father would say.

"Mostly adjectives," was her reply.

"You don't think he would approve?"

"No, I am quite certain he would not."

"Would you object to their coming here?"

"I don't think it would be a good idea to circumvent your father's wishes."

It was some time later that her cousin informed Maresa that she had reconsidered. "Since your father never comes to Hampton Manor, I don't suppose it would hurt anything if your aunt and uncle were invited, but you must bear in mind the fact that the war is still going on. I know that is difficult for you to comprehend living here, in the North of Yorkshire, but until Napoleon is stopped, travel between Italy and England is nigh impossible. And do not forget that the letter might not reach its destination. But, write your letter if it pleases you, and invite them to visit, with my blessings."

"I suppose it was a foolish idea," Maresa said, but later that night, after thinking back over it, she wrote the letter anyway.

For a time after she ended her engagement to Stephen, Maresa felt her heart was truly broken—not because of Stephen, but because she was certain she had lost, for all time, Percy's friendship.

Twice, when she sent word to Danegeld that she wanted to see him, she received a reply that Master Percival was away on business with his father.

For as long as she had known Percy, she could never recall a time when he went out of town on business with his father. Consequently, she began to doubt that was the truth. Yet it was not like the Percy she knew, to hide behind a lie.

But, what else could it be, for Maresa could think of no other reason for his refusal to answer even a note.

It never occurred to her that Percy's absence from Danegeld might have been the truth, any more than it would ever occur to her that he had a life and future that did not include her.

Hurt and disappointed at his rejection, she swore she would hide her feelings, and send no more messages to Danegeld Hall. Whatever the reason for his withdrawal, she would never let him know how deeply it affected her.

And with a head held so lofty it threatened to touch the stars, she vowed he was no longer her friend, as if standing on her dignity would serve to elevate her.

Her newfound dignity was all but forgotten a week later, when Lucy ran breathlessly into the garden where Maresa was planting daffodil bulbs and said, "Mr. Bronwell is here, milady."

"Mr. Bronwell?"

Lucy tried to hide a smile as she dipped in an exaggerated curtsy. "I believe that would be Mr. Percival Bronwell," she said.

Maresa almost ran over Lucy to get inside. So much for lofty pride!

She rushed down the hallway and stopped short of the door, overcome suddenly with embarrassment for acting so eager, and for accusing him so shamelessly in her mind. Then fear entered in, and her heart plummeted to lie silent and cold in her chest.

Why is Percy here now, she wondered, after ignoring her all this time? Has he come to tell her it is time to break the bond of their friendship, or that he simply wanted to ease himself out of it?

Stop this foolish self-doubt, she thought, mentally chiding herself. Think of the person Percy is, and how long you have known him. He would never stoop to such and you know it.

With relaxed ease, she walked into the

room, totally unprepared for what she would find.

Inside her father's library, Percy awaited her. Oh, my Lord! she thought. Percy, what have you done?

She observed him with silent regard, while she searched for a word to describe him and the mood that held him fast. She settled on *pensive,* although she was not completely satisfied with that choice. Was there a better one she could have selected? *Serious? Contemplative? Thoughtful?*

Preoccupied, perhaps?

She decided one word would be inadequate to describe his present disposition, for he appeared calm and careful, slow and deliberate, as he gave a matter serious regard. And over all clung a sweet mist of melancholy.

She thought immediately of the poet Byron.

Something inside her chest gave a sharp twist, and she believed for an instant that she was never closer to him, or held him more dear, than at this very moment. It was such a curiously atypical sensation, and quite unlike any she had ever felt heretofore, that she allowed it to pass without further consideration, so she might focus her attention on the way his finger moved slowly over the globe that stood beside him, as if he were tracing some imaginary route.

With an expression of obvious wonderment, all she could do was stare mutely, for he was wonderfully handsome and splendidly dressed in a blue naval tailcoat, lined with white silk and adorned with gold buttons. Beneath his coat, his waistcoat of white nankeen was spotless, as were the white breeches and white stockings.

Tucked beneath his left arm was a three-cornered hat.

Percy, with his regal height and slender build, was someone she had always considered to be very good-looking. His brown hair, streaked with gold, and his green eyes did nothing but add to his attractiveness. But now, in his uniform, she could only call him staggering, and she would wager he would have to step over women from now on, so eager they would be to throw themselves at his feet.

Truly, at this moment she was so completely astonished at her own gushy thoughts, that she could only say, "Oh, my goodness, gracious and saints above!"

"I hope that was an approval." He gave the globe a spin and came to stand before her. "Did you miss me?"

Green eyes met blue, and at that moment it struck her that she was staring stupidly, not at Percy, but a lieutenant in the Royal Navy. "Oh, my Lord, Percy, what have you done?" she cried, and forgot all her previous intentions of never speaking to him again.

As quickly as lightning strikes, she threw herself against him, and hugged him so ferociously, he had to pry her arms from around his neck.

"I don't want you to fight Napoleon. Truly I don't."

"All right, I won't."

"You promise?"

"I don't know why I can't promise such. As far as I know, Napoleon is a soldier and not a seaman, so the chance of our meeting is, at best, remote." His smile chased away the air of melancholy, and he held up his hand as if he were swearing. "I promise I shall never fight Napoleon. His navy, perhaps, but never the Little Emperor himself."

"Oh! Do be serious," she said, knowing she sounded too fretful.

He laughed and held her at arm's distance so he could look at her squarely. "Here, now! I thought you'd be glad to see me."

"I am more than glad," she said, aware that she sounded sickeningly petulant, but the deed was done, and she went on. "I truly thought you had abandoned me."

"As if I could ever forget you. You look on the verge of tears. What's amiss?"

"I thought you hated me, that you never wanted to see me again. How could you be so mean?"

"Mean? Here now, confusing my actions with your thoughts. Didn't anyone tell you I went to London with my father to get my commission?"

"I was only told that you were away on business with him."

"And you see the result." He took a bow. "Lieutenant Percival Bronwell, of the Royal Navy, at your service."

Her heart began to pound. "You will be leaving soon."

"Not for two weeks, then I'll be sailing on the HMS *Beatrix*."

"Oh, Percy," she said, and hugged him again. "Whatever shall I do without you?"

"Grow up?" His grin was wide and boyish—the kind of smile that took her back to their earliest years together, and made her wish with all her heart that things could be, once again, the way they had been back then—easy and uncomplicated.

Why, she wondered, do feelings always have to get in the way?

With a half smile and a tender expression in his eyes, he gazed at her upturned face and kissed her lips softly.

It was not the kiss of a friend, but neither was it the kiss of a lover. It was a kiss that lingered somewhere in between, like a question that waited to be answered.

Maresa dipped her head shyly.

"What's this? Surely not shyness?" he asked, and lifted her chin, as if needing to see the expression on her face and the feeling, always so expressive, in her eyes.

She thought for a moment he would say something else. Instead, he continued to look into her eyes, studying her face before his hand trailed downward, over the curve of her throat.

She felt both a rush of feeling and a blush of confusion as color settled across her flushed face.

"Maresa..."

She studied the sharp contours of his face,

the slant of cheekbone, the strong jaw. She always thought him a fine-looking boy.

When had he become a man?

How was it that she had continued to see him as a boy for so long, when it was so obvious to her now that he had been a man for some time? Why, she wondered was the mind so slow to absorb what the eyes had so long ago seen?

The concept of Percy as a man, and the uniform, stood between them—a barrier that prevented him from being the idol of her childhood. She felt a mixture of pride at the man he had become, and disappointment at the friend of her youth she felt was now hopelessly gone. It was as if a piece of something deep within had been ripped out. She could almost feel a part of her flowing outward, from the gaping hole that was left.

"Oh, Percy, why? Why did you have to do this?"

"You knew it was what I wanted to do. It should come as no surprise. I expected you, of all people, to be happy for me."

"How can I be happy at the very thing that will take you away from me and break my heart because of it?"

He grinned and put out a hand to ruffle her hair. "Such a beautiful woman, yet still so inexperienced. How can you doubt my affections? Don't you know I will always be with you?"

She took a step back and looked him over critically. "Not for long, looking the way you do."

"Do you mean what I think you mean?"

"Forget it. It's nothing," she said. "Absolutely nothing, and that is why it's so heartbreaking."

"Maresa, you are speaking in riddles. What are you talking about?"

"You, Percy! You're enough to set any woman's heart atwitter. I daresay you will be married within half a year's time, and I will be as lost as this morning's sunrise."

His mood turned serious. "Would that bother you?"

She focused on one of his shiny brass buttons, against the smooth fabric of his finely cut coat. The room was uncomfortably warm, in spite of the low-cut linen gown she was wearing. When she stole a glance upward, he was close enough that she could see the individual lashes of his eyes, the pores of his skin. She could smell the newness of the fabric of his clothes and the scent she had known for some time, so familiar to her that it identified only him. Her head began to spin. She wanted to lie down. She wanted...

Her breath caught. She shook her head and the moment that might have connected them, passed.

"You did not answer my question. Would it bother you?"

"Yes, you know it would! Faith, can you not believe I would not hesitate to scratch out the eyes of any woman who dared to take you away from me?"

He seemed amused, and it struck her it was because he did not want to reveal what he truly felt. If he had remained silent, she might

77

have thought along this line a bit longer, but he erased the memory of it when he said, "My mother always said, 'you could put a uniform on a broomstick, and a woman would flirt with it.' "

For someone who was never at a loss for words, Maresa did not understand why she suddenly could not speak.

Was it because she was leaving her youth behind? Did becoming an adult mean nothing was as simple as it was before?

Everything was so different, and complicated, she was not certain she even wanted to grow up.

She decided that if this was what growing up was all about, she would just as soon never have another birthday. So far, about the only advantage to reaching adulthood she had seen was that her cousin no longer demanded she eat everything on her plate.

Long after he returned home, Percy continued to think about Maresa's reaction. He was aware the uniform had come between them, and because of that he made a special point to see her every day, but by the time the end of his two weeks came, he was not certain anything had changed between them.

He understood the change from Percy to Lieutenant Bronwell was a difficult one for her. Yet something had altered between them; something besides the uniform, and although he had waited for years to see a change between them, this was not what he meant or wanted.

He wanted her to see him for the man he was, not simply as her friend. The problem was, he decided, that he was a man, with a man's wants, needs and desires, while Maresa... Well, she looked every inch a woman, but her thinking had not kept up with the rest of her.

In some ways, he found that part of her charm, but in other ways, it went beyond exasperating.

He found himself thinking of the past winter, and the snow that had brought such intense quiet, and of the almost exaggerated sense of solitude that came with it. That is how he felt inside, cold and intensely quiet, with a sense of solitude he had never felt before. He wondered how it was that the impressions of winter could so completely describe the way he perceived himself—small beneath a threatening sky, and surrounded everywhere by the white silence of nothing but space.

Perhaps this time at sea, away from her, would be good for them both, and he began to wonder then, if he could be the cause of her slow maturing ways.

Was she too dependent upon him?

He looked at his watch and saw it was time to dress and go after her, for he had promised to take Maresa on a picnic on his last day in Yorkshire.

Eight

Thy friendship oft has made my heart to
    ache:
Do be my enemy for friendship's sake.

William Blake (1757-1824)
English poet, painter, engraver

Maresa sat silently beside Percy in the carriage as they drove across the moors toward Whitby, where the town and harbor met in a ravine at the mouth of the River Esk.

They chose a place on a cliff top, near a ruined abbey, where they could look down upon the quaint streets and narrow alleys that wound their way down to the busy quayside.

She remembered once, long ago, when they were no more than children, when they had come here, and they had counted the number of steps from the streets below, up to the parish Church of St. Mary, and the number was 199.

Her mind snagged on that for a moment, and she found herself wondering why they didn't go ahead and add one more step to make it an even 200.

"There's a bug on your dress."

She glanced down at the pale-blue linen skirt, and gave the bug a thump. It landed in the plate of biscuits. She forced a smile and looked at him, and the smile he returned was equally forced.

She decided to stop forcing anything further, for it was too much an effort for such a poor result. Her head had begun to ache, so she sat stiff and erect on a blanket across from him during the remainder of their meal.

She simply did not feel very hungry or talkative today, either of which was quite unusual for her. But then, it wasn't every day that Percy was leaving to embark upon a new life and a future that did not include her, while she was left to continue on, to try to make something of a life that she feared would never be quite the same without him in it.

He was leaving and she could not bear to think what it would come to mean in the days ahead.

She had barely eaten anything, or as he said, she "picked at her food," yet she was surprised when he spoke and she realized the meal was not only over, but that he had packed everything neatly away in the basket.

"I'm sorry, my mind was wandering. What did you say?"

"Nothing important." Like her, he fell into silent regard for a while, before he stood and held out his hand and said, "Come, walk with me."

They walked along the cliffs toward the old abbey, and climbed among the ruins, as they had when they were children.

"Do you remember the time we were caught in that terrible storm and had to take shelter in one of the shops in town?" she asked.

"Yes, and I had no coin to purchase anything,

and the shopkeeper was worried that we were in there to pilfer something."

She gave a shiver and rubbed her arms.

"Are you cold?"

"No, I was only remembering something. You know, to this day, I don't think I have ever been so cold, or so wet as I was then."

He did not smile, but the corners of his mouth did threaten to. "Do you recall that day when we found that small bronze cross?" he asked.

"Yes, we buried it near the altar, because we thought it should remain here."

"Do you think we could find it again?"

"Oh, let's do try," she said, and they walked toward the place where the altar would have been.

"It was here," they said in unison, but each of them pointed to a different place.

"Uh-oh," Maresa said, "it seems our memories fail us."

"Or at least one of our memories does."

"I am sure you are right," she said, "so let us dig where you thought it was."

Percy took out a knife and scraped away the dirt in the place he had indicated, but the cross was not there.

"I lose. Let's try your spot," he said, and they moved to the other side, and the place she had chosen.

The cross was not where Maresa remembered, either.

Percy scraped away the dirt in several more places near the place where each of them

82

remembered burying the old bronze cross, but they never found it.

"Well, I guess it is lost for all time," she said. "As lost as our childhood."

"Yes, I suppose it is. There are some things you cannot return to, no matter how hard you try."

She nodded. "A lot like life, I think."

"Do you have regrets? Are there times or places you would like to go back to?"

"Only the mistakes."

"The mistakes? Why? So you could make them all over again?"

"No, so I wouldn't make them in the first place."

"No mistakes, no discoveries. It is better not to go back, I think."

They walked back to the carriage, and after helping her into the seat, Percy sat beside her and took up the reins. With a slap, he started the horses toward home. They rode along without speaking for almost an hour, each of them preoccupied by their own thoughts, and she wondered if the painful lull in conversation was as uncomfortable for him as it was for her.

At last, feeling on the verge of melancholy, and knowing she did not want to succumb to it, she forced herself to ask, "Why aren't you wearing your uniform today?"

"I decided this would be my last official day in civilian clothes. Starting tomorrow, I'll be wearing my uniform every day."

"Yes, I suppose that is one of the requirements, now that you are a lieutenant," she said.

He stopped at the edge of a rise to look out over the purple moors and rolling hills of their home. "Let's stretch our legs a bit," he said, and came around to help her down.

He put his hands to her waist and lifted her into the air. His hands slid upward, until his thumbs caught at the swell of her breasts. Her feet touched the ground, but he did not release her. He leaned his forehead against hers and whispered her name. "Maresa, Maresa... how difficult it is to leave you."

Her head flopped against his chest like a rag doll. "I think it is more difficult to be left, than to leave."

"Not true," he said, "if you only knew..." He stopped himself and did not finish his sentence.

She tilted her head back. "If I only knew what?"

"Nothing."

"What? I want to know."

"It is gone. The sentiment has escaped me," he said, but she had a feeling that was not quite true.

There was such a sense of space and solitude here, where ridges and hills of purple heather moorland extended as far as the eye could see. She knew the deep secret valleys that cut across the plateau as well as she knew the streets in the red-roofed village, lined with white cottages. And now that it was spring, everywhere the valleys were alive with the bright-yellow of daffodils.

He gathered a few and handed them to her. "Yellow as lemons, and they will last about as long."

"I shall press one in my journal. A memory to hold on to, so..."

She turned away and looked out over the valley, and never finished her sentence.

He came to stand behind her with his hands on her shoulders. "What is wrong? Are you worried about anything? Has something happened? Have you received any bad news from your father? Do you feel well? Have you affianced yourself again?"

She sighed deeply. How could she tell him she was feeling so miserably downhearted— a vague longing, a separation from reality, and a tendency to be the cynic? In short, her insides were a jumble. "No, nothing like that," she said, "although I do wonder sometimes if I will ever see him again."

"Your father?"

"Yes. He has been absent from my life these many years, and not by accident, as you well know. Do you suppose he will ever send for me, or put in an appearance at Hampton Manor, or will I live out my days here, in exile on the moors?"

"There are worst places," he said, speaking in a way that said he was trying to lighten her mood. "You could be in Liverpool."

"Ugh, you know how much I hate liver, so how could you even mention a place like Liverpool?"

"Because I always liked the way you wrin-

85

kled up your nose whenever you heard the word." He released her and stepped forward to stand beside her.

Hands thrust deep into his pockets, he gazed out over the moors, much in the same manner she was doing.

"Here we stand, like two matching obelisks," she said, "marking the entrance to the valley."

"You still haven't told me what is wrong. It will make leaving much more difficult if I am worried about you."

She did not want him to leave at all, but it would not do to send him off in a worried state. He was going to war. He would need his wits about him in the coming months at sea. She did not want the weight of that responsibility hanging over her head. "I would tell you if I knew. Cousin Augusta says it is growing pains. Perhaps she is right."

"Growing pains? I don't know if I agree with her. Do you?"

She shrugged. "I suppose it is as good an explanation as any," she said, then changed her mind. "No, it isn't something I agree with. Not really, for it isn't pain I feel but confusion. I feel so lost, Percy, as if I no longer know who I am, or what I want from life. I miss the way things were when I was younger, without a care or worry, but I have no desire to go back there. I am not, as yet, comfortable with my role as a woman, and I worry about what lies ahead. Will I make the right choices, or will I forever be making the same mistakes? I feel as if I'm standing at a crossroads and I haven't a clue as to which direction I should go. I can't stay where I am, but I'm terrified of going in the wrong direction. Was growing up this difficult for you?"

He threw back his head with a shout of laughter. "Well, thank you for the compliment, but tell me, who it is that says I've grown up?"

"You were born grown, for I have never seen any of the anxiety in you that I have felt."

"That only means I do a supremely better job of hiding it. You do love to vocalize your misery, I must admit."

She gave him the point of her elbow. "Always the teaser! You know what I mean."

"Yes, I know, and I think everyone experiences, at one time or the other, precisely what you are going through right now. In the end, we all arrive at the same destination, but we take different routes."

"If that is the case, I must be going to France, via South America."

He chuckled and hugged her to his side. "There will come a time when we look upon this day with fondness."

"I look upon it with fondness now." She turned toward him. "Do you think we shall always be friends?"

"Of course, unless you decide otherwise."

"Even when we are married?"

"To each other?"

She gave him a shove. "No, silly, we are best friends. That, I think, is even better than being husband and wife. How could we marry?"

"The same way other people marry, I suppose. Get engaged for a time, and then stand at the altar, etcetera, etcetera...."

She had a vision of them married—man and wife living on a tropical isle with sunsets behind palm trees and a cozy garden beyond the kitchen door—all painted in the pale hues of illusion, for that is all it would ever be. Why, she wondered, did everything seen in the mind and in the future, become poetry set to music?

A breeze rippled about her, loosening a skein of hair and draping it across her face to tangle in her lashes. She reached up to push it away, but Percy caught her hand.

"Here, let me," he said. "This may be the last time for several months that I will be able to do such as this."

"Do not remind me, please."

"Sorry."

"Are you not afraid of the war?"

He tucked the hair back in place. "No, things are relatively quiet right now. The blockade is working."

"With Napoleon still hating the British as he does, they will never remain quiet for long. I cannot help being frightened. I don't want you wounded, or..."

When he saw she had difficulty finishing the words, he took her arm and they began walking back to the carriage. "Nothing will happen to me, and I'll be back before you know it."

"I know, and I look forward to it already.

You know, I simply cannot imagine being here with you gone. It seems so strange. What will I do?"

"Get engaged again, more than likely."

"You will notice I am ignoring that ridiculous comment," she said, and hastily changed the subject. "Will you write to me?"

"As often as I can."

"I shall write you every day."

"At least until you get yourself affianced again."

It was a teasing remark that carried a lot of weight, and hit uncomfortably close to the mark, but it had never been her way to look too closely at her own shortcomings, and today was no different. "Will you stop? You are being unkind to tease me so, especially when I don't think I will ever fall in love again."

Percy's response was a laugh born of doubt, while he handed her into the carriage.

On the way home, Maresa was her old self, animated, full of talk and laughter, stricken by attacks of silence only when she succumbed to bouts of reminiscence.

Once they reached Hampton Manor, he stayed long enough to play two games of chess. It was a noisy game, with much laughter and teasing, but then it was her time of triumph, for Maresa won the first game.

A more somber mood settled over the room as the second game progressed, and much of her cheerfulness and playful mood did not last, and by the time Percy declared he had bested her, it was completely gone. He began to put the chess pieces away, and when they were almost finished, he stood to go.

"Wait a moment," she said, putting the last chess piece away. "I will walk to the carriage with you."

When the carriage was brought around, he kissed her lightly on the cheek.

She looked at him crossly. "Is that all the kiss I get?"

"You would have gotten more, if you'd let me win both games," he said.

"Or if you had let me win both."

"No, it's much better the way it was," he said.

"Yes, one game for you, and one game for me. We are perfectly matched."

"In everything but love," he said, and kissed the back of her hand, which sent ripples down her spine.

Nine

Love is a mousetrap. You go in when
    you wish,
but you don't come out when you like.

Spanish proverb

Upon his return to Yorkshire a few months later, Percy learned Maresa had affianced herself again. According to gossip, it was to Squire Threadgill's son, Teddy.

When he was able to separate himself from his family for a while, he paid Maresa a call at Hampton Manor.

When he first saw her, she seemed to go weak with relief, and he wondered if it had anything to do with her most recent engagement.

She was quick to fill him in on the details, even quicker to say, "I did not tell him I would marry him. I said I would think about it. The next thing I knew, he was telling everyone we were engaged. I don't love Teddy. And he acted abominably toward me when I was a child. Always chasing me. Calling me names after church. How can I marry him?"

"I wondered about that the moment I heard you were to marry him."

Maresa dismissed that with a frown. "Well, what's done is done. Oh, Percy, I seem to be in another mess. I don't know how to get out of this entanglement."

"Tell him the truth, like you did Stephen."

"Teddy is such a sweet person, I hate to hurt him."

"You have to hurt him sometime. Better now than later."

"Everyone will think I am breaking another engagement. No one will believe Teddy jumped to conclusions."

"What do you care what they think? Go to Teddy and explain what happened, how it was nothing more than a misunderstanding."

"Would you..."

"No."

"But..."

"I told you before, Maresa, I'm not going to involve myself in any of your entanglements. I wouldn't do it with Stephen."

"Stephen was your brother. This is different. It isn't like you are best friends with Teddy."

"No. I won't do it now. I won't do it, ever."

"You are horribly mean and unfeeling."

"Well, I am sorry you feel that way. Perhaps, in time, you will change your mind about it."

"I seriously doubt I will ever feel differently."

When Percy returned to Yorkshire two months later, the rumor was that Maresa would soon be engaged again. This time, she was the darling of Baronet, Sir Pettigrew Hollifield's son, Braxton, whom she met at the wedding of the Earl of Penworthy's daughter, Regina, only a few months before.

"I suppose another engagement is forthcoming," Percy said.

"As a matter of fact, it is not, and I think you are quite unkind to insinuate I affiance myself to every man who comes along."

"I have been taught to expect nothing else."

"You are mistaken this time."

"I hope so."

"I do have a problem, though."

"Which is?"

"Braxton is a very nice person, and I know he is overly fond of me."

"Of course he is. I went to school with him, remember."

"Yes, I had forgotten."

"So what is the problem?"

"I cannot see myself married to him, so I think it best to tell him so."

"Then tell him soon, before he grows more fond of you and asks you to marry him."

"I have tried, but each time, I weaken."

"You aren't going to ask me to become involved in this, are you?"

"You wouldn't have to involve yourself. You could casually mention to Braxton that I am far too young to marry."

"You could mention it to him as well as I."

"He will be terribly hurt if I tell him such."

"He will get over it." He saw the pleading look in her eye. "No, don't ask. I won't involve myself with Braxton, or any of the others that follow. I have not changed my mind in this."

"What can I do?"

"Try growing up. Try telling him the truth. Sooner or later, you are going to either marry, or grow sick and tired of ending entanglements and engagements."

"The way people are talking, I may not have the opportunity to engage myself again. My reputation, I fear, is in shambles."

"Yes, I have heard, but cheer up. People tend to forget when you've got a pretty face."

Every time Percy looked at her the way he was looking at her now, she knew he saw nothing more than a bundle of adolescent longing and confusion, who dreamed of a great romance. He probably would never understand why it was so difficult for her to be cognizant of the fact that dreaming about romance was easier than making it a reality, any more than she could understand that deep inside, she needed someone to love, and someone to love her in return.

Her goal to be loved and married was something exclusive of her goal to love and be loved deeply, by the man she would marry—a man who could not choose to let her die.

To her, marriage had to be perfect, and she saw the attainment of perfection as a way to justify her mother's sacrifice. She feared failure, and consequently, everything she did was to the exclusion of everything else. When things did not go her way she tried harder.

Yet, in the back of her mind, there was always that afternoon, when Percy kissed her.

Sometimes she would close her eyes and lay her fingers to her lips, and recall what he said that day, when she said they were so perfectly matched.

"In everything but love."

Ten

Had sighed to many, though he loved but
    one.

> Lord Byron (1788-1824)
> English poet

A letter from Aunt Gisella arrived two days after Percy's departure.

A letter! A letter!

Her heart cried out with joy! It filled her with such anticipation that she took the letter and tucked it under her sleeve, to avoid having to share it right away.

A letter such as this screamed to be read in solitude, so she walked outside to the garden and sat upon a stone bench behind the fountain. She sat there for a few minutes, staring down at the fabric of her blue dress, while she smoothed the skirts and flicked a leaf that had settled in her lap.

She glanced at the lace trim of her cuff, well aware that the letter was still tucked safely away.

She knew she should stop being so silly about the contents of the letter, and that she should simply read it. But she could not help asking herself, what if it is a disappointment, or so full of joy that I shall be sad I no longer have the reading of it to look forward to?

At last, she decided there were no assurances of anything in life, and that she might as well read the letter, good news or not.

She pulled the envelope from beneath her lace-trimmed sleeve, and read the name and address on the envelope one last time, before she tore it open and extracted the letter.

Dearest Maresa,

With the situation with Napoleon being as it is, I do not know if this letter will reach you, but I have prayed to St. George, the patron saint of England, that it would arrive safely and without too long a delay.

Your Uncle Tito and I were delighted to receive your invitation. There is nothing we would like better than to see you. However, after much discussion, Tito decided we should not come for several reasons. First, we could not, in all conscience, go against your father's wishes, and then there is the war to consider.

There has been much fighting in the various provinces of late, with the villagers arming themselves to fight any small groups of French soldiers they encounter. The resistance here is strong, and grows stronger every day. It is simply too dangerous to consider traveling at this time.

I have prayed for years to the Blessed Virgin that this horrible occupation of my beloved Tuscany will end. I have not given up hope, but for now, our paying a visit to Hampton Manor, or your coming to Tuscany must wait.

Do not lose hope. I know there is a

time in our future when we will be together. In the meantime, we must be patient.

Tito and I send you all of our love, and your cousin Serena said to tell you her English is coming along to the point where she will pen a letter to you soon.

With loving affection,
Aunt Gisella and Uncle Tito

Percy's absence only added to her disappointment over the letter she received. It seemed to her that everyone she cared about continued to be at arm's length.

Why must I always be alone, she wondered?

Maresa had difficulty falling asleep that night, for her mind was crammed with thoughts of Percy, which was a rather common affliction. She feared for his safety, she worried about what might happen to him, and what all that could mean if he were hurt. Dear solid, dependable and constant Percy, the ballast to her flighty nature. What will I do without you?

She thought of what he would answer to that question: "Get engaged again, more than likely."

She wiggled deeper into the soft bed as she remembered his words. He didn't know her as well as he thought. She wasn't interested in being married.

Not in the least.

Upon Percy's next return to Yorkshire, it was Olympia who broke the news to him about Maresa.

"She has been engaged to Lord Brimley's son, Edward, for two months now," she said, and then cautioned him. "Don't mention it in any of your letters to Stephen," Olympia advised. "His heart is still tender and easily pained at the sound of her name."

"I won't, of course."

"Do you think she will carry this one through, or will it go as the others?"

"Who is to say, but judging from past experience, I would be so inclined to say she will probably break this one as well."

"Poor dear, she does not know what she is looking for."

"No, she doesn't, and worse yet, she is not aware of it. Perhaps I will ride over and pay her a visit after a while."

"I know she would welcome the opportunity to see you, and perhaps you could give her a little advice while you are at it."

"As if she ever listens to me."

When Percy rode over to Hampton Manor later that afternoon, Maresa told him about her engagement to Edward, which sounded remarkably like the others, to Percy's way of thinking.

"Haven't we already been here? Why did you accept his proposal if you didn't love him?"

"I thought I loved him at the time," she said, with a hint of defensiveness in her tone. "It isn't like I set out to break hearts intentionally."

"Why you do it isn't important. It's the fact that you do."

"Oh, I don't know what to do. People are talking about me like I enjoy collecting engagements."

"They will forget, in time."

"I daresay my father won't forget, if he should ever catch wind of this."

"And if he does? What then?"

"My father and I have never gotten along as you well know. Each missive the mail hack brings raises my temper to the exploding point. If he were here, I am certain we would be locked in constant battle."

"It's probably good you don't fight then, for it is said that you must not fight too often with one enemy, or you will teach him all your art of war."

"Spoken like a true military man."

"Appropriate, since it was Napoleon who said it."

"Wasted advice, I fear, for my father cares not enough to wager even a small battle with me. He would have to put in an appearance to do that, and I am someone he does not deem worthy of an appearance."

"You know the real reason he shuns you."

"Oh, yes, I know, and it is such a comfort to understand why you are hated."

It pained him to see Maresa like this. If given the choice, he would prefer the other Maresa, who was a bundle of longing and confusion who dreamed of a great romance.

That night, he discussed it with his mother.

"I suspect she always carries in the back of her mind the idea that there is someone out there waiting for her, if she could only find him. So she is continually searching until she finds someone she thinks is the one."

"And then she never allows them to stay around long enough to find out if they are the one or not," Percy said.

Deep in thought, Olympia drummed her fingers on the table. "Oh, I don't think that is the problem at all. I have a suspicion that her idea of marriage is perfection. It must be faultless."

Percy mulled that over. "Hmmm. Perhaps you're right. It would be like her...to see faultless perfection as a way to justify the sacrifice of her mother."

"Of course. She abhors disappointment, and consequently, everything she does is to the exclusion of everything else. If I've learned anything about her over the years, it's when things don't go Maresa's way she simply tries again, and harder."

Percy shook his head. "She is doomed for failure and doesn't realize it."

"Alas, I fear you are right. It is such a pity, for she is so lovely, and deserves far more than that."

"So lovely, and so innocent in the ways of the world."

Olympia smiled, her affection for Maresa obvious. "And prone to flightiness in everything...save her devotion to you, that is."

"Speaking of devotion, that will be put to the test again in two weeks."

"When it comes time for you to leave?"

Percy nodded.

"She has never taken separation lightly. A person, who is utterly devoted, expects selfless affection and dedication. Yet, I cannot fault her in that. Her life has been filled with loved ones held separate from her. Her tenacity to hold on to what little she has is admirable, although misguided at times."

"My being gone is something she will have to accustom herself to."

"And you, Percy?"

"Me? What do you mean, Mother?"

"Maresa has been in love numerous times, while you have only your affection for her."

"I would say I haven't met the right woman."

"Or you are hopelessly in love with the wrong one."

"Is it that obvious?"

"To me, it is, although I have never heard anyone else speak of it."

"Why do you think Maresa is the wrong one for me?"

"Because she does not love you in return. Adore her as I do, you are my son. Your happiness is of the utmost importance to me. I want to see you happily married. I want to bounce your children on my knee. I don't want to see you waste your life waiting on someone who will never reciprocate your feelings."

"There is always a chance she will change."

"And an equal chance that she will not. What then? Shall you grow a long, white beard in the meantime?"

He grinned. "No. When I grow tired of waiting, I shall marry someone else."

"I only hope it happens before your eight-ieth birthday."

"I shan't wait forever, Mother."

"I am relieved to hear that." Olympia sighed. "Two weeks! That is such a short time for you to be here. I wish it were longer."

"Napoleon calls and duty awaits."

"What news of Napoleon?"

"We have word that he intends to launch a massive invasion of Russia. It is rumored he intends to take the French army all the way to Moscow."

Olympia could not hide her agitation from Percy, although he knew she did try.

"You are worried about Max," he said. "When was he home last?"

"Not long after you left, but he only had a few days. He always seems to be in the worst part of the fighting."

"He hasn't changed, then, for Max always liked to be in the middle of things."

"Yes, he still does. He was never as sensible as you or Stephen, and far too prone to taking risks."

"I am sure he has outgrown that now."

"I pray he has."

Percy did not have the opportunity to speak with Maresa after all, for he was called back to his ship the next day.

When he arrived back at the *Beatrix,* he learned they had orders to sail into the Mediterranean, under the command of Lord Cecil Harrington.

The morning of their departure, Lieutenant Bronwell walked the quarterdeck, dodging the seamen darting about as they readied the ship for sea. If this war lasted much longer, he wasn't certain how England would fare. More and more, the Navy had to rely upon untrained and inexperienced seamen, or the men kidnapped and forced to serve by impressments, and most of them were Americans and did not have England's best interest at heart.

He watched while the supplies were loaded and he found he was quite anxious to put out to sea again, where he could settle into the solitude of ship life, and leave his other worries back on land. Even now, the thought of leaving his worries about Maresa behind held a certain amount of appeal.

He checked the wind, which began to pick up, and he hoped it would continue, so there would be enough to fill the sails and take them out to sea.

He walked past the sentry, who stepped aside, as he entered his sleeping cabin on the half deck. It was a small cabin, made smaller by the stash of ship supplies stored there.

Percy removed his tricorn and placed it on the table, then hung his coat on the back of the chair. He picked up the oiled pouch lying on the table and pulled out the documents that contained his assignment to the Inshore Squadron, Western Mediterranean.

They were to sail with a convoy of transports and warships to the coast of Spain.

After reading his orders, he put them away, and returned topside, as they set sail.

A week passed and now they were nearing their destination, when Percy went belowdeck and took a short nap. Later, when it came time for his duty, he went on deck and took over the watch from Lieutenant Sheridan.

Shortly after his watch began, he noticed the flagship had begun to shorten sail, so Percy gave the order to do likewise.

"Bring in the royals," he said, and took up the glass to have a look at the flagship, *Windsor Castle*. She was the lead ship of the convoy, and the farthest to port, about two miles away.

"Land off the larboard beam," Mr. Whatley called out, and Percy shifted his glass in that direction, to gaze out over the starboard quarter, and saw the blue-gray hump of land. They were approaching the Strait of Gibraltar, and once through it, they would be sailing the Mediterranean to the Spanish port of Malaga.

An hour after they dropped anchor, Percy was about to return to his quarters, when he saw the ship's captain approach.

"Lieutenant Bronwell, will you join me ashore this evening?" asked Captain Pennebaker. "They are sending a boat for me at half past six. Can you be ready by then?"

Percy nodded. "With pleasure, Captain."

"We will be dining with the Conte López de Davalillo."

At the striking of six bells, Percy was in his quarters preparing to dress.

Once he had everything laid out on his cot, he surveyed the pile of clothing, amazed that he would find a place on his body to put everything. The heavy white stockings went on first, then the fine linen shirt, white kerseymere breeches, a cravat of Chinese silk, shoes with gold buckles, and a fine blue broadcloth coat.

All that remained were his cocked hat, sword, white gloves and cloak.

When he was dressed at last, he had no more time than to take a quick survey of himself before he picked up his cloak and returned topside as the boat arrived to take them to Malaga.

It was a short trip to shore, and when they arrived, the boat pulled up beside the jetty at Malaga's main dockyard. Percy waited until Captain Pennebaker stepped onto the companionway, then he followed, with one hand on his sword, and the other holding his cocked hat secure on his head.

They were met by a small man with a big voice, who spoke perfect English. "If you will come with me, a carriage is waiting to take you to the home of the Conte de Davalillo."

Captain Pennebaker nodded. "Lead the way," he said, and motioned for Percy to follow.

Once inside the carriage, the footmen took their places and the horses sprang forward. They drove along the harbor for several minutes, before they turned up a street lined with trees, passing a cathedral on the way.

Some fifteen minutes later they pulled into a courtyard of the Conte's palace. Lights glittered from a dozen windows, and Percy noticed an equal number of carriages had already arrived.

The Conte de Davalillo was slim, elegant, aloof, and obviously a man with a long, illustrous pedigree and an overabundance of pride because of it.

After introductions to the members of the Spanish nobility present, there came a time of drinks and discussions of the war, after which, Percy was surprised to see they were joined by six ladies, each of them an articulate conversationalist, excellent flirt, and quite beautiful, each in her own unique way.

After the women, who all bore titles, were introduced, there was little time for private conversation, as dinner was announced almost immediately.

Don Pedro de Castilla, whom Percy met earlier, joined him. "The women of Spain are quite lovely," he said.

"I have seen none to compare," Percy replied. "It must be difficult to concentrate on other things, with so much loveliness about."

Don Pedro's dark eyes warmed and his thin lips parted with a smile. "Ahh, I see you are a man who appreciates the finer things."

"Wine, women and horses," Percy said, feeling absurdly stupid for handing Don Pedro such a schoolboy's line. However, Don Pedro did not seem to take it as such, for he said, "In that case, you will partner the Contessa Maria Teresa Helena de Prada at dinner, Lieutenant."

Percy nodded. "With the greatest pleasure," he said, not having any recollection as to which of the sloe-eyed beauties was the contessa with half a dozen names.

He was given a quick reminder when a voluptuous beauty took his arm, and spoke in flawless English, "I had hoped you would be the one, Lieutenant Bronwell from Yorkshire."

Percy wondered how much more the Contessa knew about him. Although the Spanish were now their allies against the French, it had not been that many years ago when England and Lord Nelson battled it out against the French and Spanish at the Battle of Trafalgar.

But they were allies now.

Castlereagh and Parliament had given it their blessing, so with the air of a man determined to serve his country in whatever way he was presented with, he offered the contessa his arm, glanced at her magnificent bosom and escorted her into the dining room.

The Contessa de Prada was truly the most beautiful woman at the dinner table; in fact, Percy was fairly certain she was the most beautiful woman he had ever seen. Her face was heart-shaped, her bosom like crushed pearls as it rose and fell with each breath above the daring décolletage of her fashionable court dress. But it was her eyes, liquid pools of suggestive glances and consuming fire, that captured his attention and held it throughout dinner.

From time to time, Percy would glance in Captain Pennebaker's direction, ready to join the conversation, but each time he saw Captain Pennebaker was knee-deep in admiration over the raven-haired beauty seated at his side.

Champagne and conversation was followed by caviar, dinner, more champagne, dessert, and more champagne with conversation. By this time, considering the quantity of champagne consumed, the evening, as well as the conversation, was quite lively.

When it came time to retire to another room, the contessa let it be known that she was available for more than conversation.

As they emerged from the dining room, she took his arm. "Shall we take some air, Lieutenant?"

"It would be a pleasure to escort such a lovely lady. Do you have a wrap?"

"I would not want to spoil the view."

The most extraordinarily bold expression came into her eyes and she pressed herself closer against his arm until he could feel the softness of her breast.

"Nor I," he said, wondering how this predicament was going to end.

The countess curled her arm through his. "This way, Lieutenant."

He felt like a lamb being led, where, he

did not know, but he had a pretty good idea how it would all end up.

She led the way, down a corridor and up a staircase, then down a long hallway. At the end of the hall, she stopped and opened a door. Percy saw at once it was her private apartments.

She stepped inside.

He followed her into the room as he listened for the sound of bleating.

She closed the door behind them. The click of the lock went off in his head like a rocket.

Percy saw her sultry look, the moist pout, the splendid bosom that gleamed in the soft filter of moonlight coming through the window.

His head began to whirl, and he was thinking he had had far too much champagne for this. What an idiot he had been.

He could not get drunk while in uniform, and with Captain Pennebaker downstairs.

And yet, he had.

At this point, Percy made two startling discoveries: One, that the contessa's dress was held together by two hooks, which she undid rather quickly, and two, that she was wearing absolutely nothing beneath it.

By the time the dress fell about her feet, he added a third discovery: she had a magnificent body that was made for loving. He would soon discover she knew how to use it.

He was about to make his excuses and an apology, when she put her hand on him. The combination of champagne, too long an abstinance and the contessa were more than he could battle.

As she led him to her bed, he had a vision of the *Beatrix*—flying a white flag.

A stabbing pain in his head awoke him the next morning and he slowly rolled over with a groan. His mouth tasted like cotton and something else...perfume?

The previous night came rolling into his mind like a cannon volly. He should have declined the third...or was it the fourth glass of champagne?

He most assuredly should have declined the contessa's advances.

He tried to think back to the night before and the return trip to the *Beatrix*. For the life of him, he could not remember Captain Pennebaker being with him, but then, he did not remember coming alone, either.

In fact, he could not remember coming back at all.

Percy groaned again. If he made a fool of himself last night, he made a fool of the Royal Navy, and England. He had visions of a military trial, and being stripped of his commission and sent home in shame.

It was in the midst of such thoughts that he heard a knock at his door. "Enter!" he said a little louder than he intended.

Immediately he put his hands to his temples to massage the reverberating boom.

Captain Pennebaker came in, looking much like Percy felt.

"What time did you return to the ship last night, Lieutenant?"

Percy tried to sit up, fell back, and made it on the second try.

He swung his feet over the side of his cot and answered weakly, "Truthfully Captain, I vaguely remember returning at all, and I have no notion of the time."

Captain Pennebaker parked himself in one of two chairs beside the table. "Pardon me if I don't laugh. My head aches damnably. Did you drink the champagne?"

"More than my share, regrettably."

"Remind me to stay with coffee or tea, next time around. How was your contessa?"

Percy felt his face grow warm.

The captain smiled. "Mine, too." He took a deep breath, obviously still feeling the effects of last night. "I only ask, because I daresay she could not have been any better than mine. Damnably talented woman, that contessa. I've never known such hands."

Percy had a flash of a similar memory.

"Take a shower-bath. It will restore some of your good health. I will have Claverly bring you whatever it was he gave me, for your head. Worked damnably fast."

Percy was certain his flesh was turning green. "It couldn't work fast enough to suit me."

Captain Pennebaker laughed softly. "I knew you would be a good sport, Lieutenant. I am pleased to discover that, since I received another invitation only moments ago, to dinner with the Conte de Davalillo again tomorrow night. I shall send word that we will both be honored to accept his invitation."

After Captain Pennebaker left, Percy hoped their stay in Malaga was to be a short one, for he did not expect that his call to serve his country would be taken so literally.

Eleven

All farewells should be sudden.

> Lord Byron (1788-1824)
> English poet

The day before her birthday, Maresa was up early.

After breakfast, she took the dogs and wandered out onto the moors for her daily walk. These amblings had become a habit, and truly something that she could hardly avoid, considering the invitation that awaited her from almost every window in the house. Each time she glanced out the casement, the ridges and valleys called out for her to seek the beauty of their summits, and to walk the deep valleys.

It had rained for the past three days, and when the sun burst forth from behind gray clouds, and seemed to drive them almost instantly away, Maresa was unable to stand her confinement any longer.

She grabbed her bonnet off the hook by the back door, and was about to go out, when her cousin called after her to say, "The weather will not last, and you will get a drenching if you go out overlong."

Maresa tied her bonnet strings and took a peek upward, where the sky was a lovely robin's egg blue, and said, "It is lastingly fair, Cousin, but promise I shan't go far."

"Take the dogs with you," she reminded, "you never know what sort of unsightly characters might be about, and up to nothing but the wrong sort of mischief."

"I was planning on taking them with me," Maresa said, and hurried down the steps before her cousin could call out any more orders.

The change in the weather was especially appreciated on this day, being the eve of her birthday, and she looked upon it as a gift, since there were never many gifts coming her way on this occasion, or on any other, for that matter.

And so it was, that on the afternoon of Maresa's seventeenth birthday, she returned from her lengthy walk, never suspecting that anything out of the ordinary awaited her.

The moment she stepped inside the house, she heard loud voices coming from the library. An agitated Mrs. Brampton stood at the end of the hall. As if waiting for her, she motioned for Maresa to come quietly.

"What's amiss?" Maresa whispered when she reached Mrs. Brampton. "Who is shouting in the library with Cousin Augusta?"

She asked this, although she knew who it was who was doing all the shouting. What she did not know was, why. Why was he here now, on her seventeenth birthday, when he had missed every birthday for almost ten years?

" 'Tis the viscount. He has come to take you to London."

The words she had been about to speak caught in her throat. Of all the millions of reasons Maresa could have heard as to why her father was here, this was the one answer she was not prepared for.

London...

Her first thought was, why? Why London? Why now?

He has come to take you to London.....

London, London! Her mind was suddenly cluttered with a dozen imaginings. It was the city she had dreamed of seeing, and had given up hope that she ever would.

She was both thrilled at the prospect of going there, and at the same time, terrified of being taken there by her father. Slowly, suspicion began to form in her head, followed by numerous questions.

Why would he suddenly appear after so many years and want to take her to London? Surely he had not heard of her engagements, or even if he had, why were they something he even paid attention to?

He did not care about her.

So, why would he care how she lived her life? That was the reason he sequestered her here in the first place, wasn't it?

So, he did not have to see her, or be involved with her on any level?

She did not know her father well, that was true, but from what she did know, she knew he was not the sort to take her to London out of a kind and charitable heart. Lying at the back of her mind was a premonition that her father had to have something to gain by this, or he would have never put in an appearance at Hampton Manor.

At last, she was able to collect enough composure to say, "Do you have any idea why he is here? Did my sisters come?"

"His lordship came alone. All I have been able to gather is, word of your broken engagements has apparently reached London and his lordship is furious."

Maresa's spirits sank. So, that was the reason after all.

Mrs. Brampton went on. "At the present moment, he is in the process of blaming Mrs. Rightly."

"Yes, I heard the commotion when I arrived."

"What shall you do?"

The call to duty settled over her like a lead cape. "Dread it, as I do, I mustn't let her take the blame for something of my own doing."

"I am sure she—"

"Mrs. Brampton!" a voice laced with exasperation called out. "Send someone to find my daughter. Now, if you please."

Maresa took a deep breath, smoothed the folds of her skirt, then removed her bonnet, and handed it to Mrs. Brampton. She paused a moment in front of the hall mirror, to smooth her hair, and tuck the trailing wisps, loosened by the wind, back in place.

With a quick glance in Mrs. Brampton's direction, she said, "I am here, Father," and she headed down the hall, totally unprepared for the changes in her father over the past years, or, for that matter, his reaction to the changes in her.

"It's about time! Where have you been?"

Maresa stepped into the room. "I have been for a walk, Father."

She immediately saw her father's stricken look. "Teresa...my God!"

It shocked her to hear the sound of her mother's name upon his lips, and it sounded like a sacrilege to hear it said in such a manner. However, she could not deny that the thought that she favored her mother so much, or the fact that she might have caused him some discomfort, sent a ripple of joy pulsing through her.

It had been such a long time since she had seen him.... She was shocked to see he had grown so much older. His hair was almost completely gray now, and his skin no longer reflected much time in the sun, but his eyes were the same eyes she remembered, cold and silver-gray, like the inside of an oyster shell.

She looked around the room, her gaze alighting for a moment on the globe, and she remembered the afternoon Percy had stood there, with his finger on the world, and how different it all felt with him, than it did now, with her own flesh and blood.

She wished he had said something to make her feel he was glad to see her, but perhaps it was better that he did not. After all the years of absence, anything positive would have been hypocritical. "Hello, Father."

He turned his head away, as if the sight of her frightened him. "Dear God in Heaven. Must you look so much like her?"

"I am sorry if I am a reminder of that which you have sought to forget. I fear I cannot help the way I look. If it pains you to see me, I can leave, or perhaps I could put the canary cover over my head," she said, thinking perhaps a little levity was called for.

"I will not tolerate disrespect."

"I fear I must hasten to laugh, Father, so that I do not weep. Shall I leave now?"

"Stay where you are, I will have a word with you, when I finish with Augusta."

"You should not be angry with Cousin Augusta."

"When I want your input, I will ask for it. So many broken engagements before your seventeenth birthday, and you see no reason to be angry with Miss Incompetence?"

"She did not accept any of those offers of marriage, Father. The fault is all mine."

"I am well aware of that, and will deal with it later. Of that, have no doubt. Suffice it to say, your wild-running days are over. I have given Mrs. Brampton instructions to have your things packed. I am taking you to London."

"And Cousin Augusta?"

"She will not be needed in London."

Maresa saw the distressed look on her cousin's face, and she knew what a horrible jolt it would be to her, to suddenly find herself tossed out like yesterday's paper, without any regard to her welfare. That she was a widow with no other means of support, Maresa had not forgotten.

It seemed to her, that if Cousin Augusta accompanied her to London, she might have ample time to find another position, before they both found themselves out on the cobblestone streets.

"I have been deprived of a mother, father and family ties. I will not suffer the loss of my long-time companion and the closest thing I have to family. Over the years, I have forgiven much and asked for nothing. Now, I am asking to have Cousin Augusta accompany us to London."

Her father opened his mouth, and then shut it.

Everything was suddenly hushed and eerily quiet. For a moment she felt as if she sensed another presence in the room—a calm current that settled silently over everything.

Maresa was never certain what it was exactly that made his tone soften somewhat. "Very well, she may accompany you to London...at least for the time being."

Maresa gave a curtsy, wishing all the while he was the kind of father she could rush to and have him take her in his arms, while she planted a kiss upon his cheek. "Thank you, Father."

He did not look at her when he said, "You are dismissed. Have your things ready. We leave at first light. I have affairs to attend to in London, and do not wish to stay here overlong."

"Excuse me, your lordship," Augusta said.

"Now what?" the viscount asked, his exasperation back.

"It is Maresa's birthday, today, your lordship."

"Yes...well, I knew that, of course. Blast it, why do you think I chose to come today?" he asked, and gave Maresa a look that bordered on apologetic. For a moment it looked as though he might say "Happy Birthday," but then the look passed, just as another birthday would pass without her father's well wishes.

At that moment, all Maresa felt for her sire was pity. Out of respect, she called him Father, but he had never been a father to her. Still, she could not help thinking that if things had been different, he might have been a good father; if her mother had not died; if she had not had the misfortune to look remarkably like her mother; if her father had been a stronger man.

The first week after she arrived in London, the fog was so dense that the Prince Regent, having set out for Hatfield House, was forced to turn back at Kentish Town.

The fog persisted for almost a week after that, being found to be so thick one morning that the mail coach from London to Birmingham took seven hours to reach Uxbridge.

The coal tar smell of fog penetrated the houses, and when Maresa looked out her window, she could not see the row of town houses across the street. The morning paper said the number of deaths attributed to the bad air in London alone, was up forty per cent above normal, the worst affected area of London being the East End, where the density of factories and domestic dwellings was greater than almost anywhere else in the city.

If that was not bad enough, word came that the United States had declared war.

Away from her home, missing Percy, stuck inside from bad weather, surrounded by wars and rumors of more wars—it all served to make Maresa terribly homesick, and she longed for the days of long walks across the Yorkshire moors, where she could see for miles from atop almost any ridge, and where the sun did not hide its face behind a thick, smelly cloak of fog for weeks at a time.

Maresa met all four of her sisters shortly after her arrival in London, but it was a week or so later when they all gathered for a family dinner. It was not something she looked forward to, and by the time everyone had arrived, she understood why she had felt such dread.

Her first thought was, she was truly thankful that she had been given those years in Yorkshire. She no longer thought of it as punishment, but a blessing. Faith! She did not think she would have maintained her sanity living in this house. No wonder poor Beatrice stuttered.

Three of her sisters, Jane, Anne and Fanny, who were at least ten years older, were married. All three of their husbands had declared earlier that previous engagements, although regrettable, prevented their joining them for dinner. Or so Maresa was told, but if the truth were known, she suspected the poor, henpecked husbands probably leaped at the chance to have an evening away from the women they had so unwisely married.

Twenty-year-old Beatrice was the closest to Maresa's seventeen years, and the only one of Maresa's sisters who was unmarried, and the only one Maresa found likable.

In fact, as the evening continued, on and on, Maresa found herself drawn to Beatrice with a mixture of pity, and true regard.

As a group, her family was formidable, and she supposed it was no accident that they came across that way.

It did not take her long to learn a great deal about her sisters, mostly through quiet observation, for Maresa decided it best to remain silent and thereby lessen the risk of saying the wrong thing. Not that anyone in the family noticed, or seemed to mind. Not in the least.

Jane, the oldest, was the most prone to gossip and tale carrying.

"I heard today that Lady Woodmere has taken a lover...a much younger man, mind you."

"B-b-but Lady Woodmere is quite y-y-young herself," Beatrice said.

Jane ignored her. "I heard, only today, mind you, that Lady Tallmadge saw the two of them secreted away in the back of a carriage near Convent Garden. Can you imagine anyone so brazen? I cannot help but wonder what Lord Woodmere must think."

"I think Lord Woodmere stopped thinking about twenty years ago, on his eightieth birthday," said Anne, who possessed the most wit among the family.

"That is just like you, Anne, to make light of a sinful situation," Fanny said, as Maresa declared her the pious one. "I always thought she had a rather wicked look about her."

"Well, we can't all be married to a minister and white as next year's snow, now can we?" asked Anne.

"Enough!" the viscount said. "I would think you would be mindful of your manners, at least the first time you dine with Maresa present."

Anne smiled at Maresa. "Perhaps it is best this way, Papa, for Maresa can see how we really are, without putting on any airs."

"Oh, yes, please be yourselves," Maresa said.

"You haven't said much," Fanny said, settling her gaze upon Maresa.

"I am so taken aback at the sight of so many family members gathered around the table at mealtime...I suppose I am stunned into silence."

"Yes, I would imagine you ate alone in Yorkshire," Fanny said. "Or did you dine in the kitchen with the staff?"

"At Hampton Manor, dinner usually consisted of Cousin Augusta and myself. From time to time, Percy Bronwell would join us, and of course there were many, many times when I dined at Danegeld with the Bronwells. Their many kindnesses toward me knew no bounds."

"Yes, that is what I heard. You were especially fond of one of them, I understand... enough to affiance yourself to him...for a time, that is," Jane said.

"I adore all the Bronwells, including Stephen."

"Yes, I understand you have quite an attachment for the younger brother, as well. What is his name again?" Jane asked.

"Percy."

"I am sure he has gone into decline over your leaving for London," said Fanny.

"Not really, since he does not know. Percy is a lieutenant in the Royal Navy, somewhere in the Mediterranean. I would think that would hardly make him a boy," Maresa said, "but it is true that I am immensely fond of him. He is my dearest friend."

"How very odd to declare a member of the opposite sex your best friend," said Fanny. "I would be careful about making that declaration, if I were you. People love to talk, you know."

"Yes, I've noticed," Maresa said so sweetly, that no one caught her meaning, save Anne, who smiled and ducked her head.

"There are not a lot of choices for friends when you live on the North Yorkshire moors, as you must well know, so one must take their friends where they find them," Maresa said. "The Bronwells were our closest neighbors, so we were bound to form friendships."

Maresa noticed Beatrice had only contributed one comment toward the conversation throughout the meal, until her father said, "Bea, where are your manners? You have not said two words since we gathered for dinner."

"S-s-sorry, Papa. I w-w-was listening overmuch, I s-suppose."

"Well, you need to acquaint yourself with your sister, since you are closest to her age. I want you to join her and your cousin for a tour of London tomorrow."

"Y-y-yes, Papa."

"If you will excuse me," the viscount said. "I have some figures to go over before retiring." He stopped just short of the door, turned, and said to Beatrice, "On the morrow, see to it that Maresa is taken to a mantua-maker. Her clothes are abominable. I'll not have her going about London looking like a rag man's daughter."

Maresa's first reaction was embarrassment over her country clothes, for dressed even in her finest gown she knew she would look, at best, like a destitute relative.

She felt like an odd piece of furniture, a chair that did not match the others, an irrelevant thing, a note tossed aside, an unfortunate apparition, a haunt of conscience, a shadow that lurked in the attic as a dreaded reminder.

"You do know what a mantua-maker is, don't you?" asked Jane.

"I am familiar with the term, although I was never fitted for clothes by anyone from the city. All my clothes were made at Hampton Manor."

"Apparently," Fanny said. "One would think that even in the country, the daughter of a viscount would take some pride in the way she looked."

"One might also think that even living in London, the sisters of a viscount's daughter might come to pay an occasional visit to their youngest sister, and offer to advise her on the latest fashions in London, since she had never been allowed there, and had no way of knowing her clothes were terribly out of fashion," Maresa said, not bothering to temper either her words or her tone.

At this point she didn't care what they thought of her. If this was an example of what the soft life in London did to a person, she was most thankful that she spent her early years in Yorkshire.

Before anyone else could comment Beatrice suddenly became quite lively and animated, and to Maresa's surprise, spoke with hardly a stutter, which made Maresa wonder if she only stuttered around their father.

"Oh, we must make a stop at Mrs. Gordon's dress shop. She is the best mantua-maker in London." Beatrice said.

"Heaven forbid," Jane said. "You aren't going to take her to Mrs. Gordon's to be fitted? That is most uncivilized. You know Mrs. Gordon always comes here."

"I thought her shop would be something Maresa would enjoy seeing," Beatrice said.

Anne nodded. "You are right, of course. Mrs. Gordon would be perfect, although I must warn you, Maresa, a day in London can be terribly exhausting. After your initial visit, we shall have Mrs. Gordon make her calls here, which is the usual way."

"Befitting the daughter of a viscount," Fanny added with her nose slightly elevated.

Maresa wished she had a cruet of vinegar to pour in that haughty nose.

Immediately after the *Beatrix* docked in London, Percy hired a post chaise that was horsed and waiting by the quay. He had only one week, and his father was ill, but he wanted to stop by and see Maresa before he left, since his mother had written that Maresa was now living in London with her father.

He had not received a letter from her since she left Yorkshire, but then his ship had been on the move about the Mediterranean and the Tyrrehenian Seas. He suspected the only reason his mother's letter had reached him was due to her giving it to Commodore Thackerly at dinner one evening.

The strength of the Royal Navy was being sapped by the need to maintain a tedious blockade of the key French ports where

Napoleon's warships waited for an opportunity to escape into the Atlantic.

Because of Napoleon's Russian invasion, French troops were being pulled out of Spain, which meant the Duke of Wellington and his army was advancing farther into the Spanish peninsula. Consequently, the *Beatrix* was rarely in any port for more than a few days.

Having frequently engaged the enemy, they had captured three French vessels two weeks ago, and now had put into the Port of London for repairs, having taken a cannonball in the hull, just above the waterline.

While he waited in the receiving room of her father's town house, Percy's thoughts were upon Maresa and how she was faring in such close proximity to the viscount. He knew how impulsive she could be, and he worried what she might do, if things were not going in the direction of pleasant.

He found he was a bit curious about her, and wondered how she would look now that the city had an opportunity to take its hold upon her. He wondered too, if she was engaged again, or was she simply the darling of the ton and being squired about by every dandy in town?

He heard the light tap of a slippered foot, the soft rustle of delicate fabric, and Maresa came into view, like the sun rising over Mount Etna.

"Percy," she said, as she made her entrance. "How I have wished to see you again."

She took his hands in hers, and he kissed her, on one cheek, and then on the other.

"Maresa…" The words he planned to say caught in his throat at the sight of her, dressed in a fine morning gown of delicately flowered cotton. His gaze dropped to the fashionably low décolletage, and he found it did not please him to see she had given in to the dictates of style so easily. "You look…"

"Different?" she said, and twirled around. "Isn't it lovely?"

"Yes, quite the loveliest thing I've ever seen," he replied, while never taking his gaze from her face. "You've changed."

"For the better, I hope."

"I don't know. How can you improve perfection?"

"Oh, I have missed all the lovely things you used to say. Do tell me you shall be here for at least a fortnight. I have so many things to tell you."

"No, I am only here for an hour or so. My father is ill, and I am on my way to Danegeld Hall. I could not be in London without coming to see you," he said.

"I am so happy you did, but tell me about your father? Is it grave?"

"No, mother wrote that he has had repeated occurrences of influenza, which weakened him, of course. She told me not to worry, that the doctor thinks he will be over it soon. She assured me it was nothing life-threatening, just something he cannot seem to put behind him."

"I am very sorry. Please give him my love, and tell both him and your mother how much I miss them."

"Mother wrote that it is not the same with you gone, and how much they miss your cheerful visits."

"I cannot believe you are here" she said. "Why did you not write me?"

"I did," he said, and pulled a pouch from inside his coat. "Only I never had an opportunity to mail them."

He handed a bundle of several letters to her. "I thought about tossing them overboard, since the news is old."

"I would never have forgiven you if you had. I treasure every letter you write, and your visits even more."

"How are you enjoying London?" he asked.

"I love it...but I also hate it. There are so many parties, and I have the loveliest clothes, and so many of them! I am trying to adjust to the ways of the city, but it is so vastly different than Yorkshire."

"Yes, it is different, but don't let it change you too much."

When Maresa's father walked by the drawing room and saw Percy, Maresa introduced them, and was surprised to see him become more animated than she had ever seen him.

"Welcome to London, Lieutenant."

"Thank you. I hope you don't mind my dropping by like this, but I am on my way home. I haven't much time, but I did want to see Maresa."

"No, I don't mind, not in the least. You are always welcome. I am certain Maresa is delighted you are here. How goes it with the war? Do you see an end in sight?"

"I am guardedly hopeful. One good sign is that we are picking up large numbers of recruits fleeing from Napoleon. There are over two thousand de Meurons who have joined the British army this year in Malta. They joined to fight Napoleon, rather than be drafted by conscription to fight for him. The peninsular war is draining the French coffers and diverting money needed to fight the Russians. Napoleon is moving troops from Spain to Russia, which benefits Wellington. The French allies are falling away, one by one."

"Is it not difficult for the British, as well... concerning the situation we are faced with, fighting Napoleon and the Americans?"

"We have a strong navy, for which I am thankful, and excellent leadership. However, I won't say it isn't difficult to maintain the blockade of the French ports, patrol the Mediterranean, and fight the French and the Americans. We pray for a turn in our favor."

"Well, I am late for an appointment, and regret I must leave. Do what you can to end this bloody war."

"Yes, sir. I am trying my best, sir."

Maresa and Percy stood together and watched her father leave.

"He can be quite charming," Percy said.

"Yes, although I never knew that until this very moment."

"Well, perhaps that is good news."

"In what way?"

"He could start being charming to you, as well."

"No, that is not possible."

"Why not?"

"Because I have a face that he cannot bear to look upon—a face he can never forget."

Twelve

Love is blind; friendship closes its eyes.

English proverb

Although Percy's comments about the war were optimistic, the war only seemed to get worse, and the fighting in Spain and Russia continued. Two days ago, the papers were filled with the news that Napoleon had reached Moscow, but the Russians had burned the city before fleeing.

In his last letter, Percy wrote he was now assigned to the *Nottingham,* still part of the Mediterranean fleet, under Captain Otway.

My dearest Maresa,

It seems like an eternity since I stood in your home in London, and I fear it will seem even longer before I have the opportunity to do so again.

We received orders to intercept two French frigates, which sailed from Toulon, and we sailed immediately through the Straits of Bonifacio, between Corsica and Sardinia, but could not locate the French vessels. We then learned the French were sailing through the Piombino Pass between Elba and the mainland, so we headed in that direction, and we sighted the enemy at dawn, a little windward.

We took the *Celeste,* a fine frigate-built ship only five months old and carrying twenty thousand shot and shells, and ninety tons of gunpowder.

We suffered six casualties, including Midshipman Mr. Henry Moore.

We saw action again yesterday at dawn. It lasted until two in the afternoon. The *Nottingham* ran the gauntlet twice through the French lines, with no less than three ships upon us at one time. By the grace of God, we were able to make them strike to us, and we managed to sink two of their ships, one with eighty guns and one with seventy-four. This time we lost twelve good men, including the son of Lord Chiswick.

I fear I bore you with details, but you asked in your last letter for me to enlighten you in regard to the war, and you specifically asked for details. I appreciate your concern for my well-being, but I do not want you to worry about me. I promise you now, that I shall return. After several battles, I have suffered only a minor burn and a small cut on my wrist.

There is never any danger of my forgetting you or what our friendship has meant to me over the years. I only hope it has been the same for you.

As always, I think of you often, and hope you are adjusting to your new life. I don't know when I will be in England again. The war dictates, and I am England's loyal servant.

Pray for me.

Your loving friend,
Percy

Maresa read the letter twice, in hopes that she would absorb some of the jargon, so she would be better prepared to discuss the war with him when she saw him next, but all she could recall later was twenty thousand shot and ninety tons of gunpowder, and had not a clue what kind of question she could ask about such as that.

She sat down almost immediately and answered his letter. She told him of the dress she wore to a ball at the home of Lady Halifax, and how many times she was asked to dance, and asked him, as she always did, to be especially careful. She ended by telling him about her many confrontations with her father.

Dearest Percy,

Your letter arrived when I needed it most, for I was sorely missing your presence in my life.

Things have not been going as well as I hoped with my father. We argue overmuch. Each time it happens, I promise myself that is the last time I will lose my temper with him, but I always forget.

It is just that my father's lack of understanding, his opinionated, overbearing, controlling ways began to bear down upon me, and I always lose my resolve. How I wish you were here to temper my words and advise me.

I know you told me I must not fight too often with one enemy, or I would teach him all my art of war, but I never seem to remember that until after our confrontation.

On a brighter side, you will be happy to know, that I have not affianced myself to anyone, although I have had several callers, most of whom my father approves of. He has made it known to me that he wishes me to make a good marriage, so I will be happy and well provided for, but I know the main reason is so I will no longer be his responsibility.

I now feel that it wasn't because I had so many offers of marriage in Yorkshire that he brought me to London, but that I did not follow through with any of them.

You remember you told me your mother

said you could put a uniform on a broomstick and women would swoon? Well, I think my father would happily see me wed to that broomstick, if it meant I would be out of his powdered wig!

Always your devoted friend,
Maresa

Maresa was an overwhelming success during her first season in London, at least according to the gossip that circulated by the ton. But after two broken engagements, tongues stopped wagging about her in a complimentary way.

There were times when she was aware she was being criticized because she would flirt outrageously with one suitor, and then reject him, only to set her sights on another. What hurt Maresa the most, was that they did not understand that this was not something she set out to do intentionally.

During her first year in London, Percy had managed to see her twice, but never for very long. Stalwart, ingenious, engaging, and true as they came, whenever he was present, he commented upon her nature of impatient impulsiveness, and her stubborn unwillingness to be pushed.

Watching the two of them dance one evening Anne, the only one of her sisters to notice this, said as much to Cousin Augusta. "You know, I have been watching them whenever they are together. When he is around, Maresa is at her very best. He is the perfect counterpart, I think, and her equal in every way."

"I am delighted to hear you say that, Anne, because I have always thought that very same thing," Augusta said.

"It is a shame she cannot see what is before her very eyes."

"Yes, especially when she is constantly tripping over the evidence."

"I have a suspicion."

"Tell me, do."

"I think," said Anne, "that Maresa doesn't see Lieutenant Bronwell in a romantic light, simply because she cannot obtain what she wants from him by wheedling, persuasion, flattery or guile—wiles that she uses to such advantage over the others."

On the dance floor, Maresa was embarking upon a similar discovery, when Percy trod upon her toe for the second time. "You are not the best dancer I have ever danced with. I swear you are worse than you were in Yorkshire."

"I'm sure I am. I've been aboard ship long enough that my sea legs don't function too well on dry land."

"Oh, Percy, I don't know why I like you so much."

"Well, at least we know now that it isn't because of my dancing. My guess is we have been able to remain friends for so long, because you respect me."

"Of course I do. I respect you because you are my friend, though, not the other way around."

"No, you respect me because you cannot dominate me utterly and effortlessly as you can all the others."

Maresa did not respond to that, and soon Lord Peterson cut in, and Percy went on to dance with Lady Barbara Marshall.

By the latter part of Maresa's second season, news of the war began to escalate.

In June, Wellington defeated the French army in Spain at Vitoria. The forces of Austria, Sweden, Prussia and Russia expelled the French from Germany in the Battle of Leipzig the following October. Although the Mediterranean fleet had been allocated to operate against the east coast of Spain from the summer of 1812, they had made little progress until May of the following year, when Wellington advanced and brilliantly outmaneuvered the French, and won a crushing victory over the army of King Joseph and Marshal Jourdan at Vitoria, which effectively settled the outcome of the Peninsular War.

Wellington pushed on against what remained of the French forces in Spain, now unified under the command of Marshal Soult, who made great efforts to bar the Allies' path through the Pyrenees, which hinged upon the border fortresses of San Sebastian and Pampona.

After Sorauren, one of the bitterest battles the English won, San Sebastian was taken in a violent assault. On October 7, 1813, Wellington forced the crossing of the River Bidasoa against outnumbered French defenders. As the British crossed over the Pyrenees they were, remarkably, well-behaved as they moved across France. Napoleon's imposition of conscription had become so hated, that

Wellington's army received much better cooperation from the French civilians than the French army.

From that point on, Napoleon's days were numbered.

Maresa did not know at the time, that she had that, at least, in common with the little French Emperor.

That Christmas was the most miserable holiday in Maresa's life, for her father gathered the entire family together on Christmas Eve, for the sole purpose of informing her that they were ashamed and tired of her many broken engagements, and all they wanted for Christmas was for her to be married, and at this point they did not particularly care who the poor fool was.

"You are clearly a woman in need of rehabilitation," the viscount said. "Your reputation grows worse with each passing day. You are known from one end of London to the other, as a woman who plays at love. People gossip about how you toy with a man's affections. You develop passionate attachments too easily and conjure up romantic images that no one could live up to. It has been said that you and Lady Caroline Lamb have a lot in common, and I am ashamed to say I agree. The only thing different between the two of you is you have not, as yet, thrown yourself at Lord Byron."

This was a devastating insult, for Maresa, although fond of Byron's poetry, was crushed that her father compared her to Caroline Lamb. Maresa might flirt, but she never chased a man, and she was as chaste as the day she was born, whereas Caroline Lamb was notoriously immoral, and flagrantly had an affair with Byron, while married and the mother of a small child.

That her father would compare her to someone of such low moral fiber and unsavory behavior hurt her, and hurt her deeply.

The viscount ended by saying, "In English society, if you do not conform there is something wrong with you."

"There is nothing wrong with me. It's the English men. Weak-willed, ineffectual, milksops, every one of them!" She was about to add, "and that includes you," but decided against it, out of respect, if for no other reason than he was her father.

"Regardless of your immaturity and refusal to see the truth of the matter, people are talking and it is beginning to have an effect upon the rest of us," her father said.

"I haven't seen any evidence of that!" Maresa shot back.

"Say what you will, but I have grown tired of your nonsense, and I am now negotiating with Lord Hatfield concerning a betrothal between the two of you."

"No! You cannot do this! I shall not marry Lord Hatfield. He has been turned down by every woman in London for the past ten seasons."

"I did not ask for your opinion, Maresa. That will be all. You may go now."

Maresa was so furious she could not think

of anything to say so she said, simply, "This is not over!" and ran from the room.

She did not stop running until she was in her room and had slammed the door behind her.

Bea came in to see how she was a few minutes later. "I heard what Father said to you. I am so sorry."

"Don't be, for I would drink hemlock before I would marry Lord Hatfield. His very name makes my skin crawl."

"I have never heard Papa so angry."

"You may hear him even more angry before this is resolved. I am thinking quite seriously of accepting the Earl of Ramsford's proposal, just to spite him."

"Ramsford! He is Father's arch enemy!"

"But he does have the loveliest blue eyes."

"Shhh! Don't say that so loud. If Father hears you..."

"He is a divine dancer. Have you ever danced with him?"

"Never, and if Papa ever finds out that you did, he will lock you in your room and forbid you to go out. You cannot go against your father's wishes. You know that isn't the way it is done. There are laws..."

"Archaic laws that should be changed."

"Well, do not think to take it upon yourself to change them. You are in enough hot water as it is. You know it is Papa's right, and his duty, to see you well married, and once he has arranged such, it is your responsibility to encourage his choice and to impress him with your wifely instincts."

"Discussing this is going to make me ill. Can we not talk about something else?"

"You cannot ignore this, for it will not go away."

"I do not love Lord Hatfield."

"This is not a matter of love. Papa does not consider love a bona fide reason for marriage. Love and marriage are two different things—like a business arrangement."

"Our mother loved our father when she married him, although I cannot imagine why. You told me that yourself."

"That was one of those rare, unusual things."

"Then I shall have a rare and unusual marriage as well."

"You cannot."

"Oh, I wish I were the daughter of a chimney sweep, and then I would be free to marry whomever I wished. Why is it, that when you are the daughter of a man with a title, you are held in lower regard than the servants who empty your chamber pot?"

"I don't know."

"Well, that makes two of us then, doesn't it?"

"What are you going to do?"

"I am thinking about it. I wish something would happen to change his mind, but I realize that is not very likely. Still, I cannot help but hope and pray for a miracle."

"Sometimes miracles happen at the most opportune time."

"Yes," Maresa said, "and sometimes they do not."

After taking a short walk for a bit of fresh air, Cousin Augusta returned home with the tell-tale beginnings of a dandy bruise around her right eye.

Beatrice, who was coming down the front stair about that time gasped, then exclaimed, "D-d-dear Cousin Augusta, whatever happened to your poor eye?"

Quite methodically, Augusta removed her muff, her cape and her hat. By the time she finished, the viscount was giving her eye a serious inspection.

"How did this happen?"

"It's nothing, your lordship."

"I will have an answer," he said.

"It was a simple disagreement."

"Details, if you please."

"I was waiting on the corner for a draper's wagon to pass. Agnes Meade and Hannah Lawson were waiting to cross the street as well."

"Who are Agnes Meade and Hannah Lawson?" the viscount asked.

"They are in the employ of the Whitbys, your lordship. Agnes is the cook and Hannah is the upstairs maid."

"Go on."

Maresa came down the stairs at that moment and opened her mouth to speak, but her father quickly said, "Don't say a word." Then to Augusta he said, "Continue."

"Agnes and Hannah were speaking loud

enough for me to hear, and when Agnes said she had heard it upon good authority that Maresa had spoiled her reputation to the point that no respectable man would dare ask for her hand in marriage, I foolishly said that was nothing but malicious gossip, and the two of them ought to be ashamed if they couldn't find something more pleasurable to do."

"And?"

"And Agnes said I was right about that, and she hauled off and smacked me in the eye, then turned to Hannah and said, 'It was pure pleasure to do so.' "

That night was the worst of Maresa's young life. Nothing but threats and ultimatums from her father, criticism from Fanny and Jane, and disapproving looks from their husbands. And every time Maresa looked at her poor cousin's eye, she wanted to cry.

To think her foolishness had brought this upon such an unsuspecting lady who had sought to do nothing, save to uphold her. This did nothing but add to Maresa's discomfort and feeling of dejection, because her problems were now spreading to encompass others.

Two days later, Cousin Augusta told Maresa she had found a position as governess to the two young daughters of Sir Reginald Tewksbury. "I will be joining them at their country home near Maidstone, in Kent."

"I am relieved to hear you will be leaving London, for I know you have not enjoyed being in such a large city."

"No, I am a country girl at heart." She took Maresa's hands in hers. "I cannot thank you enough for the recommendation you gave me. I have truly been worried of late that the viscount might grow tired of my presence here and send me packing. Without a recommendation from him, I was doubly worried that I would be unable to find a suitable position. Thanks to you, I have been able to circumvent your father, and find a position with your recommendation."

"I am relieved," Maresa said, "for I have been concerned about your future, especially if my father has his way and marries me off to anyone who will have me."

"You must not say such, Maresa. No matter what your father says, you are a worthy person and a woman any man would leap at the opportunity to have."

"When do you leave for Kent?"

"Four days hence."

"I shall miss you."

"And I you."

After Cousin Augusta left, Maresa felt truly alone. First Percy, and now Cousin Augusta.

To make matters worse, Maresa received a letter from Mrs. Brampton a few days later.

My dear Maresa,

The countryside has been in upheaval of late. I don't know if you heard that Percy's brother Stephen was engaged to be married at Christmas, but his fiancée's family has postponed the wedding, because of rumors that you and Percy were lovers and that is why your father took you to London.

I write you about this, only to prepare you in case you hear of it elsewhere.

The Bronwells do not believe a word of this, including Stephen. They are not upset with you in the least, and I have that directly from Mrs. Olympia Bronwell herself—dear sweet lady that she is to make a personal call to Hampton Manor to inform us of the situation, and their undying support of you.

She did say the postponement of the wedding was only a temporary measure, to allow some time for the rumor to die down, so that Stephen and Tess would not have such a dark and malicious cloud hanging over a day that should always be remembered with fondest regard.

Your most humble servant,
Mrs. Brampton

At this point, Maresa was beginning to wonder how things could get much worse.

It was her darkest hour, a time when she had nothing save her mother's necklace and Percy's letters for solace and comfort, not realizing these things sometimes prevented her from facing her problems on her own.

That evening when Viscount Strathmore returned home, he immediately called Maresa into his study. It was an understatement to say he was furious. "I have only this minute come from White's. Do you have any idea how people are talking about you? The latest snippet is, 'Falling in love with Miss Fairweather proves to be all storm!' And just a moment ago, as I was getting into my carriage, Lord Hatfield wanted a word with me. He had heard the gossip, of course, and felt you were too much responsibility for him to tackle. Any plans we made are, at this point, null and void. A fact that should please you greatly, in spite of my public humiliation."

"I'm sorry for your embarrassment, Father."

"As you should be, but sorry won't fix it. Not this time. I will give you until June to be married, and if you are not, by all that is holy, I will marry you off to any man foolish enough to have you. Do I make myself clear?"

"Perfectly, Father."

If Maresa learned anything at all over the past month, it was that ill fortune seldom came alone, and bad news always took flight with the wind.

Why then, was comfort like a cripple that crept forward, ever so slow?

Reminders of her plight were everywhere. There was no escape, and she found her life was beginning to resemble the earlier years of her life in Yorkshire, for people whispered and pointed, while some took special delight in talking just loud enough for Maresa to hear the hateful things they said about her. She was beginning to feel more maligned than Byron, who, at least, deserved some of his criticism.

There seemed to be no escape, not even when

she tried to lose herself in a book of Richard Barnfield's poetry:

My flocks feed not,
My ewes breed not,
My rams speed not,
All is amiss.
Love is dying,
Faith's defying,
Heart's denying,
Causer of this.

Normally not a woman prone to tears, Maresa gave in and began to sob uncontrollably. Bea came into her room and asked, "What is the matter, Maresa? You look so terribly sad."

"Oh, I do conceive myself the *miserablest* person ever in existence. I am being beset by legions of gossip, and battalions of horrible things that happen to myself and those around me."

Dear, gentle Bea came to sit beside her and patted Maresa's arm. "You are unlucky, it would seem—like the unlucky fellow who got hurt on the nose when he tumbled backward. But, if it's any consolation at all, it would seem that even if it's bad luck, you clearly have a lot of luck."

Maresa stopped crying long enough to look at her, trying to find the message of comfort she was certain must be hidden there.

Then she began to laugh, and laugh, until she was crying again, but at least this time, they were tears of laughter.

She laughed until Bea began to laugh, and the two of them sat side by side, arms around each other, weak with laughter, until they heard a knock on the door.

"S-s-someone is knocking," Bea said,

"I know," Maresa answered, and then the two of them doubled over with laughter again.

When they finally had laughed until they were too weak and exhausted to laugh anymore, they realized that a good part of the staff, as well as Jane and their father were standing in the doorway, gaping at them.

Lord Strathmore shook his head, and said, "I worry about the likes of you two. I truly do."

When everyone was gone, Maresa managed to push herself into an upright position. "Whew! I feel like someone has bled me with leeches."

"I am as weak as potato water," Bea said.

"You know what?"

"What?"

"I feel so much better."

Bea's eyes grew round with surprise. "Why, so do I."

Thirteen

Thou Paradise of exiles, Italy!
Percy Bysshe Shelley (1792-1822)
British poet

The feeling did not last, for the next morning Maresa awoke and remembered her father's threat.

Be married by June or he would take the matter into his own hands.

She did not know what to do. She wished Percy would suddenly appear, not only for her own solace, but so she would know he was all right.

This morning's paper was filled with the reports of casualties of the escalated fighting to end the war, not only with Wellington's forces moving across France, but also of ships and crews lost in the Mediterranean.

She decided not to write him, because she did not want to be the cause of any distraction. If she did not write at all, she would not be tempted to tell him of all her woes, and how even her buttered bread always fell dry side up.

Apparently, not everyone had the same concern about distracting Percy, for a week later, Beatrice came running into her room to announce, "This is your luckiest day ever, Maresa. You've got a letter from Percy."

Maresa ripped open the letter, desperately needing Percy's comforting words.

Dearest Maresa,

Most profound apologies for not writing sooner, but we have just this day anchored off the coast of Sicily, so I have a moment to take pen in hand to write this letter to you.

It is often said that he who paddles two canoes, sinks, and it would appear that you are desperately close to doing just that.

I have received word of the grave situation you find yourself in there in London. I am sure by the time you finish this letter, you will feel my chastisement of you is like a double betrayal.

Believe me when I say, that I would not undertake to be so firm with you if I did not love you so much. Try to remember this as I tell you it is time to realize that you are the primary cause of all your woe. Whatever ill befalls you does so because of the choices you make, which are universally poor ones.

My advice to you would be to forego any further engagements, until you have known the young man in question for quite some time, and have at least maintained some high level of affection for him for at least six months.

Above all, know that my thoughts and prayers are always with you, and your face is constantly before my eyes—the

first thing I see each morning, and the last
I envision at night.

Your most loving friend,
Percy

P.S. I have just received word that the Duke
of Wellington has entered France from
Spain. It could be that victory is within
our grasp, at last.

Maresa was so hurt over Percy's criticism,
that she ignored everything he said. Instead,
she wadded up the letter and threw it into the
corner. "The primary cause of my woe! Is
that the talk of a friend?"

Beatrice, looking panic-stricken, shook her
head violently, stuttered a hasty, "N-n-no!"
before she remembered something she needed
to do, and hurried from the room.

Maresa watched her go, and supposed Beatrice had it worse that she did. Afraid of her own
shadow, she was, and shy as a moonbeam. Her
greatest hope was to be a spinster, and their
father loved to say, "If that is your wish, you
are heading in the right direction. I cannot
understand why you refused a season any
more than I can understand why Maresa affi-
ances herself to every man she meets."

Maresa ignored his comment about her,
but as for Bea, she could not understand why
her father could not figure that one out, especially since he was the one mainly responsible
for Beatrice being afraid of her own reflection.

Maresa sat cross-legged on her bed and

thought, her situation could be worse. She could be Beatrice.

She caught a glimpse of the wadded-up letter and forgot about her sister for the time being.

"The cause of my own woe! Humbug! It's the milksop men! If only I had somewhere to go...a place where men truly were men...a..."

A flash of inspiration lit up her face. If Wellington was in France, then that meant the war would surely be over soon, and if the war ended, there would be no reason why she could not go to Tuscany!

Further thought was put aside, for it was announced that Lady Radcliffe had arrived for tea.

Oh, dear me, she thought. I completely forgot Lady Radcliffe was coming.

Maresa rushed through her toilette, not convinced she looked terribly refreshed, but there was nothing to be done about that now. She leaned closer into the mirror, gave her cheeks a pinch or two, and decided before she went down to join Lady Radcliffe that she would leave thoughts of Percy, Tuscany, and the war here in her room.

"Have you heard the latest news of Napoleon?" Lady Radcliffe was asking Beatrice, when Maresa entered.

"I heard yesterday that he suffered massive losses in Russia and had abandoned his troops to return to Paris," Beatrice answered.

"My dear, that is old news. I have just heard from Mrs. Hollowell, whose husband,

Admiral Hollowell informed her only this morning that Napoleon has abdicated."

Maresa sat down in the nearest chair with a loud thump. Napoleon has abdicated? "Are you certain about that, Lady Radcliffe?"

"As certain as taxes. It is the latest thing being talked about all over town. I am surprised you have not heard it yourself."

"We..." She glanced at Bea. "My sister and I have not, as yet, been out of the house today."

"Well, you must rectify that immediately. There are all manner of celebrations being planned. People are pouring into the streets. Bands are playing. I've never seen such celebrating."

A burden of tremendous proportions seemed to evaporate inside her, as if some horrible demon had been cast out. Relief, joy and a feeling of incredible lightness settled into the void. "Thank God, the ordeal is over," she said, still unable to believe the war she had known since she was a child would no longer dictate their lives. She felt a sudden burst of what it must be like for a prisoner to suddenly be granted freedom.

It was true that Maresa had known nothing but the threat of Napoleon for all of her young life. It was a name she had come to hate, for Napoleon had kept her, year after year, from going to Tuscany, and prevented the Italian side of her family from coming to England to see her.

She hated Napoleon as much as she detested

153

the war. She could not fathom what life was like before Napoleon, any more than she could visualize what it would be like with him gone.

Lady Radcliffe had no problem in either area.

"Just imagine! Our borders will open and our men will be coming home. I cannot help but recall the way it was before the threat of Napoleon changed our way of life. To think, that after twenty years of warfare, we shall not only have peace, but also access to the continent, which has been closed to us since the break in the Peace of Amiens. Do you realize I have not had the privilege of owning a Parisian gown for over eleven years? I have been starved, I tell you, literally starved of Gallic fashion and culture!"

At this point, she must have noticed the blank look on the faces of both Maresa and Beatrice, for she said, "Oh, my dears, do you have no inkling of what this means?"

Bea said simply, "I suppose it means Maresa will finally be able to go to Tuscany to visit our aunt and uncle."

Lady Radcliffe's face brightened. "Why, Maresa, you sly little fox! I had no idea you had relations in Tuscany! Such a delightful place, and the people... La! What I would not give to be there at this very moment, but do tell me of your family."

"I fear I do not have a great many details beyond their names," Maresa said, and then told her what little she knew.

"How sad to think you have never met

them. Well, we shan't dwell upon that. Now is the time to make plans to pay them a visit. I would think you might want to do that soon, for I know there will be an absolute flood of the English heading across the channel. Paris gowns! La!"

"I have been thinking of arranging passage when the war was over for quite some time now, but I did not know how to get a letter to them safely. I have written many letters in the past that did not arrive."

"Oh, fie! I can help you with that. Admiral Hollowell will be returning to duty in the Mediterranean two days hence. He had to return to London, you know. Had a bout with his gout. Hmmm. That rhymes, doesn't it? Well, anyway, Lady Hollowell was certain it was brought on by the inclement weather. He is much recovered now, and most anxious to return to duty. I am sure he can see to it that your letter reaches your relations. Where do they live?"

"They have a villa near Florence."

"Ahh, Florence, the jewel in Italy's crown. How I do envy you, my dear."

Lady Radcliffe finished the last of her tea. "Lady Fortescue is giving a small dinner party for Admiral Holloway tomorrow night. If you can write your letter and have it delivered to me before then, I will personally give it to him."

Maresa leaped to her feet. "Oh, Lady Radcliffe, how can I ever thank you?"

Lady Radcliffe stood. "Why, you can invite me for tea when I come to Florence!"

Maresa smiled. "It would be a pleasure."

Lady Holloway glanced at Beatrice, as if only just aware she was even in the room. "Thank you for the tea, my dears, but now I must be on my way. I do so love being the bearer of glad tidings!"

Maresa and Beatrice thanked her for paying them a visit, and walked with her to the door.

"You won't forget about the letter?" Lady Radcliffe asked. "At my house before tomorrow evening?"

"I shall write it straightaway, and dispatch it immediately after," Maresa said.

"It might get there before you do, Lady Radcliffe," Bea said.

"Delightful!" Lady Radcliffe stepped outside and opened her parasol with a snap. "A French gown," she sighed. "My heart is all aflutter at the thought. You simply must tell your Italian aunt to take you shopping in Paris. Lovely. Simply lovely. *Au revoire,* my dears."

Maresa and Bea each hid a smile as Lady Radcliffe disappeared behind the doors of her coach.

True to her word, Maresa went straight upstairs and sat at her writing table. Flipping open the inkwell, she plunged the nib of the pen into the ink and began to hastily write a letter to Aunt Gisella and Uncle Tito, inviting herself for an extended stay.

When she finished, she read over the last paragraph twice.

Once the arrangements for my travel are planned, I shall write again to tell you of my agenda. I do so look forward to seeing each of you, and my mother's childhood home, after so long a wait.

I had begun to wonder if I would ever have the opportunity to use the Italian I have studied all these years.

Your loving niece,
Maresa

Once she dispatched the letter to Lady Radcliffe, she went in search of her father. She took her time, in order to mentally prepare herself for a battle of wills.

The battle of wills existed only in her mind, for her father voiced no opposition. He readily agreed to give her one year in Italy, if her aunt and uncle responded favorably to her letter, and with the condition that she find a husband during that time—or he would have her home and married within a month after her year was up.

Maresa stood there looking at him.

"Was there something else?"

"No. No, that is all."

He returned to the book he was reading, and left Maresa to wonder why she had even thought for a moment that she could say something that expressed hope that they might reconcile. It was impossible and she knew it.

In the Saturday paper, Maresa read that Louis XVIII was restored to the throne of France, and that Napoleon had bid his generals farewell at Fontainebleau, before being taken to the Island of Elba, on the HMS *Undaunted,* whose captain, Thomas Usher was quoted as saying, "It has fallen to my extraordinary lot to be the gaolor of the instrument of the misery Europe has so long endured."

By the end of the month these sentiments did not express the general feeling, however, for it was reported that English visitors, out of extreme curiosity, were sailing to the island in quite large numbers, in order to call upon the exiled emperor, or at least catch a protracted glimpse of him.

Apparently, the grand tours Lady Radcliffe had spoken of so fondly had been resurrected.

Things began to move quite rapidly after that, with Maresa beginning to wonder if she would ever get everything done.

A letter from Uncle Tito arrived two days before she was due to sail for Leghorn, expressing the delight of the entire family upon receiving the news that she was, at last, coming to Tuscany.

> Your cousin, Serena, is a bundle of nervous energy in anticipation of your arrival. She has set herself the task of preparing your room, which is adjacent

to hers, of course, while your Aunt Gisella and myself are most anxious to welcome the other daughter we always wanted.

Angelo is...well, Angelo is Angelo, and you will understand that when you meet him.

Most affectionately yours,
Uncle Tito Bartolini.

When the day arrived for Maresa's departure, the London paper officially proclaimed the "Grand Tour" had indeed resumed with a flourish. The English, it was reported, were "going across the channel in large numbers."

As Lady Radcliffe put it, "Everyone is going to the continent. Where you go—France, Germany, Italy—is not important. As long as you go!"

And go is what Maresa did.

Fourteen

I love the language, that soft bastard
   Latin,
Which melts like kisses from a female
   mouth,
And sounds as if it should be writ on
   satin
With syllables which breathe of the sweet
   South.

Lord Byron (1788-1824)
English poet

The crossing was windy and rough, and it caught Maresa unprepared for the violent bout of seasickness that struck her almost immediately after they set sail.

She remembered little of her journey after that, save a moment when she doubted Percy's sanity at choosing a life at sea. Surely he was not bothered by the same affliction. She also wondered why anyone would go on the "Grand Tour" if they felt this miserable during the entire journey.

When the shores of Italy were in sight, the sickness began to ease, and soon she felt well enough to venture forth, albeit on wobbly knees.

Soon she found her way on deck, and settled her gaze on the sails that snapped and whipped in the breeze above her, while she listened to an amicable lady standing beside her, who was from Kent.

Mrs. Applethorp was on her way to Lucca, to visit her daughter who had married an Italian doctor several years before. She was the grandmotherly sort, soft and plump, ample bosom, sturdy shoes, and the oddest little hat trimmed with a lone daisy. But its stem was too long—frightfully close to her eye it was—and it bobbed up and down each time she spoke.

Quite distracting.

After Mrs. Applethorp introduced herself Maresa asked, "Are you going to Tuscany, or will you be traveling on to another location?"

"I am going to Tuscany—Lucca, actually. Due to the war and subsequent blockade, I have not been able to pay even a short visit, until now. I have been heartsick because of it. Can you imagine my not being able to see my daughter or my lovely grandchildren in several years?"

"That is one of the hardships I found so grossly unfair about this never-ending war. Truly, I thought it would never end. I am so sorry for you, Mrs. Applethorp, for I can only imagine how devastating it must be to be separated from your daughter and to miss the loving interaction with your grandchildren while they are young."

"Oh, dear me, I cannot tell you, Lady Fairweather, how difficult it has been, never to see any of them. My dear husband died two years ago, and I blame that French monster for the sadness that he lived with, never able to see the grandson that was named after him.

161

The end of this horrid war is a blessing...and long overdue."

"It is truly a blessing," Maresa agreed, "and most definitely overdue."

She searched the coast for a glimpse of her destination. Leghorn, she had learned, was a town situated on the Ligurian Sea, not far from the islands of Elba and Corsica, on the western edge of Tuscany.

"Did you know Livorno was once known as 'the port of the de Medici family'?" Mrs. Applethorp asked. "It was once a seaside resort favored by many British travelers before the French up and ruined everything."

Maresa smiled inwardly, as she remembered the time her cousin went to such great lengths to find information on the de Medicis after Maresa had inquired about them. "Livorno?" Maresa repeated, suddenly remembering something that puzzled her.

"It's what the Italians call it—Livorno. Leghorn—that is the way it translates into English, I suppose, much in the same way that Roma becomes Rome. Firenze is Florence, and Toscana changes to Tuscany."

Toscana. How lovely the sound of it was. Toscana... Toscana... Toscana... She closed her eyes and imagined what it must be like.

In her opinion, Toscana was a far lovelier word than Tuscany, and for that matter, Firenze outshone Florence by a mile, especially when she remembered there was an old plow horse at Hampton Manor named Florence.

Maresa was perplexed; unable to understand what was wrong with keeping the names the Italian's used, considering it was their own country. Why, she wondered, would we take it upon ourselves to change it?

The ship drew nearer to land, passing landscape that varied from sandy beaches and rocky coves, to groves of pines, before, finally, the sails came down with a rattle and a loud snap, and they entered the Medici Port Mrs. Applethorp had spoken of.

By the time they docked along the quay, near the *Monumento ai Quattro Mori,* which Mrs. Applethorp referred to as, the Monument to the Four Moors, Maresa was fair to bursting with excitement.

For someone who never left the moors of Yorkshire until she was seventeen, it was hard for her to believe that she was about to set foot on Italian soil, only two years later.

Her attention was drawn to a particular coach waiting along the esplanade.

Three people stood next to it and Maresa wondered if they could be her aunt and uncle. A preposterous thought, certainly, since she told them she would arrange passage from Leghorn to their villa near Florence.

She was about to ask another question of Mrs. Applethorp, when one of the three people by the carriage began to wave. Almost immediately, the other two joined in.

Maresa glanced around, but did not see anyone who looked in their direction, or returned their wave, so she decided those

163

people must be waving at her. Still, it was a tentative hand that she lifted to wave.

They promptly waved back, this time with renewed vigor.

Certain now, that it was indeed the Bartolinis, Maresa began to wave with the same excited dedication.

Mrs. Applethorp smiled and said, "Aha! It would appear that you have found your long-awaited family. Good luck, my dear. I do hope you enjoy your time here, in this loveliest of places, although I do not know why I say that, for I have never encountered anyone who did not love it, and many of those were most reluctant to leave. But I will not say any more, so I won't spoil any of the excitement of discovering Italy's magic for yourself."

"Oh, thank you, Mrs. Applecore," she said, blissfully unaware she had completely missed the ending to Mrs. Applethorp's name. "I do believe it is my aunt and uncle, and perhaps my cousin, Serena, although I am not positive." Maresa's insides were fairly humming a tune of delight. "I want to wish you a most blessed time of reunion with your daughter and her family, and I know you will spend your first few days with them with a grandchild in your lap."

Soon, she was in the eager embrace of Aunt Gisella, Uncle Tito and Cousin Serena, with everyone talking at once, and Maresa was so overjoyed, she feared she might cry.

She never expected her Aunt Gisella to look so much like the paintings of her mother. Even when Maresa figured in the fact that her mother's portrait was painted when she was a young woman, the resemblance was remarkable.

"Dear, dear Maresa, you look so much like your beloved mother, God rest her soul," Aunt Gisella said, and crossed herself. "The moment I saw you, it was as if the years had fallen away, and for a moment I thought it was Teresa coming home again."

She hugged her niece once more, and put her gloved hands on each side of her face as she said, "You are even prettier than I expected, and so grown-up! How happy we are to have you here after waiting so long to see you."

She was a small woman with warm brown eyes that reflected all the feeling expressed in her words. The soft lavender gown she wore must have been one of the latest Parisian fashions Lady Radcliffe spoke about. A gypsy hat, of white chip and heliotrope ribbon, had just enough white ostrich plume that curled on the left side to be perfectly stunning, and still provide a glimpse of dark curls.

Maresa liked her immediately.

"I cannot believe I am here," she said, gazing at each of them. "But, where is Angelo?"

"Oh, that rascal cousin of yours is wrapping up everything with his studies at the university in Bologna," said Uncle Tito. "He should be home by the time we arrive."

"I do hope it will be a long visit, before he must return."

"Oh, he won't return," Serena said. "He graduated last week."

"He remained another week to see to the packing of his belongings and settle his affairs before he returns home," Aunt Gisella said.

"Truly, I can never thank you enough for allowing me to come. I feel at home already. It is a dream come true."

"Thank us...for allowing you to come? Nonsense! We are the ones who wish to thank you—the saints be praised," Uncle Tito exclaimed and crossed himself. "Now, Serena will be happy, for she will have the sister she has always wished for. I, on the other hand, shall be even happier, for I shall have peace of mind."

Uncle Tito entered the conversation with the air of an admiral whose rank puts him in command and speaks to make his presence known, but has no true desire to enforce rules or lay down orders, and manages to earn respect, rally his troops and win battles without ever firing a shot.

"Oh, Papa, I do wish you had found a way to bring Maresa long before now," Serena said with obvious affection, but when she spoke to Maresa, it was with the heart of a true thespian. "Dearest Cousin, I am sorely grieved to think of all the years we missed that we should have spent together. We shall dedicate ourselves to making up for time lost! We shall be just like sisters! The war is over and we are liberated. It is time to celebrate!"

So much for society's conventions that women should be modest and reserved, Maresa thought. I have found my place!

"Two daughters, double the trouble. I think I shall stop by the monastery and talk to Father Ignatius," Uncle Tito said with a wink, and Maresa thought he looked exactly like his name, for in truth, she could not imagine him being called anything other than Uncle Tito.

"We shall do our best to make up for the lost years," Maresa said.

"Yes, we shall be even closer than sisters!" Serena replied with such feeling, it was stage worthy.

Smartly dressed in a dark-blue carriage dress, this stylish cousin of hers obviously went through life with a dramatic flair, and the exotic turban she wore seemed to validate Maresa's impression of her.

"Oh, my dear," said Uncle Tito to his wife. "I fear we may be in for it now. Do you suppose it is too late to send her back?"

There was a lull in conversation after Uncle Tito announced it was time to start the journey home, and he handed them into the carriage one at a time, while the two postilions saw to the loading of Maresa's luggage.

Soon everyone was tucked away inside the carriage, where they resumed their conversation, until Uncle Tito fell asleep, and the three women smiled at each other and fell into silent contemplation.

As for Maresa, she had her face to the window, and thought it fortunate that her arrival in Leghorn was so early in the morning, which meant she would have the opportunity to see a great deal of the Tuscan countryside before darkness covered it for the night.

She was in Italy, and the excitement of it began to settle in.

Italy!

She bit her lip, as if trying to decide if what was happening, if what she saw, was real. Here she was, on her way to Florence. The same Florence she had studied when she was younger. Florence, so crammed with history.

Those are Italian trees, and I am breathing Italian air. Tonight I will sleep in an Italian bed, and tomorrow morning I will eat my first Italian breakfast.

A carriage passed and the driver cracked his whip and said something in Italian to the horses. She had not thought about that, but of course it would be, that the animals here understood Italian. Intelligent beasts.

Maresa inquired about Pisa—would they be going near it?

Aunt Gisella said they had already passed it some time ago, and promised they would bring her back another time to see the leaning tower.

The road, as it ran along the Arno River, tinged a muddy brown, was respectable without too many potholes, and the countryside as lovely as any she had seen in England.

They left the Arno, and the road began to wind its way through varicolored patches of soft colors spread over the landscape like a collection of incongruous bits of fabric, yet nothing more than the contrast between meadows, woods and cornfields, grapevines and olive trees.

It was Maresa's first glimpse of the vines that produced wine, and she was surprised to see they were not planted in neat rows, as crops in England, but were left free to twine around the trees in the hedgerow.

Her gaze followed the curve of a stream as the carriage began to climb a steep hill. The road had narrowed considerably, and on Maresa's side, she could see over the edge of a precipice to where the land unfolded to a flat, rolling plain.

It was a fast-paced trip, with one stop to sleep and a few stops to rest the horses before they turned through an ancient iron gate and traveled up an avenue that ran between two rows of tall, slender cypress trees, that led, as Serena pointed out, "to the main entrance, the villa and the ancestral chapel, as well as the lemon-house, servants' quarters, and the gardens and fountain."

Hugging the top of a hill was Villa Mirandola, an ancient villa of noble ancestry, surrounded by a balustraded terrace, with sweeping views from all four sides.

When the carriage stopped, Maresa stepped from the warm confines of the coach into the cool shadows of a stone-flagged archway, lined with lemon trees in terra-cotta pots almost hidden beneath a cascading abundance of flowers.

She paused a moment, before following

her aunt and uncle into the villa that would be her home during the coming year.

Accustomed to the lovely country homes and palaces of England, Maresa was totally unprepared for the understated beauty of such a home. She looked back over the landscape, her gaze following the straight lane of cypress trees that the coach had traveled down only moments ago. On a rise in the distance, the square tower of a monastery reached into the heavens, not far from where the towers of a medieval city clung tenaciously to a hill.

"Welcome to Villa Mirandola," Aunt Gisella said, as she joined Maresa. "It is the home of your ancestors, and it has been in the hands of the Antonari family for centuries."

"Antonari. That was my mother's name before she married?"

"Yes, that was both our names."

Maresa remembered asking what her mother's Italian surname had been before she married, but no one at Hampton Manor knew the answer, and asking her father was out of the question.

"Maria Teresa Antonari," she whispered, hearing the sound of her mother's Italian name on her lips for the first time.

This was the house where her mother was born, and where she married a young Englishman she promised to love until the day she died, never realizing that day would come much too soon.

Aunt Gisella and Uncle Tito lived in the hills of the Tuscan countryside, an hour's drive from

Florence, where the earth was hard baked and rocky, a mix of limestone and clay, scattered with the smooth round stones of marl and alberese.

Grapevines and olive trees did not seem to mind the thin, fertile layer of soil, in this place of struggle, that was older than the medieval battles between the provinces of Siena and Florence.

"Are you coming, *fioralina?*" Aunt Gisella asked.

Maresa smiled and said, "Yes, Aunt."

Fioralina...little flower. How dear this place and these people were to her already, and she had yet to set foot inside the villa.

At that moment, Maresa felt tremendous sadness for her mother who died so young, but sadder still that she had to leave the sun-warmed beauty of such a place, for the cold and barren loneliness of the Yorkshire moors.

"Take Maresa up to her room," Gisella said to Serena. "I will find Anna and Patrizia and send them up to help."

Gisella was looking at Maresa in a reflective manner. "Dear child. I see the shadow of my sister across your face. You are so very much like her."

"I never knew that until my father came to Yorkshire on my seventeenth birthday, and when he saw me, he looked as if he had seen a ghost. He called me by my mother's name. I'm glad I look like her. She was very beautiful."

"Yes, she was."

"Well, you look like her, too," Serena said.

Gisella smiled. "Well, yes, I suppose I do."

"Was your resemblance strong when you were my age?"

"Of course it was, silly!" Serena said. "They were twins!"

"Oh, my dear, I can tell by your face that you did not know that," Gisella said.

"No...no one told me that."

"I am sure that is largely the reason why your father never invited us to visit, and why he did not tell us of Teresa's death until after she was buried."

"I suppose that would make sense," Maresa said, still stunned to learn her mother was a twin.

Aunt Gisella said, "I thought you might like to be in your mother's room, which was a good thing, because Serena wanted you next to her. I believe I wrote you about it."

"Yes, you did, and I cannot think of a place I would rather be."

"Why don't you take Maresa up to see her room, then?" Aunt Gisella said to Serena.

When they walked into the chamber that belonged to her mother, Maresa was reminded that this was where she slept until the day she married Maresa's father. She could not say anything, for she could not find the words to describe the flow of emotions that swept over her.

The walls were covered with *trompe l'oeil* pastoral scenes, with birdcages and statues against a backdrop of Tuscan scenery. A four-poster bed of wrought iron stood against one wall, next to a large window, with the shutters thrown open to let in the afternoon breeze.

On the opposite wall, next to the fireplace, stood a chair Serena identified as a "Louis Seize wing chair and ottoman." Along another wall, in a deep alcove, stood a Thonet chair and washstand with an earthenware jug and basin.

"My mother kept the same furniture and carpets that your mother used," Serena said, "but the white draperies and the coverlet were replaced because they were too old and subject to tears. I know you would have liked it best if everything had remained unchanged."

"That would have been wonderful, surely, but in truth, I am so overwhelmed with the thought of simply being in my mother's chamber, among so many of her things, that I cannot imagine any more joy than this."

Serena swallowed and looked off. "Although I never met you, I always prayed for you, and asked the Virgin Mary to watch over you. From the time I was old enough to know you existed, and to hear my mother tell me the sad story about Aunt Teresa, I was sorry you never had the opportunity to know her as I know my mother."

Maresa reached out and took Serena's hand. "Thank you. I know already that you and I will be close as sisters."

"Closer," Serena said, "and now we share the same mother, which is basically what we do anyway, you see?"

While Maresa was trying to "see," Serena went on.

"I say that because our mothers were twins, and exactly alike, so that means they were the same. One was a copy of the other. Now, whenever you look at my mother, you see yours."

Maresa understood where she was going with all of this, but she did not have the heart to tell her it wasn't the same at all.

When Anna and Patricia arrived to do the unpacking, Maresa dug through her reticule to find the keys to unlock her trunks. When she came to the portmanteau, she exclaimed, "Oh, no! I cannot find the key to this one."

"Not to worry. I shall open it," Serena said. "Wait here, I'll only be a moment."

With a frown of puzzlement, Maresa watched Serena hurry from the room.

She returned moments later, with a small object that looked like a leather crafter's tool.

A look of utter astonishment froze upon Maresa's face, as she watched this lovely cousin of hers hoist up the skirts of her fine gown, get down on her knees and begin to pick the lock of her portmanteau like the most practiced thief.

The lock popped open with a loud snap!

"Wherever did you learn to do that?" Maresa asked, lowering her voice considerably, so that Anna and Patricia would not hear.

"Angelo taught me, but you mustn't tell Mamma or Papa. They would disapprove quite strongly."

"Yes, I can see how they might."

"It is a skill worth knowing. How else could I have opened your portmanteau?"

Maresa opened her mouth to answer that, but Serena must not have needed an answer, since she went on with her line of thought. "If you like, I can ask him to teach you, too."

Maresa frowned. "Thank you, but I don't think so."

"Where's the harm?" Serena asked.

"I don't know, but it does not seem right, somehow."

"Just because you know how to do it, doesn't mean you have to use it. It isn't the knowledge, but what you do with it."

"Yes, I suppose that is true. However, I do not think I will ever have a need for such a skill."

"Of course it's true, and besides, one can never be too certain it is something they will never use. My motto is, one can never be too prepared."

Much later, after Maresa and Serena had overseen the unpacking of most of the things in her trunks, which now lay in neat little piles, scattered about the room, Serena dusted her hands.

"There now, I think that is enough for now. Let the two of us be off and leave the maids to finish everything else."

Fifteen

What men call gallantry, and gods
  adultery,
Is much more common where the climate's
  sultry.

Lord Byron (1788-1824)
English poet

Serena took Maresa by the hand and pulled
her out of the room and down the hall.

"Where are we going?"

"To find Angelo."

"Oh, yes, Angelo. Tell me about him."

Serena paused. "Oh, Angelo is...Angelo!"
she said, and continued on her way.

That was almost the identical thing that Uncle
Tito said, and Maresa had to admit her curiosity was roused. "Do you know where he is?"

"Of course not, but he is around here somewhere. He likes to get himself lost."

"Why?"

"So he can seduce a maid here and there and
no one will be the wiser."

"You know, so he must not get himself too
lost."

"Angelo and I have no secrets."

"How fortunate you are to have a brother."

Serena laughed at that. "I don't...not in
the real sense, anyway. My parents found
him—a tiny baby left on our doorstep—when
I was quite small. They were certain gypsies

left him there, but it did not matter, for my mother fell in love with him and refused to give him up."

"He is like your brother, then."

"Worse! Papa says he is the embodiment of the gypsy thief and the Italian nobleman all rolled into one. Mama says, '*Lui ha il cuore da gypsy e l'anima Italiano!*' He has the heart of a gypsy and the soul of an Italian."

"And you? What do you say?"

"I say he is a clever charmer, a scene stealer, part hawker, part promenader, an interpreter of dreams, and he is as mischievous as they come. He is persuasive as the devil, rebellious one moment, and then he turns as agreeable as St. Agnes the next. You must become the best of friends with him, otherwise things will be beyond miserable."

"In that case, I hope I do as well, although you make him sound positively frightening."

"He isn't, though. He is fiercely loyal, and would lay down his life for those he loves."

"Angelo sounds perfect, which I find strange, since I was not aware men attained perfection. I thought that was reserved only for women."

Serena laughed, obviously enjoying that comment. "Oh, he is perfect all right...a perfect snoop! He loves to go prowling about and pry into the private affairs of others. He can move as quiet as a cat, and you may never know he's around. He's excessively inquisitive and, of course, a natural-born picklock."

"And you all obviously adore him."

"How could we not? Papa is fond of quoting

Falstaff's tribute to Prince Hal, 'I am bewitched with the rogue's company. If the rascal have not given me medicines to make me love him, I'll be hanged.' "

It had been a hot day, and now the sun was riding the crest of a distant hill. Soon it would disappear altogether.

Already, Maresa could tell it had cooled considerably now that the Tuscan sun was not burning down upon them, and they left the villa and walked down the tree-lined avenue. While they walked along, Maresa noticed how they kicked up tiny puffs of red earth that clung to the hem of their dresses.

She took in as much of her surroundings as she could. "It is so lovely here, and so completely different from England."

"*Sì*, it is very beautiful... *Come é bella la Toscana!* It is not so warm in England, no?"

Maresa laughed. "No, and we would definitely not call this warm in England. Faith, I daresay the sun today was boiling hot!"

"We call it *il sol leone*, the lion sun. It is both loved and quite necessary, in order to ripen the grapes and olives. Where would we be without it?"

How accepting these Italians were—accepting and appreciative, Maresa thought, for already she was beginning to see signs of their patience and tolerance everywhere. In England, everyone would be complaining profusely if the weather dared turn so hot.

But here, at Villa Mirandola, where they treasured every crumbling piece of plaster, each crack that traversed the ceiling, every inch of faded frescoes, everything remained unchanged as it had for centuries, an age-old observance, respected because of its long endurance.

Serena held her hand up to shield the last rays of sun from her eyes. "There! I think I see him."

Maresa looked toward the undulating lines of the horizon, distracted for a moment by the vivid earthy colors, the bright-blue sky, the neat plots of landscape where vines mixed with olive trees and the baked earth turned to a molten gold by the red rays of the sun.

Maresa found her reverie interrupted by the silhouette of a figure walking toward them.

As he drew closer, he waved and called out to them. *"Buona sera!* Your cousin has arrived."

From the moment she first saw him, Maresa saw that a mischievous grin was only one of Angelo's many charms.

Serena introduced them and filled him in on their trip from Livorno and the unpacking in Maresa's room.

"So, you would like me to teach you to pick the lock, eh?"

He was obviously surprised when she said, "No, I don't think that is a skill I need to develop."

"Why not?"

"One lock picker in our midst is enough, I think."

"And Serena?"

"Two lock pickers, then," Maresa amended, only to learn Angelo was not one who took no for an answer, and by the time a week had passed, Angelo and Serena declared her to be as proficient at lock picking as either of them.

Maresa did not see that in exactly the same proud vein as they did. "I pray to Heaven that I don't ever have to use this newfound talent of mine," she said, and knew somehow, that the three of them would be inseparable from here on out, and she was right.

Maresa and Serena were on their way back to the villa, after gathering wildflowers, when they saw Angelo come riding up the avenue.

He dismounted and handed his horse over to the young boy who came running toward them.

"Where have you been?" Serena asked. "Have you been trying to win Bianca Orsini's affections again?"

"I do not need to try. It comes natural, and Bianca is mad about me."

"She must be mad, if she cares for the likes of you," Serena said.

Angelo folded his arms over his chest. "You will never get a husband with a tongue like that."

"Who said I want a husband—most of the men I see make spinsterhood seem heroic."

A week ago, this sort of banter set Maresa on edge and made her uncomfortable, but she hardly noticed it now, having become so accustomed to it, since it was Serena and Angelo's favorite form of communication.

When the three of them returned to the villa, they were greeted by the infectious laughter of Aunt Gisella coming from the orangery, which the Italians called *limonaia,* or lemon-house.

"You see? Your mother does not mind being married and obedient to her husband."

"That is because she is not married to someone like you, Angelo."

"What is wrong with me?"

"You are so...so Italian! You chase a woman until she cares for you, then you avoid her to make her suffer. You are not happy until she is totally devoted to you."

"The most beautiful virtue in a woman is devotion. It is their pleasure and their destiny."

"There you go, equating innocence with ignorance. Maresa and I are not stupid."

"No, and you are not married, either."

Serena pulled two hard, little green olives from a tree and threw them at Angelo, who grabbed her and swung her around, both of them laughing.

"I cannot help but wonder how this is all going to settle down," Maresa said.

"Oh, it won't," Serena said. "We enjoy the verbal challenge too much." She paused to take a stone from her shoe. "Hold these for me," she said, and thrust her wildflowers into Angelo's hand.

They walked through the rooms lit by the late-evening sunlight lazily filtering through the closed shutters, until they stepped onto the portico, where the stone steps led down to the *limonaia*.

There, among the intoxicating scents of flowers, Aunt Gisella and Uncle Tito sat upon a stone bench, arms entwined, with Gisella's head lying on Tito's shoulder as he whispered into her ear.

Something warm seemed to flow into her and Maresa knew she had found the love, affection and the sense of familial belonging so long absent in her life.

"I have been wondering if you were going to be back in time for dinner," Gisella said, when she caught sight of the three of them standing on the steps of the portico.

"We've been picking flowers," Maresa said.

Aunt Gisella and Uncle Tito both looked at Angelo.

"Yours look a bit wilted," Uncle Tito said to Angelo, just moments before he almost threw the flowers at Serena.

"I don't gather flowers."

"I am glad to hear that," Uncle Tito said. "Where there were two, there are now three. What say you to that, Angelo?"

"Twice the women—twice the headaches!"

"Oh, I almost forgot. Come Maresa, I have something I want you to see," Aunt Gisella said, and rose to her feet.

Maresa followed her through an archway into a small courtyard, where the last long rays of sunlight lingered on walls covered in a yellow-ochre wash. She could hear the low murmur of a narrow stream of water splashing from the mouth of a *mascherone* that decorated an antique fountain.

Gisella stopped next to the fountain. "See your mother's name scratched into the stone next to mine?"

Maresa pressed her face closer to examine the markings.

"We were six when we escaped the watchful eye of our governess and carved our names on the fountain. Papa threatened to punish us and have it removed, but of course he never did."

Maresa put her finger in the grooves. "Maria Teresa," she whispered, feeling as close to her mother as she did when she held her mother's necklace. She was glad she came here, where she could add substance to the shadow of her mother.

Gisella put her hand on Maresa's arm. "Come Maresa, let us go inside and ready ourselves for dinner."

"I will be along in a moment, Aunt."

Gisella looked at Maresa and then at the fountain, where she and her twin made their mark so long ago. With a knowing smile, she said, "Of course, but don't be overlong."

"I won't, Aunt."

After everyone had gone, Maresa sat beside the fountain, while she trailed her fingers through the water and thought of her mother.

It was almost dark when she stood to return to the villa, and saw Angelo walking toward the arched doorway.

"You are still here," Angelo said. "I was sent to find you. Dinner is ready."

"I'm sorry. I lingered overlong."

He stopped in front of her. "Do not be sorry, *fiammetta,* for it gives me a chance to speak to you alone."

Fiammetta? He called me "my flame." Maresa wondered why. "You wish to speak to me? About what?"

"Love...love has made me speak to you, *fiammetta.*" He took her in his arms and kissed her with passion.

She shoved him away. "What is wrong with you, Angelo? Is this the way you greet every woman you meet?"

"No *bella,* only the pretty ones."

"I'm not that pretty!"

"*Fiammetta,* you did not like it?"

"Stop calling me that! Really, Angelo! I am not your flame, and you cannot desire to speak to me as such...we only met a week ago. Go try that impassioned display on Bianca."

"I cannot help it. Love guides me...my words, my actions. Bianca is a child."

"This is absurd. I know that you, Serena and I shall have a deep and long-lasting friendship. Unfortunately for you, that is all we are going to have. Ever!"

"You do not have any feelings for me beyond friendship?" he asked, not looking particularly embarrassed or upset over her declaration.

She shook her head. "I am sorry, but there can be nothing beyond friendship."

"You love another?"

"No, but I am certain I will soon."

"All right. Let us go eat, then."

As quickly as his fiery intensity of feeling swept over him, it seemed to vanish. There was something unsettling about a man who could shift his affections from a woman to food as quickly as he had done, and she was left to wonder if this was the way with all Italian men, or was it simply something particular to Angelo.

As they walked along together, Maresa's curiosity got the best of her, and she could not help asking, "Can you explain to me, what got into you back there?"

"What do you mean?"

"How can you explain your actions...calling me *fiammetta,* and taking such liberties?"

He shrugged. "I am Italian."

I am Italian.

She mulled the words over. *I am Italian...*as if that was all the explanation necessary. Italians, she decided, were most assuredly creatures of impulse.

From that moment on, they were the best of friends.

185

Sixteen

A little still she strove, and much repented,
And whispering 'I will ne'er
consent'—consented.

> Lord Byron (1788-1824)
> English poet

Here, in the land that gave birth to the Renaissance, Uncle Tito did his best to carry on the traditions established by Cosimo de Medici, and looked upon the land as not only a place to live in peace, but as a good source of investment and profit.

He was not the first to do so, for Michelangelo and Dante had at one time lived here, and Machiavelli's home in Sant'Andrea in Percussina, was not very far away.

Galileo too, forgot his battles with science and the accusations of heresy, to take pleasure in drinking the wines and caring for the vines, which he pruned himself. "Wine," he said, "is like the blood of the land, the sun captured and transformed by such a complex structure as the grape berry...composed of light, it expands the soul and comforts the spirits."

And so it was, that in this rocky, hilly agrarian land called Chianti that was so unsuitable for agriculture, Uncle Tito planted rows of vines that hugged the hills and slopes, and lovingly tended his grapes to produce his beloved Chianti.

"A cask of wine works more miracles than a church full of saints," Uncle Tito said one afternoon after they returned from a walk through the vineyards.

"My Tito loves his Chianti, can you tell?" Aunt Gisella asked.

"Oh, yes," Maresa replied. "And now that I have tried it myself, I understand completely. I look forward to the fall, when the grapes are ready to pick, so I can see how they transform themselves into wine. Then, all I need is an occasion to drink it!"

"We are never at a loss for reasons to drink Chianti," Aunt Gisella said.

"There are five reasons for drinking," Uncle Tito said. "The arrival of a friend, one's present or future thirst, the excellence of the wine...or any other reason."

By the time Maresa had been in Tuscany a few months, she had two offers of marriage, but came close to accepting only one of them.

"Why did you decline both offers?" Angelo asked.

"I've grown weary of being engaged and then crying off."

"Just how many engagements did you break in London?"

"Two."

"Two broken engagements is not so bad," Angelo said.

"That is two broken engagements in London," Maresa added, sounding a bit remorseful. "There was another one in Yorkshire…and one misunderstanding."

"Well, you should be getting good at it, *cara. Sbagliando s'impara.*"

"My Italian isn't that good!" she said, feeling somewhat dismayed.

"*Sbagliando s'impara!* It means, we learn by our mistakes."

"What are you two talking about?" Serena asked as she came into the room. She did not wait for an answer. "Mama sent me to find you. It is time to dress. Papa has ordered the carriage for eight o'clock, and he said we mustn't be late. Everyone comes to the balls during the carnival season, because they know there won't be any more for a whole year, once Lent starts. We need to start dressing now, because it will take some time to get ready."

Even in England, Maresa had heard of the famous Italian masquerade balls that were held during the carnival season, but never did she dream she would actually be going to one.

So it came as a complete surprise when Aunt Gisella stopped by her room a few days ago. Maresa, sitting on the bed, was delighted her aunt decided to join her there. She spoke about the carnival season, which consisted of customs that dated back to the time of the ancient Romans. It began at Epiphany, or Christmas to mark the season for entertainment and festivities, and would continue until Shrove Tuesday, the beginning of Lent. It was a time when social barriers between the classes and the sexes were shamelessly ignored, power was mocked, and every inhibition released in the search for the wildest of pleasures.

Maresa was immediately informed that no one in the Bartolini household would be taking part in these inhibitions, since they attended only one masquerade ball each season, and that was at the villa of the Marchesa Dionisitti, between Florence and Fiesole.

"In my opinion, it is the most civilized function during Carnival," Aunt Gisella said, "although there have been rumors, from time to time, of occasional wickedness in the past."

"What exactly, happens during carnival to make it so wicked?" Maresa asked.

"I must point out, that since Napoleon, things have changed somewhat. However, you will still find those who have something dishonorable to hide, have the most to fear. Groups of revelers would stand beneath the windows of those known to be guilty, and mock and ridicule them without mercy. It did not matter who you were, or how influential you had become. This meant adulterous husbands, tavern owners who served watered-down wine, corrupt notaries and lawyers, priests who had not remained celibate, drunkards, loose women, and the like... they were all subject to disdain and humiliation. The bad part was, they were unable to speak in their defense, for to do so, only made their mockery worse."

"But, how do they get away with it?"

"The mask, my dear, the mask! It is something to hide behind...something to guarantee anonymity."

Maresa was thinking about her broken engagements, and wondered if she might be likewise singled out. But how would they know? she asked herself, and gave it no more thought.

"Now, when your mother and I were little girls, *Epifania,* or Epiphany was our favorite time of year, for that was when our father would tell us stories of the old woman, *La Befana,* who would come at night to fill the children's shoes with the gifts they had wished for, and they would discover them on the morning of the Three Kings." She sighed and seemed so wistful, Maresa did not move.

Aunt Gisella shook her head, as if chasing away a spell, and drew her feet upon the bed, and locked her arms around her knees. "I remember our father taking Teresa and me to the Epiphany Fair in Florence, so we could buy little glass trumpets. And then he had to listen to their shrill noise all the way home."

Maresa laughed. "It must have been a wonderful time to be a child."

"Yes, it was, except for the illness that claimed so many of them, before they reached adulthood." She dropped her arms and swung her feet off the bed. "Well, I suppose we better get dressed, or Tito will start to pace the floor."

Maresa followed her aunt out into the hallway, and went next door to Serena's room.

The maids had already placed Maresa's *Queen Isabella* costume on the bed by the time she arrived there. She was about to start dressing when Anna came in to help her.

Soon, she stood before the mirror in a regal gown of coral brocade, overlaid with black lace and beautifully embroidered with gold thread. Then came the worst part, sitting still while Anna dressed her hair and secured a gold crown Aunt Gisella had given her to wear.

Dressed now, she picked up her embroidered shawl, and the mask of black and gold and went to see how far along Serena, the shepherdess was.

"Oh, Maresa, you are stunning. Mother was right. The colors are perfect on you."

Aunt Gisella poked her head through the door. "Come, my darlings, Merlin is standing at the bottom of the stairs with a crystal ball in his hands and promises to turn us all into frogs if we don't hurry."

Down the stairs they went, Aunt Gisella a beautiful Guinevere in a deep-blue velvet, Serena a shepherdess in red and white, and Maresa.

And there, at the bottom of the stairs, standing beside impatient Merlin was Angelo. "You are absolutely the most perfect Harlequin I could ever imagine," Maresa said, while thinking he looked very handsome in his costume of diamond-patterned, multicolored cloth.

"We call him *Arlecchino*," Angelo said. "He

is the witty character who was supposed to have been the leader of a band of demons. As a remnant of his half-devilish origin, he still wears a black mask."

"I think you should have been *Punchinello,* with the big yellow nose—very appropriate," Serena said. Then to Maresa she added, "It looks like a big chicken!"

"My nose is not big."

"It is big enough to hold up your mask, and that is a good thing," Merlin said. "Now, may we all proceed to the carriage, so we can arrive before it is time to leave?"

It had stopped snowing, and the pale light of late afternoon captured the feeling of winter as Maresa took in the overcast sky. Quiet tranquility seemed to pervade everything.

She sat silently in the coach, listening to the occasional bursts of conversation as she looked out the window to take in the rich orchestration of subtle pinks and mauves, or the occasional cold teal of a gate.

Soon, the angle, length and color of the shadows on the snow would announce the arrival of night, and the beginning of Carnival.

"Have we passed the Capponis' gate?" Aunt Gisella asked.

"A moment ago," Uncle Tito said. "How could you miss that long, brown façade?"

"I fear my mind was elsewhere," she said, and Maresa wondered at the knowing look that passed between the two of them.

"There is the Alloris' country house," Serena said. "It won't be long now."

Aunt Gisella looked out the window. "You know, I do believe they have added more porticos and lengthened the balcony."

Maresa pulled her gaze away from the window and leaned back, enjoying the documentary that she saw unfolding, and the way her relatives added their own interpretations and observations to define the relationship between culture and nature. She was beginning to notice the intimate relationship Tuscans seemed to have with their surroundings, for not only did they enjoy adding their individual touches to the land, but they appeared to take great pleasure whenever they noticed familiar landmarks, or a well-known crossroad as they traveled.

The coach left the sunken road, cut deep into rock by use and the passage of time, and drove through a tall gate bearing the Dionisitti coat of arms. To the right of the gate, a dozen lit candles illuminated a small shrine to the Virgin Mary.

The carriage passed through the gate and continued up the lane that led to the marchesa's villa. Between the tall towers of cypress, Maresa caught an occasional glimpse of silver-gray olive trees, but by the time they reached their destination, it had grown too dark to see much of anything.

Villa Dionisitti boasted as ancient and noble an ancestry as the marchesa.

By the time they arrived at the marchesa's

villa, Maresa knew the first two verses of an old Carnival song, *Una Volta Anticamente*.

Her heart was racing when the carriage stopped, for she had never seen costumes like these. Each one was like a piece of art. She knew she would never be able to pick a favorite, for every one she saw was her favorite—until another one came along.

As they entered the villa, Maresa could hear the music coming out of the ballroom greeting them with gay notes, effervescent as champagne.

"We must hurry," Serena, said, "the quadrilles are going on."

The ballroom of the villa was unlike anything Maresa had seen in England. Two-storied, and frescoed with quadrature, it appeared enormous, even when filled with people. And the people were everywhere, laughing and dancing, while Maresa could only stand there and stare.

Le Maschere! The mask!

They were everywhere, for no face was visible, and soon Maresa found she was beginning to like the idea of being completely incognito and unidentifiable. Now she could understand how Carnival could become a time for mischief and wickedness.

"Come, my queen, dance with me." Maresa recognized that voice. "Angelo," she whispered, "I do not know if I can dance in this. The brocade is so heavy."

"If you fall, I promise to help you up."

"I am relieved to learn you have a chivalrous side."

"Of course. I almost came as Sir Lancelot."

"That would have been nice, too. What made you change your mind?"

"I do not know how to behave like the English. They are too reserved and cold."

"No, they aren't...well, not all the time."

"You see? Even you cannot deny it. If I were Sir Lancelot, I would be standing stiffly along the wall talking, like the English minister over there, but since I am Italian, I am dancing with Queen Isabella."

"Well, you should not lump all the English together like that."

"Why not? It is true. When I go to bed at night, I have a woman! The English have bed warmers."

Maresa laughed. "You are incorrigible, but I cannot imagine you any other way."

The music ended and Angelo asked if she would like something to drink.

"I think I need a glass of champagne," she said.

"Will you topple over in your heavy dress if I leave you here a moment to go after your champagne?"

"You could prop me up against the wall over there, with the English minister."

"I like you here. I'll be right back."

Maresa watched him, and smiled when a woman in a domino mask pulled him into another quadrille that was just beginning. She was about to set off for champagne herself, when she was captured in the arms of Henry VIII, and found herself dancing the quadrille as well.

After several dances, she went in search of Serena and Angelo.

Certain they were no longer in the ball-room, she began to thread her way through the smaller rooms adjoining the ballroom.

Before long, she found herself in a deserted room, dimly lit by single candelabra. She must have made a wrong turn somewhere.

Her first instinct was to return the way she had come, but she noticed a large window with the protruding dome of the grotto illuminated in the moonlight.

She stepped closer, to capture the sight of the snow glistening on the grotesque masks that crowned the grotto, and the haunting statue of a slain dragon in the center.

A sudden draft, as if someone had opened a door, wafted through the room and the candelabra dimmed and went out. Maresa gasped and whirled around, but she was unable to see anything.

"Hello," she whispered. "Is anyone here?"

"*Una donna alla finestra è come un grappolo d'uva su una strada.* You are English," came a whispered, masculine reply, which was followed by the warmth of a hand that slid down her arm.

She jumped and pulled back. *Una donna alla finestra è come un grappolo d'uva su una strada,* she thought. A woman at the window is like a bunch of grapes in the road?

She shivered at the thought of being compared to a bunch of grapes, ripe for the plucking.

"Don't be afraid," he said. "In a moment, your eyes will adjust to the darkness."

There was only the light of one candle that burned on a nearby table, but it was enough to see he was wearing a favorite costume called the *bautta*.

He was dressed in black velvet, with a black silk hood and voluminous cloak called a *tabarro*. His mask was white, and covered his face completely. The three-cornered hat partially shaded his face and made his eyes difficult to see.

"Who are you?" she asked.

"A guest, like you."

"I—I must get back. My family will be looking for me."

"A moment, *dolcissimo,* and I will escort you there myself."

She tried to leave, but there was something wrong with her feet, for they were unable to move.

He put his hand on her shoulder.

His touch was foreign to her, and she stood woodenly before him, awkward and uncertain, not at all the composed young woman who had broken so many hearts, and almost as many engagements.

She wondered why she did not simply turn and walk away, but the power of the revelers from the ballroom, the spirit of *Carnevale,* the lawless power of costume and mask served to disarm her sense of propriety, and drew her into the dark ritual of merriment.

The lone candle sputtered and went out.

The lights beyond the door grew dim and she was captured in a dreamlike state. The music faded, as did the sound of conversation that only a moment ago, drifted about her.

There was no fire in this room and the air was cold. With each breath she could feel its bite, yet she felt uncommonly warm.

He removed her mask, but did not touch his own.

She was beginning to tremble, not from the cold, but from the audacious direction of her thoughts. The vision of his mask as it danced in her head, and her own unmasked state touched her in some unfamiliar way, and she could feel herself being drawn forward into the power of masquerade and shadow, and unrestrained night.

Her mask gone, she could no longer hide behind its pretense. Not that she wanted to. Perhaps this was what she wanted all along, this unrestrained freedom to give in to the unknown world where those things forbidden reside; a purgatory of wants and needs and desire.

She tilted her head back, unable to see him, but she knew he was quite near. She could feel the warmth of his body reaching out to her, and she thought he must have just come inside, for his clothes smelled of fresh air and pine.

Something warm and gripping filled her, urging, and she hovered on the brink of unmasking all the rigid philosophy, the restrictions, the chains of conformity that bound her so tightly.

"I have thought of nothing, *cara,* since I first saw you, far more fair than any queen, even fair Isabella."

"But, I am Isabella."

"Are you? Or is it because this is the night when no one is who they are, and everyone is someone they are not?"

She could feel his breath, the smell and heat of his words that spread over her, mind numbing, and calm as the snow that comes, quiet as fog, to settle over a field.

"I must go back."

He pulled her with him, deeper into the room, into the unknown, and she followed, blind and trusting, when she knew she should not go. "I cannot."

A rustle of fabric in darkness; she knew it was the sound of him removing his own mask. Blindfolded by the surrounding darkness, she could see little more than dark shadow and shades of light.

He pressed against her and she felt the wall against her back. His hands were on her face, her throat, her shoulders, and then skimming lightly over her breasts to encircle her waist. His arms went around her, and she opened her mouth and drew in a breath of air, only to feel the shock of surrounding warmth of his kiss.

She felt every point of pressure of his body, knew the places where naked skin touched naked skin and two people meet as equals, in desire and lack of pretense.

She was shocked, first by his sheer audacity, and later by the pleasure that had no name, the absence of shame, and the thrill of anonymity that coursed, silent as an underground river.

She had a vague thought that she should run from the seduction of this place, but it was a thought never put into action. He kissed her again, more firmly this time, and with a question she was afraid to answer.

New awareness. Transformation. A flowing inward, into herself, spiraling and hot, hotter still, melting wax held over a candle.

She knew the warm texture of his mouth, his taste, the smell of his breath, the curl of sensation at his touch and the spirit of the night came into her and swept her back, far back, into the primitive world where two people stood, naked and full of new knowledge in a long-lost garden.

The kiss was long, longer than her thoughts of resistance, but not as long as her desire for more. Everything about him, this house, the very idea of *Carnevale* was surreal, a room of mirrors, a villa swimming with ghosts and mysterious undercurrents. Nothing seemed real.

Nothing except the kiss that left a burning reminder imprinted on her lips.

Her hand came up, to spread over his chest, a mute show of resistance, but the moment she touched him, she found her fingers clutched the silk of his cloak instead.

He removed his mouth, and by this time, she was beginning to get a pretty good idea as to the meaning of the looks that passed between her aunt and uncle on occasion, and she found the idea of it intriguing enough that she wanted to explore it further.

"You taste like almond nectar," he whispered while he kissed her throat and shoulders.

Maresa shuddered. "I don't think…" Her head ached with the effort expended as she searched for the words.

"Good. I prefer it if you don't. *Carnevale* is not a time for thinking."

He kissed her again, and Maresa began to grow afraid, prompted by the cold water of thought, afraid not of what he would do, but of what she might allow him to.

"Please," she whispered, "I cannot…"

"Why can't you? At a masquerade, no one knows you, and you can do what you like, for everywhere you go, mystery and the black of night cover you. When you are unknown, you are never gossiped about, for all your desires and dalliances are like the creation of Gothic art, conceived in passion by persons unknown. So, there you have it, my shy, mysterious love—hidden meaning, hidden beauty, hidden fires."

"I have never known anyone so bold." She pulled back. "You are…shameless."

"Bold and shameless men are masters of half the world," he whispered, placing little nibbling kisses along her throat.

"*A mali estremi, estremi rimedi,*" she said, and hauled off and kicked him on the shin. Hard.

She grabbed her heavy skirts and tried to run,

but the bulk of fabric slowed her to a fast walk, however it was enough to get her away from him and out of the room.

"Extreme situations call for extreme remedies," he translated. "You will have to do better than that, *cara*."

She did not look back, but somehow she knew, he was still there, in the dark room, watching her, his face hidden in shadow.

She secured her mask, and started off again.

This time, she walked faster down one hallway, and turned down another, until she came to a long corridor and a flight of stairs. She turned around and around, looking for something she recognized, but saw only the blurring of candlelight from the candelabras overhead, mirrored and bright.

She heard a woman's throaty laugh, and headed in that direction, and soon she was surrounded by the revelry once again, and was absorbed by others like herself, masked and in costume, while seeking to throw off the restrictions and injustice of life in the wild abandon of celebration lasting only one night.

Seventeen

Lord! I wonder what fool it was that first invented kissing.

> Jonathan Swift (1667-1745)
> Irish author and clergyman

Maresa did not realize until much later, after they arrived home, that something had changed, or was it that she had changed?

The long-locked door to awareness had been thrown open. Her unknown admirer had given her a glimpse into another world she only thought she knew existed, but he had stopped there, and now she would never know the rest of what he might have shown her.

She was aware of her body as something other than a shrine on which to hang clothes, and was left uncertain as to which she felt more, a desire to chastise him for the doing of it, or her eternal gratitude for leading her out of the Middle Ages and into another era, enlightened and aware.

As she lay sleepless in her bed, she thought about the man she had no name for, and knew that he would not be as easy to forget as she hoped.

She may have rid herself of the man, but her heart still clung to his memory.

The next evening, she stepped in the snow-dusted tracks where others had walked before her, on their way into the theater to attend the performance of the ballet, *Apollo and Terpsichore.*

Once inside, Aunt Gisella commented on how quiet Maresa was.

"Do you feel well, dear?" Uncle Tito asked.

"I'm fine, Uncle."

"She is probably still tired from last night," Aunt Gisella said. "We were out much later than I intended."

"Oh, but it was such a grand evening," Serena said. "I danced holes in my slippers."

"It is not you we are worried about," Uncle Tito said. "You have never had a quiet day in your life, Serena. I have never known anyone who lived up to her name any less."

"I know," she said with a sigh. "There are so many things that bear repeating, or new thoughts that cannot wait to be given life. How does one resist the urge to speak?"

"When we discover the secret to that, you will be the first one we tell," Angelo said.

If the truth were known, Maresa was a bit melancholy, for she still could not shake the memory of the kisses she shared with the masked stranger. Tonight, she hardly saw what was being performed on stage, for she was too occupied with allowing her gaze to scan the audience, as if by doing so, she might catch a glimpse of the faceless, nameless man.

She could not help wondering if he thought of her at all. Did he know who she was? Had he singled her out intentionally, or was it simply a chance meeting?

Would she ever see him again?

No, she knew she would not. It was one of the rules of *Carnevale,* as well as the mystery.

Her thoughts spun backward, to that night, after she left him, and how she learned that all decisions have their good and bad sides. Even now, she could feel the frustration she felt then, when all her inquiries about him turned up nothing.

Few had seen him.

No one seemed to know who he was.

Not even Angelo, who always knew everything about everyone.

There were no clues as to his identity. No proof that he even existed at all, save in the fires of recalled moments.

It did not change the way she felt, or lessen her desire to see him again. It only made it more difficult to realize she was aching for a man she did not know and probably would never see again, based solely upon the mystery of his kiss, and the wonderful things it did to her.

Admitting this made Maresa wonder about a lot of things, one of them being her criteria for falling in love.

That was when she began to wonder if all the times before, when she fancied herself in love, if she had simply been in love with the concept of love, for this was the first time she could recall her attraction to someone being based upon the lure of desire, and not the more superficially defined things.

By the time they were all gathered together in the carriage for the journey home, Maresa was beginning to accept the fact that she would not be able to change things, and she might as well learn to live with it.

When she told Serena about it, and confessed some of her frustrations and feelings to her cousin, Serena was sad along with her. "I am so sorry, Maresa. I truly wish you could have been better strangers."

Two days passed, and Maresa went about her daily routine, but always before her was the memory of the masked guest. His memory transformed her, at least inwardly, but on the outside, she did not seem all that different. She still wondered if she would ever come to her senses and put this man out of her mind.

Monday was her day to write letters and, on this Monday, Maresa was doing just that—sitting by the fire, writing a letter to her sister, Beatrice. She paused to reflect upon the latest gossip Beatrice reported being said about her in London: that Maresa had been sent to Italy to have a baby.

Her first reaction was outrage, but that soon died away.

Let them think and say what they will, she thought, as she gazed out the window. Somehow, looking at the world outside changed her perspective. Before long, she forgot about the things being said about her, and began to notice that everything outside was dressed in shades of brown, ochre, gray and blue, with splashes of white—something that hinted at the intense cold.

She caught a glimpse of movement out of the corner of her eye, and upon closer inspection, noticed the distant figure of someone riding up the road near a screen of chestnut trees, and how his gray horse and black cape seemed absorbed into the enveloping landscape of winter. I do hope the poor fool doesn't have far to go, she thought, and turned her gaze away.

When she finished the letter she placed it in an envelope, then turned it over to write the name and address on the front when Aunt Gisella came into the room, wearing a dress of soft gray wool, which seemed to go perfectly with the weather outside.

She paused and rubbed her arms and drew her shawl more snugly about her. "Dear me, aren't you cold in here? Shall I have Italo bring in more wood for the fire?"

"Thank you, Aunt, but I am almost finished here."

Aunt Gisella smiled. "I will send Italo to build up the fire. You have a visitor, and I would not want him to freeze."

Maresa's face registered surprise, for visitors were not something that was either ordinary or expected. She mulled over the possibilities and gave up, since there were no real possibilities. "A visitor? Now, who would be foolish enough to brave such wretched weather to come here on a day like this?"

Aunt Gisella smiled, with an expression

that said she was really enjoying this. "Someone who thinks a great deal of you would be my guess. Of course, if you are not interested in having a visitor, I will be glad to inform him."

Maresa sprang to her feet. "Where is he?"

Amusement settled over Aunt Gisella's face so easily, it was obvious it was an emotion she felt frequently. "In the receiving room. Wait here and I will send him to you."

Maresa still had no idea who it could be... unless... No, that was impossible. "You will not tell me who it is?"

"No, I like the idea of it being a surprise."

Maresa hated surprises. More than enough of them had been played on her as a child and even now, the bitter reminder of it was never far away, and would come flooding back with all the sharpness she felt back then.

She had learned the more one knew about what went on around them, the better prepared they were to deal with it. Her aunt was acting strangely and, even more odd, she seemed to be enjoying it.

Truly baffled now, Maresa was challenged to figure out who the man was before she saw him, for she did not want to be caught off guard. "Won't you at least give me a clue, Aunt?"

"No, it is much better this way, believe me."

Maresa knew it could not be the man from the marchesa's ball, because she had not mentioned it to her aunt. But, what if he simply showed up and asked to see her, stating they met the night of the ball?

That was ridiculous and she knew it. Even if he did know who she was and where she lived, he would never be so bold as to ride up to her door and ask to see her.

Aunt Gisella smiled warmly and put her hand on Maresa's cheek. "Stop fidgeting and relax. Surprises are delightful...especially this one! I will be back in a moment."

Off she went, with an extra bounce in her walk, or so it seemed to Maresa, who took a deep breath and willed herself to relax, since that was one of her few options. Thankfully, she would not have long to wait.

She ran her hand over an old wooden box, with the top and sides handsomely carved with scenes of the Creation. She was about to pick up an icon of the Virgin Mary, when she heard the sound of approaching footsteps.

She turned toward the door as Percy walked into the room, followed by Italo with an armload of firewood.

Thrilled as she was to see him, she feared she did a poor job of hiding the disappointment that filled her, for she had secretly hoped her visitor was the black-caped Lothario from the marchesa's ball.

It only took a moment for it to register on her that this was Percy she was looking at, and she hurried toward him.

"Dearest Percy!" she said, and embraced him. "I cannot believe you are here! How did you manage to get away? Oh, I have sorely missed you," she said in sincere honesty.

"And I you. How have you been faring?

You look even better than I remembered, if that is possible."

"I have been well," she replied, pushing aside the memory of another man, to enjoy the presence of someone who had always been dear. "I cannot believe you are here. Why didn't you tell me you were coming, you scoundrel?"

"I was in Sicily, awaiting my new orders, and decided to pay you a visit, even though it will be a short one. I do not have much time."

"How much time is that?"

"Only two days."

"Two days! Oh, I do wish it were longer."

"As do I."

"Well, we shall make the most of it. Compared with not seeing you at all, two days are wonderful."

He did not seem to be listening, but preoccupied with careful scrutiny of her face. "How have you been? Are you enjoying Tuscany?"

"I have never been better. I am truly happy here. As for Tuscany, I never imagined I would love it or feel at home as much as I do. You will fall in love with it here though, so I might as well warn you."

Serena and Aunt Gisella came into the room.

"You have met my family?" Maresa asked.

Percy nodded. "I did, and I had a nice visit with Serena while your aunt went to find you."

Serena blushed slightly. "Mama told him you read his letters until they are fair to crumbling," she said, obviously itching to cast herself into the conversation.

Without taking his gaze from Maresa's face, Percy said, "I shall make it a point to write more often, then."

"You could write to me, as well," Serena said, and everyone laughed.

"Hmmm," Aunt Gisella said as she gave Percy the once over, "I wonder. Is it the man? Or is it the uniform?"

"Oh, it's both!" Serena said, so eagerly that everyone broke into fresh peals of laughter.

Maresa joined the laughter, for she understood an eligible man was often considered to be a fair conquest for all the daughters in a family, and frequently, if a young man pursued one daughter with no avail, another daughter quickly let it be known that the young man might have better luck with her.

It was the first time Maresa truly thought about the idea of Percy falling in love with someone, for she had always thought of him as her personal friend and confidant, and childishly must have expected him to spend the rest of his life in that capacity.

She was greatly surprised to realize that she did not receive too well the idea of Percy with another woman. When she approached it logically, she understood he was her friend. Nothing more. And that meant it was also logical that he would at some point, want to marry and have a family. But, there was still that little bit of selfishness within her that did not own up to the thought of him as hers.

"I do hope you will plan to stay with us while you are in Tuscany," Aunt Gisella said, her voice full of warmth and sincerity. "We will not think of you leaving to stay elsewhere. Think of this as your home anytime you are here, Lieutenant. Our doors are always open to you."

"Thank you for your kindness and the generous offer of such hospitality," Percy replied. "I would be greatly honored to be a guest in such a lovely home. I have often wished for the time to come here and acquaint myself with the family Maresa writes about in her letters with such fondness."

"Then let me extend an invitation to you to join us for Christmas."

"I am most grateful for the invitation, and would be honored to accept, if I did not have to report back to Palermo three days from now."

"Is there no way you could extend your visit?" Aunt Gisella asked.

"I'm afraid there is not. The *Nottingham* will be docking at Palermo three or four days from now, and I must be there before she sets sail. Unfortunately, it is not something I can change."

"Nor would you want to," Aunt Gisella said, "but do keep in mind that your company is always appreciated and you are welcome here whenever you can arrange it."

Aunt Gisella invited him to lunch, and they all proceeded to the dining room. "I am sorry Angelo and Tito will not be here until later. They rode to Greve on business yesterday. We are expecting them back this evening, so hopefully they will arrive in time to join us for dinner tonight. I know you would appreciate having some men about."

"I look forward to it," Percy said, "but with three lovely ladies to dine with, I cannot truthfully say I am in distress."

"Maresa, you did not tell me your friend was so charming."

"I did not want to spoil the surprise of discovering it for yourself," Maresa replied.

Lunchtime opened the way to the relaxed repartee that was the usual accompaniment to family meals at the Bartolinis'. As for Maresa, she tried to follow the conversation, but it was useless. Her mind wandered too much, and she was only aware of a bit of conversation that hovered momentarily in her conscious mind, before it floated away.

Tell me about your family, Lieutenant.

Most of the wine that we produce here is sold to vendors in Florence.

I wish you could have seen Maresa at the Marchesa's ball the other night.

Yes, I have considered remaining in the Royal Navy when the war is over.

Remind me to show you the portraits of my mother hanging in the gallery.

This is delicious; what do you call it?

My husband was born into a family of bankers with an aptitude for agriculture.

I could sit here talking for the rest of the evening.

Maresa did not know why she suddenly found Percy so much more interesting to observe than partaking in the verbal exchange going on around her. It was not something she decided to do, but was rather the result of seeing him in a new light.

She had never really considered the easy charm, the equal measures of polish, education and interest he displayed during discussions such as this. Nor had she been completely aware of the respect and admiration he won so easily from others.

As she listened and observed, she began to learn more about him now than she had in all the time she had known him. That he spoke more than passable Italian she was not too surprised at, since it was to be expected he would pick up the language after spending so much time in Sicily, as well as other Italian ports, but when did he become conversational in French?

She did not dwell overlong upon these things, for they were still talking and she dared not miss anything more.

Almost immediately after turning her attention back to their conversation, she began to look upon him with a charmed gaze that was a mixture of awe and astonishment. A moment later, she was unable to hide the bedazzled expression on her face, when he fell into deep discussion with Aunt Gisella about the state of affairs in the Italian provinces since Napoleon had combined all of them under his rule.

While she was still considering the numerous benefits to Italy that came as a direct result of French occupation—for in truth, she had heretofore given them no thought whatsoever—she realized they had already shifted their thoughts to analyze *The Decameron*. That topic led them quite naturally to another classic in Italian literature, *I promessi sposi,* and they spent a few minutes to lightly debate its ideological position concerning the Catholic Church.

Shortly thereafter, they fell into a discussion of the Renaissance, Dante and the de Medici's, and from there, went on to touch on the ruins of Pompeii, the rule of the Roman Emperor Augustus, and the might of Pisa's long-forgotten fleet.

When, she wondered, did he become such an ardent student of history?

It struck her as strange that one could spend a lifetime around a person, only to discover there was so much about them one did not know. How very odd she felt. Almost as if she were attracted to him, which she knew was preposterous. She decided it was nothing more than the fact that she was impressed with his knowledge; in love with his mind.

"Oh, my goodness, just look at the time!" Aunt Gisella said. "My dear Lieutenant, I must apologize for taking so much of your afternoon, when it is Maresa you came to see."

Before Percy had an opportunity to respond,

she arose and said, "I am certain Italo has the fire burning by now."

Maresa laughed and said, "It's been long enough to have it burning, let it burn out, and then get it burning again."

Aunt Gisella suddenly looked at Serena like she was seeing her for the first time. "Serena, I only this moment realized, I do not think I heard you utter a single word during our meal. That is quite unlike you. Did you not have anything to say?"

"I had a few comments, but I never could seem to find a place to wedge them into the conversation."

This time, everyone laughed.

To Maresa, Aunt Gisella said, "Serena and I will see to some household matters, so that you and Lieutenant Bronwell might have a few words in private. Angelo and Tito should be home before dinner. I know he will be delighted you are here."

Maresa stood with Percy and watched their departure. "I like your aunt very much."

"And Serena?"

"Her, too," he said with a smile directed at her, "although I did not hear too much from her."

"I know, and I was amazed, since she is quite fond of talking. I think it was not so much that she did not want to speak as she said, but rather that she could not find an opportunity to do so. Truly, I do not think I have ever heard Aunt Gisella talk so! Uncle Tito would say she was 'wound tighter than his pocket watch.' "

"She is a most interesting woman to talk to. Very knowledgeable and obviously educated, which, as you know, is rare for Italian women."

"Yes, she told me once that her father believed very strongly in the education of women."

"Coming here has worked wonders. You have changed a great deal since you came here."

"Do you really think so?"

"Of course."

"Is it that obvious?"

"It is to anyone who knows you."

"And you know me?"

"Better than you know yourself, Maresa."

"That would not be difficult, since I have come to realize of late, that I know myself least of all."

"Everyone reaches that point sooner or later."

"Enough about me and my wonderful family. I want to hear about you, Percy. Tell me where you have been and how have you been," she insisted, and gave him a light cuff on the arm.

He winced slightly and drew back his arm.

"You are hurt."

"Nothing life threatening."

She looked him over more closely now, searching for signs of his injury to tell her the truth of the state of his health. "When were you injured? Where? How did it happen? How do you feel now? Do you want to sit down?"

Percy laughed. "Easy. I told you, I'm fine.

I took a bullet in the shoulder off the coast of Spain...."

"Oh, no!"

"It was before Napoleon's abdication. They removed the bullet two weeks ago."

"Two weeks ago? You mean it was in your shoulder all that time?"

"Yes."

"Why did you wait so long?"

"There was no time then, and later, it seemed to be healing well enough. It only began to bother me a couple of months back."

"I worry about you."

"I don't suppose it would do any good to tell you not to, because it has been a part of the female character for so long, it has evolved to become an inherited trait. Still, there is no reason for you to be overly concerned. Things are relatively quiet now that Napoleon is safely tucked away in exile."

"You should not fall into the trap of over-confidence, Percy, for that is when accidents are most likely to occur. Who knows? You might fall off the rigging, or go overboard."

He laughed. "I don't climb the rigging, and if I go overboard, I pray they will leave me there to spare me the embarrassment of being fished out."

"Don't make light of it. What would I do if something happened to you?"

"You would probably get engaged."

"There is no humor in that old line."

"Truth, but no humor."

"That is not fair."

He dipped his head. "Then I apologize."

She looped her arm through his. "Do you feel strong enough to take a tour of the villa? It is the most beautiful place...like a palace, and filled with art and frescoes."

"I think I am up to the task," he said looking down at her—a look that left Maresa feeling uncertain, almost as if an inexplicable intimacy had suddenly sprung up between them.

A small slice of silence filled the space that stretched from where he stood to where she was.

Percy, looking resplendent and quite handsome in his uniform, continued to look at her, which only served to increase her discomfort. For a brief moment in time, she felt as if all her thoughts and flaws were open to him; that he knew her with far better understanding and with more vivid detail than she ever would know herself.

"Where shall we start?" she said at last, needing to break the gap of quiet that grew ever wider between them. She felt a bit distracted, and wondered at the cause of this...she could not think of a name to call the way things were between them. Not strained, exactly, but certainly not the free and easy exchange, the close understanding, the firm bond that had existed before.

Before what? she wondered, unable to find a point in time, or a particular incident that would have influenced such a change.

"Here now," he said, and stepped closer. He lifted her chin with his fingertips, higher and higher, until she had no choice but to look at him. "What are you thinking?"

"That I have never quite gotten accustomed to seeing you in uniform. Each time I look at you, I see my dear friend, but I also see a man I don't know. I don't understand. Why should that be any different?"

"Perhaps it is difficult for you to see me as a man, and not the boy you've always known."

"Is it difficult for you to see me as a woman?"

A look akin to sadness settled deep in the green eyes that studied her, then vanished with his first words, "That has never been difficult for me."

The implication washed over her. "Sometimes I think I am afraid that growing up means things will change between us. It happens to everyone, doesn't it? You grow up. You marry. You have children. Before long, you no longer remember the people and places that you once held so dear."

"It doesn't have to be that way."

"Then I shall work very hard to see that it does not. Now come along," she said, and took his hand. "I do want to show you around the place where my mother was born. Oh, and the paintings of her. She was so beautiful, Percy. You cannot imagine."

"Yes, I can, each time I look at you."

Eighteen

She burns me, binds me,
tastes like a lump of sugar.

> Michelangelo
> line written on the back of a letter
> dated 24 December, 1507

Two days passed unbelievably fast, and on his last night at Villa Mirandola, Percy found himself firmly ensconced within the Bartolini household, for he felt comfortably established as part of the family, and could, with little effort, have stayed a much longer time.

Gathered around the dining table with the members of the family, he listened to the recounting of familial stories, details of the life of Maresa's mother before she married and a full accounting of Maresa's many adventures with Serena and Angelo.

From time to time, he would feel Maresa looking at him, but whenever he glanced at her, she would look away.

"Tell us of the way of things now that Napoleon is no longer a threat," Uncle Tito said. "How is he taking his exile, do you think?"

"There are those who feel he is perfectly content with his exile, but it is also known that Napoleon believed he would be recalled to France by the allies within six months of his abdication. That it did not happen must be a terrible disappointment to him. I do not think Napoleon is a man who takes disappointment well."

"You think he has some plan of returning to power?"

"I know he has hopes of such, and if the occasion presented itself... Well, I cannot help believing he would take it. Don't forget Murat is still on the throne in Naples, and although he swears his allegiance to the allies, he has a history of changing sides to suit his personal interests. All in all, it is a situation that bears close watching."

Uncle Tito opened his mouth, but made the mistake of glancing in his wife's direction. "I see I am being reminded that the dinner table is no place for men to discuss war. Shall we leave the ladies for a drink and the continuation of our conversation?"

"I am at your disposal," Percy said.

He was unable to tell what Maresa's reaction was to the idea of his leaving with her uncle. Her expression, which seemed to hover somewhere in the wide gap between relief and disappointment, did not tell him much either.

After they retired to Tito's study, Percy discussed the war at length with him, but his thoughts were on Maresa. He had not accomplished what he hoped to accomplish by coming here, for there had been precious little time that he had been able to spend alone with her.

Angelo walked into the room. "I have been sent to fetch the gentlemen. The ladies grow tired of each other. I, on the other hand, reached that point an hour ago, and now I am running out of ideas to entertain them."

"I thought you enjoyed being with the women," Uncle Tito said.

"Only when there is one that I can seduce."

Percy and Tito laughed. "I think our visit has come to an end," Tito said.

It was much later, when Percy excused himself, due to his early departure the next morning.

"Must you go?" Serena asked.

"I leave before daybreak."

"Which is not very far off," Gisella said. "I seem to be saying this quite frequently, but I fear we have taken up far too much of your time, and given Maresa very few opportunities to visit with you."

"I shall have to rectify that by coming back again."

"Oh, yes!" Serena said. "Please do come again. Soon!"

Percy gave his thanks to everyone for a remarkable two days and excused himself. As he walked from the grand salon, he wondered if Maresa regretted not having a moment of privacy to say goodbye.

He reached the great stone staircase when he heard footsteps behind him.

Maresa called out his name.

He turned to see her hurrying toward him.

"I was afraid you had already gone up to your chamber."

"I have been admiring the art on my way."

"I wish you did not have to go."

"Do you?"

"Of course! Do you doubt it?"

"There have been times..."

"Oh, Percy, how can you say that when you know how dear you are to me?"

"Perhaps I need reminding." He stood there, watching her, and finding her so lovely his heart cracked. Look at me, he thought. Don't think of me as only your friend, when I want to be so much more.

At that particular moment, she rose up on her toes and kissed his cheek. "There, you are reminded."

He made a sudden move, before he could think twice about it, before she could realize what he was about and turn away. He put both arms around her and pulled her against him. He kissed the top of her head and felt her body tense, when he longed to feel her arms go around him. "I want more than that," he whispered into her hair. "I want more than a reminder or a kiss on the cheek."

"I don't understand."

"I think you do."

Her astonished eyes grew wide and her hand came up to press against his chest, as if she were trying to push him away, but she only clutched the lapel of his coat, and it recalled to mind another night, not so very long ago, when he had stood with her like this, when she curled her fingers into his silk cloak.

He lowered his head and captured her lips, which were opened with a gasp of surprise. With luxurious slowness, he kissed her, as if leaving on the morrow and Napoleon were the furthest things from his mind. He teased and seduced, drawing her into him and feeling her hesitancy, and knowing the exact moment when her inhibitions gave way.

This is what he wanted—had wanted since the day he was old enough to know what kissing was.

Maresa. Always Maresa. Her eyes, her mouth, her face, always before him, and blocking the image of any other woman from his view. "*Dolcissima...*"

Sweetheart... Maresa was trying to remember who called her that, but Percy was too much a distraction for her to think clearly. Still, the word lingered in the back of her mind.

He pulled away, but only to scatter a random pattern of kisses along her jaw and neck. Even then, he found he was still reluctant to let her go. "A heart rubbed raw with wanting now filled. Between two worlds I hover, like a burned-out star," he whispered.

Dolcissimo... Suddenly she pushed away. "You!" she whispered. "Oh my heavens! It was *you!*"

Wrapped in the tight coil of desire, it was not easy for him to jump to another level as quickly as she had done. "Me?"

She doubled up her fist and punched it against his chest. "It was you that night...at the marchesa's ball. It was you who kissed me. Oh, how could you!" she said and turned away.

"Maresa…"

She swiped at a tear. "Don't bother to deny it. I may not be too experienced, but one thing I do know is, you were there that night. Only I cannot understand why you did not reveal yourself. Why would someone who professes to be my friend, play such a shabby trick on me?"

"It wasn't a trick, Maresa."

"Regardless, it was cruel—and quite a terrible thing to do. I don't know you anymore, Percy. You've let something come between us and I feel like my heart is broken. Of all the people who have betrayed me, I would never have thought you capable of stooping to such."

"Maresa, listen to me. Listen to what I have to say."

She shook her head and began backing up. "No. No, I can't. I can't listen to you. Not anymore. Whatever we had, it is gone. With one stupid prank, you have destroyed a perfect friendship. How could so much love turn so quickly to hate? I don't think I can ever forgive you, Percy, for what you have done."

If he lived five lifetimes, he would never forget the sight of her running away from him as she cried out, "Don't bother to come back. I never want to see you again. Not ever!"

If they told him the moon fell from the heavens, it would not have left this night half as black.

The next morning, before the rooster crowed, before the first hint of sun tinged the cold morning sky, Percy picked up his tricorn and tucked it beneath his arm as he went quietly down the stairs.

A moment later, he was outside, and led his horse from the stable. It was better this way, he told himself, for parting should be swift and unexpected, when everlasting.

He mounted, and rode away from Villa Mirandola, chilled by swirling snow, and with a heart as cold as ice.

He was tired, his insides empty. It was time to give his heart a rest, and love a chance to breathe.

Not once did he pause, or turn to take one last look at the villa, for if he had, he would have seen her standing at the window with a candle in her hand.

From that moment on, Percy looked at life differently. He knew now that Maresa would never be his, and that knowledge made him have as little regard for his own life as he knew she had for him.

Life seemed to take a turn when he returned to his ship.

He still carried the pain in his heart, a pain that went beyond anything he could ever imagine, or explain. His heart was broken. His boats were sunk. There was no escape now. Nothing he said or did seemed to matter anymore. Happiness, as he once knew it, was over. All he had to look forward to was inner peace.

That, and the war with America that was still going on.

He gave his all to his country. He volunteered for dangerous missions, and risked his life to save that of a fellow shipmate. His courage knew no bounds, and rarely a week went by that he wasn't being commended for an act of bravery or valor. He was consumed in a rush of courage, a man fragmented, held together by inner strength, a grand sort of reckless indifference to self that some preferred to call valor.

Nineteen

Love is like linen often chang'd, the
    sweeter.

          Phineas Fletcher (1582-1650)
          English clergyman and poet

Maresa's romantic illusions and ideas of love were now nothing more than twisted bits of confusion that caused that which she wanted and that which had happened to bleed together, until she could not seem to tell them apart.

To say she was not infatuated with the man who kissed her at the marquesa's ball, would surely be a falsehood; yet, to say she was even the least bit besotted over Percy was pure fiction.

Her confusion came in knowing they were

one in the same. If she felt attraction toward one of them, then why not the other?

Oh, she thought, this is such torture. Being in love could never be this confusing. Could it?

The door opened and Serena rushed into her room, excitement hovering over her with an almost luminous quality. "I've been looking everywhere for you. Mama said we are most assuredly going to the Brancaleones' ball on Saturday. That means we haven't time to have new dresses made, so we shall have to make do with what we have."

Maresa thought that was no sacrifice surely, since they both had several new gowns yet unworn, but she felt so mopey, not even the idea of another ball could cheer her. "I don't think I want to go."

"What?" Serena spoke with such emphasis it was almost humorous. "Don't be silly. It is one of the biggest balls of the year. I do think you should wear the white gown you had made in England. I have not seen anything like it at any of the parties in Florence."

Maresa knew that when Serena got like this, with her mind all made up, folded and tucked neatly away, one might as well surrender. "Oh, all right."

Serena threw herself across Maresa's bed. "You are still sad about Percy, aren't you?"

Maresa turned her head away. "I don't want to talk about it."

"No, I don't suppose you do, but you might as well, because I shall keep prodding you about it. Besides, what difference does it make if you talk about it? You think about it all the time." She sat up, fluffed a pillow and put it behind her back. "Mama said all things are possible between a man and a woman, except friendship."

That comment caught Maresa off guard. Then, she narrowed her eyes and gave Serena a very stern look. "Serena, did you tell Aunt Gisella?"

"No, of course not!"

Maresa did not say anything, but she increased the sternness of her look until it went beyond serious. "Did you tell your mother what I specifically told you not to repeat?"

"Well, maybe I did tell her a little."

"A little? Ohhh! I shan't tell you anything ever again!"

"How can I help you, if I don't ask Mama what I should do?"

"I don't want any help, and if I do, I will ask your mother myself."

"Well, I could go mad waiting for you to decide. You may not think you want help, but you need it. I've never seen anyone as miserable as you, or anyone who needed help as much as you do."

"I'm not miserable. I'm hurt. Percy was my friend and I will never understand why he stooped to such a low-level trick."

"Mama said it wasn't a trick. She said any fool could see he's in love with you, and a man in love will stoop to desperate measures."

"Call me what you will, but I could never believe his foolishness was prompted by love."

"If not love, then what?"

Maresa's list of reasons was suddenly blank. She had no answer. Because for her, love had never progressed beyond a selfish sort of infatuation, Maresa had no idea what was hidden in the heart of selfless love.

"I don't want to talk about it anymore," she said, but only an hour later she was doing just that with Aunt Gisella.

"If I fancy myself in love with a stranger, only to discover that stranger is Percy, yet I feel nothing but hostility toward him, how can that be? They are, after all, one in the same. On the other hand, if Percy truly had feelings for me, how could he so coldly plan such a mean trick?"

"Most Italians believe that in love, as in war, whatever strategy you deem necessary to accomplish your goal is allowed."

When Maresa asked Angelo the same question, he replied, "It is impossible for a man to be friends with a woman he is attracted to. His mind is always focused on ways to get her into his bed. Desire always gets in the way of friendship. That's the way it is, *cara*, and there is nothing you can do or say to change it. So stop worrying your lovely head over it and be nice to Percy, so he can, in turn, be very nice to you. That is the way the game is played. *Capisce?*"

"*Ho capito.* I understand," she replied.

"Good."

"Angelo, would you kiss me?"

"With pleasure, *cara*. Does this mean we are no longer friends?"

231

"No, it means you are my friend and you are going to help me decide something."

"Decide what?"

"An experiment, nothing more. I want to see if I feel the same way when I kiss you as I did when Percy kissed me."

"Which Percy? The masked one or the naval officer?"

"They are one in the same."

"Are they? Then why do you not feel the same toward both?"

Maresa had to think about that for a moment, but with no answer in sight, she finally she had to admit the truth: she had no answer.

"Did you enjoy Percy's kiss as much as you enjoyed the masked stranger?"

"No! Well, that is... Oh, I suppose I did enjoy it, until I realized he was the stranger who kissed me, and then that ruined it. It ruined everything, don't you see?"

"No, I don't see, any more than I don't think you need to kiss me to answer something so obvious. He's in love with you, and a man in love will stoop to desperate measures."

Maresa frowned. That had a very familiar ring to it.

"Who told you that?" she asked.

"No one. I heard Serena tell you."

"How is that possible? Serena was in my room when she told me, so unless..."

Angelo stood there, looking as blank as a freshly painted wall.

"You snoop! Were you spying on us? And in my bedroom, no less! Oh, you are vile!"

"I was not spying in your room. I was listening outside the door."

"And you think that is all right?"

"Of course."

Well, that was abominably impertinent, she thought, and she tried to be furious. But it was difficult to lose her temper with someone like Angelo. How could you fault someone who was perfectly honest? He was a rascal of the first water and he admitted it. She put her hand to her head. "There must be something wrong with me. Why am I confiding in you? I will only end up more confused than I was in the beginning."

"What is wrong with that? I am a perfectly good confidant."

"Confidant? You are a snoop, that's what you are...a thief, a listener at keyholes, steamer opener of mail, sneak..."

"Women!" he said, then grabbed her, and kissed her with the wildest abandon.

When he finished, he released her. "Do you have your answer now?"

"It—it didn't feel the same."

"Then you have your answer. It isn't the kiss you are in love with, *cara*. It's the man. And that is the end of it, all wrapped up neatly like ravioli."

Maresa did not believe that in the least.

And yet, as the days passed, and she tried to remember how it felt to kiss Angelo, the memory of it had slipped away. But the kiss from Percy's lips haunted her night and day.

The evening of the Brancaleones' ball arrived and Maresa wore the white gown, which, according to Serena, ensured that she would not go unnoticed.

Maresa, on the other hand, did not care if she was. The last thing I need, she thought to herself, is another man!

As it happened, one man, Nicola Brancaleone, did notice her, and he wasted not a moment in approaching Angelo, to inquire about her.

"Who is she?"

"The Bartolinis' niece from England. She is here for an extended stay."

"She is lovely."

"Of course. She is half Italian! That is what gives her the smoldering looks and the boldness, and it makes her outspoken and a bit temperamental—something you will rarely find in an English woman. She is also half English, which means she has a beautiful body, a fair mind, and an immature heart, as well as periodic fits of morality, a penchant for speaking about the weather, and she absolutely detests our tradition of the afternoon rest."

"Introduce me."

Angelo shrugged. "Very well, but I did try to warn you."

"I can handle a woman of any nationality."

"She has recently come from England, so she is not accustomed to Italian men. You should remember the English have different views than we, when it comes to lovemaking without marriage."

"Who said I was not considering marriage?"

Angelo raised his brows at that and held up his glass in a toast. "It would seem an introduction is forthcoming, for I see she is looking this way, and probably wondering where I am."

"Then let it be now," Nicola said.

"Come," Angelo said, and he walked with Nicola over to where Serena and Maresa were talking. Upon arriving at their side, he introduced Nicola to her.

"A pleasure to meet you, Signore Brancaleone. I am enjoying your ball very much." She glanced around the splendid room. "It is the perfect setting for such an evening. And we noticed during our ride over here that even the weather is cooperating."

Nicola kissed her hand, completely captivated by this dark-haired vision in white. "*Signorina,* we have a rule in Italy, that a beautiful woman must dance every dance."

Her cheek colored, pale as a rose and she looked down. He caught the almond scent of her hair, and saw the way her dress hugged her curves, to flare at her feet. He had never envisioned such a goddess.

"Then I shall have plenty of time to rest," she said, and at that moment Nicola was besotted. He found her unbelievably, extraordinarily, overwhelmingly, charmingly beautiful.

He would have her.

"If you would excuse us," he said to Angelo and Serena, "I would like to have this dance with your lovely guest."

Before anyone could respond, they were in the midst of the other dancers.

"You are enjoying your visit to Italy?"

"More than I ever dreamed. I shall be sad when it comes time to return."

"And when do you leave?"

"My father gave me one year but sadly, it is almost over."

"Perhaps we can find a way to keep you here, *signorina*."

"You do not know my father."

"You do not know me."

The music ended, and when Maresa turned to be escorted back to where Angelo and Serena waited, Nicola put a detaining hand on her arm instead of walking her back. He did not ask her for another dance. He simply took it, and took her with him onto the dance floor once again.

They danced every dance.

When Maresa declared she had danced holes in her slippers, Nicola laughed and said, "Another dance, surely."

He caught the way she glanced toward a group of young women who were watching them carefully.

"I fear I have taken up far too much of your time. There are other ladies waiting...." Maresa said.

"Let them wait. None of them have captured

my interest as you do. I find you touchingly beautiful. The beauty of your face shall haunt my imagination long after this ball has ended. When may I see you again?"

"A thousand pardons," Angelo said, "but I must take Maresa to join her family. Your aunt and uncle are ready to leave."

Twenty

It is impossible to love and be wise.

Francis Bacon (1561-1626)
English philosopher,
lawyer and statesman

Later, as Maresa and the Bartolinis rode home in the carriage, Aunt Gisella said, "My goodness, I never thought I would see the day that Nicola Brancaleone's attention would be held by one woman during the entire evening. He was totally enraptured by you, Maresa."

"I am certain it was only because I was a new face in the crowd."

"No," Aunt Gisella said thoughtfully, "that isn't the reason at all."

"I do wish I had not danced so much, so I could have seen what was going on," Serena said. "Now I shall have to rely upon everything you say, instead of forming my own opinion."

"That has to be the first time you have ever done that," Angelo said.

"Regardless of what you say Nicola thinks, he has asked my permission to pay you court," Uncle Tito said, "so he must be thinking something quite serious."

"Santa Maria!" Aunt Gisella said. "Nicola Brancaleone has never paid serious court to a woman."

"Pay me court?" Maresa asked. "I hardly know the man. Pay me court, indeed. That sounds like a clever introduction to a boring play."

"What think you of him?" Uncle Tito asked.

"I have not thought of it overmuch, to be completely honest. He was very considerate. I suppose I found him quite...nice."

Uncle Tito seemed relieved to hear that. "It is a good thing then, for Signore Brancaleone was making it deliberately clear to all and sundry that he was laying claim to a certain young lady of English-Italian descent, and that any would-be rivals with similar ideas in mind were out of place and out of season."

"Do you think so, Tito?" Aunt Gisella asked. "I know he was quite taken with Maresa—that he found her chaste, charming, and of a ripe age—but what you say goes much deeper than an innocent flirtation."

Uncle Tito thought about that for a moment before he replied, "I am not certain how deep it goes. He is a pleasant enough sort, but also a seducer of women who moves quickly from one casual relationship to another."

"Nicola has a reputation with the ladies," Angelo said. "You must be on your guard around him."

"Of course I shall be," Maresa said softly, the smooth, white skin of her forehead marred by deep, thought-provoking consideration.

"Listen to the two of you," Aunt Gisella said. "Can't you see you are frightening her?" She patted Maresa's cheek. "Pay them no mind, dear. Nicola is a gentleman and a member of one of the most ancient families in Florence. He is quite capable of recognizing quality when he sees it. I am certain he will behave himself accordingly."

"That is good to know," Maresa said.

"You should have a care around his mother, though," Aunt Gisella said. "She is a daughter of a marchesa and, the way she flaunts it, you would think her father was the last de Medici. You might say she is quite jealous of her importance. Nicola is her only son, and she has been known to be haughty, vindictive and a crafty planner of stratagem when she deemed it necessary to deter anyone with amorous attachments or intentions that involved her son. It was once rumored that she was trying to arrange a marriage into the family of the Emperor Napoleon but, of course, under the present circumstances, that would be out of the question for someone with her aspirations."

"Once she has learned Maresa is the daughter of a wealthy viscount she will, no doubt, approve of Nicola's choice, for wealth offers an exemplary pedigree that is not only desirable, but faultless. I say this, because I have heard it rumored that the Brancaleones' fortune is in a state of decay," Uncle Tito added, "which would stoke the fire to fuel his search for a suitable wife."

"That is a misrepresentation, surely," Aunt Gisella said, "for you saw tonight the lavish way they entertain."

"An excellent way to hide the truth of indebtedness is to spend lavishly," Uncle Tito said.

They arrived home before Maresa was ready for the discussion to end, for she deemed it prudent to learn all she could about this man who asked Uncle Tito to pay her court. She was a wiser woman, she reminded herself, and not the foolish young girl she was in England, affiancing herself to all and sundry.

Once they were inside the villa, Maresa, Serena and Angelo continued the discussion.

"I cannot lie and say the things Aunt Gisella and Uncle Tito said about him did not make me a bit nervous," Maresa said.

"He cannot help it if he venerates a petticoat," Angelo said. "He is, after all, a man."

"That is no excuse," Maresa said. "He should practice restraint!"

"*Cara,* if a man were always to do that, none of us would be here."

"All right. I suppose I shall be forced to admit all of this attention is flattering in a romantic way," Maresa said.

"Wouldn't it be wonderful if he asked you to marry him, and then you would not have to go back to England? Now, that would be romantic," Serena said.

"Perhaps for a while, but that sort of thing never lasts for long," said Angelo.

"What do you mean by that?" asked Serena.

"Think you, if Beatrice had been Dante's wife, would he have written her into immortality?" was Angelo's reply.

"I don't understand what you are trying to say," Serena said.

"Have you not observed that marriage, which is undeniably—according to the church—the sole motive for gaining the legal right to a woman's virginity, is never enough to form a lasting bond? Marriage, preceded by desire, is always succeeded by a lack of interest that has nothing to do with love. It is easy for a man to love one woman and make love to another. I think these things must be some of the basic laws of nature," Angelo said.

"I wish you would explain your explanation," Serena said, while her face reflected her bewilderment, and the effort she had expended trying to understand Angelo's reply. Then she hit upon it. "You mean, love conquers all, and then it is over?"

"Precisely," Angelo said, "and that is why we have mistresses."

"And lovers," Serena added.

Angelo's look darkened. "That is not the same thing."

"So say you!" Serena replied. "When I

241

marry, I shall take as many lovers as my husband takes mistresses."

"Then perhaps your husband will exercise the greatest of care to see that you do not find out," said Angelo.

"Wait a minute," Maresa said. "Aren't you forgetting something? You make it sound as if this sort of behavior is not only condoned, but expected, as well as being so widespread that it occurs in every marriage."

Angelo nodded. "So far, we agree."

"But what about your own family?" Maresa asked. "Do you believe Uncle Tito has had mistresses or that Aunt Gisella has taken a lover or two?"

"That's different," Serena said.

"How so?" Maresa asked.

"They're our parents," Serena said.

Maresa turned to Angelo. "You, I notice have not commented on this. Surely you have an opinion."

"Our parents have a very rare situation and, when it works, there is nothing better. However, the notion that a man and woman can live together for twenty years and never lose interest or stray, brings to mind a herd of sheep."

It was sometimes said that the weather in Tuscany could be as changeable as a stepmother's face. The weather was not something Maresa paid a great deal of attention to, until they were blessed with two weeks of unsea-

242

sonably mild weather, for truly Mother Nature seemed to be playing some sort of satirical joke by harnessing spring in winter's traces.

Never one to argue with Mother Nature, or a blessing, Maresa was delighted to take advantage of the unexpected turn in the weather, and when Nicola called upon Maresa, as he had every day for the past two weeks, she readily accepted his invitation to go riding.

Although it felt like spring was in the air, the weather was not the herald of spring. It did not smell like spring, with the fresh abundance of new growth, nor were the birds giving vent to the verses of new spring songs. Still, it was a pleasant reprieve and reminder of the pleasures of the coming months when more outside activities could be planned.

For as many days as the weather permitted, Maresa and Nicola went for long horseback rides along the twisting country roads. Maresa could almost feel the beauty that crowned the countryside as they climbed the olive-clad slopes, and rode along narrow paths through the woods into a valley, where the towns and castles hugged the mountain.

They dismounted and strolled along a path, leading the horses behind them. The bare-branched spread of chestnut trees canopied above them, and to their right spread the dormant twigs of fruit trees that would soon transform themselves with the bright-green buds of spring. She had some inkling now, why it was that the poets always loved Italy, for there was poetry and inspiration in everything she saw.

The hills were lovely, with villas and monasteries visible in every direction, and each thing she saw charmed her. When she paused beneath the withered crown of a tree and said such to Nicola, he took her in his arms and kissed her, then said, "I too, am charmed by what I see."

One afternoon, when the weather was already beginning to turn cooler again, and they were reminded that these mild, easygoing days would soon be a thing of the past, they decided to have a picnic on the greensward beneath the lofty trees barren of leaves. They ate their lunch beneath the whispering sound of the bare colonnade of chestnut trees, where a fast-moving river cut through the valley, with a gurgle and a roar. In the distance, she could see the gray stone of a bridge arched over a gorge, almost hidden from view.

Maresa would wish then that she were an artist, so she could take out her easel and paint every detail of what she saw, and in that way, record the memory, for she knew nothing so lovely could ever be recalled in the mind with the same vivid display of reality. Yet beauty was so abundant here, in the distinct colors of the hills, the tangled thickets and fields laid bare.

It was the beginning of the third week of Nicola's courtship when Serena announced her opinion about the future of things between Maresa and Nicola. "I think he will ask you to marry him, quite soon. I know you grow tired of hearing everyone say this, but I've never seen Nicola so besotted. In truth, I think he is fully prepared and more than ready to ask for your hand in marriage."

"Oh, I think you're wrong. We enjoy each other's company, that is all."

"You better pray she is not wrong," Angelo said.

"Why do you say that, Angelo?" Maresa asked.

"Because your father is sending you a letter giving you four months to be married, or he is arranging your wedding himself."

Maresa laughed. "You are such a tease."

"I wish I were teasing this time, *cara*."

She could tell by his face that he was not teasing. Her heart began to pound. She was completely dumbfounded by what he said. "How do you know that?"

"It's here," he said, pulling a letter from Beatrice out of his pocket.

Maresa yanked the envelope from his hand and looked it over. "You steamed my letter open?"

He shrugged. "How else would I know what was inside?"

"Is there nothing you won't do, in order to pry into another's affairs?"

He shrugged. "Perhaps there is, but I have not, as yet, discovered it."

"You are a surreptitious sneak!"

"Thank you. I have worked very hard to accomplish it."

A letter from Maresa's father arrived a week later. The ultimatum was, as her father explicitly put it:

Dear Daughter,

As you know, our agreement was you were to have one year to acquaint yourself with your relations in Italy. At the end of that year's time, you were to return to London.

As you surely know, you have four months of that year left. If you are not married by the time you return to England, I will arrange a marriage for you myself, and I will see that you follow through with it this time.

Understand this is my final word on this matter. Under no circumstances will I extend the period of time for your stay there. I am writing this well in advance, to provide you ample time to make all the necessary arrangements for your travel back to England.

I expect to be informed as to your travel plans, including your expected date of arrival.

In the event that you do find yourself married by this time, I expect you will notify me of that as well, but do not think I am so foolish as to accept your word in this matter. Any report of marriage sent to me, must include an official document of marriage, or a legal document of certification. To do otherwise would not be in your best interest.

My regards to the Bartolinis,

I remain,
Your father

All the air slowly escaped her lungs, and Maresa slumped down into the nearest chair. Sometimes it felt to her as though her father had spies about, for he always knew the exact moment to make a move to thwart all her plans and to rob her of happiness. Was the man never consistent? One moment he was demanding she get married. Then he agreed to give her a year in Italy to find a husband, and then refuses to wait until that time is up before he puts her on the auction block in London. It went beyond humiliating, and she found it not only tremendously frustrating, but also difficult to understand. Why, for goodness sake, could her father not work with her, instead of always going against her?

Listless, with her appetite gone, she claimed a headache and spent the rest of the evening in her room. Her extremities were heavy with lethargy, as if affixed to leaden weights—the kind of feeling that comes when one begins to wonder if it is really worth picking up and going on. Sometimes it seemed more sensible to simply give up and give in.

She looked at the dress the maid had placed upon the bed for her to wear to dinner, and wondered if she would ever feel like wearing that dress, or any other, again.

What was the use?

Nothing was turning out as she planned. Not even sunny Italy was as rosy as she once painted it.

She glanced at her reflection in the mirror, and saw herself as undeniably plain. A woman in love is beautiful, as is a woman who is loved. She could claim neither. Even a dash of mediocre happiness would add a certain amount of color to the cheek and inner gleam in the eye, but how could she ever expect to be happy with the dismal future that awaited her, for there was little doubt that she would return to England unmarried, and then be trapped forever to do her father's bidding.

As always in times like these, she was reminded of Percy, for he was never truly far from her mind. He was always the one person she could talk to, who was levelheaded, painfully honest and yet he always wanted what was best for her. He never tried to stifle her, or push her into a mold where she would never fit, although he did reshape her thinking from time to time. But even then, it was always done with the gentleness and consideration and forethought that she would expect from someone far older.

Her soul in tumult, she needed his calming ways that passed through her like the solace of prayer. Percy believed in her; in her strength, and her ability to believe in herself, even when she felt she never could.

But what was the use? It did no good to think about these things, or to feel either, for that matter. She could not understand herself. Why did she think Percy or anyone else would or could? All her life she felt as if she struggled with whether to follow her heart, or her brain, and now she was beginning to feel she should do neither, for when had the dictates of one or the other ever given her what she wanted, or for that matter, what she needed?

The enemy was within her, looming larger, and with grander schemes, always destined to fail. She was guilty of the worst sort of deception for she had, too many times, trifled with the hearts of others and led them to believe and trust in her love and devotion, and she feared now that neither of them were emotions she was capable of. The saddest recognition of all was to learn that in deceiving others, it was really herself who was deceived. She felt like a soldier going into battle, who looks around and finds that the army that was with him has gone.

Should she bend to her father's wishes and do as countless women before her had done and walk blindly into an unfulfilling and loveless marriage with a stranger? Or should she affiance herself yet again, and marry in haste to someone she does not know well, but has at least met? Lord, she thought, there have to be other choices.

After all this thinking the only thing that was a constant was Percy, for his strength reached out to her and lent her comfort. If only he were here, she would not ask his advice this time. If only he were here so she could put her head on his shoulder, and feel, as she always did when he was nearby, that all would work out.

Perhaps, if she wrote to him, she might feel the same comfort.

She moved to her desk and took out pen and paper and began a letter to him. Half a page later, she tore it up and began another.

That one too, she tore up.

Three more letters she started, and each was ripped in two.

Maresa sighed and looked across the room at the things familiar both to her and her mother. She tried to imagine her mother sitting here, in this very same chair, at the same age Maresa was. She looked at the small, oval miniature of her mother sitting on the table. Nothing in the portrait looked familiar, save the emerald necklace around her mother's neck, and she wondered where she had been sitting when it was painted.

She focused on her mother's face as if waiting for her to speak, to give her the motherly advice she so sorely needed. What would you have done, mother? she wondered. Would you have continued to rely upon the dearness of your friend, time and again? Or would you have taken the matter under your own advisement, and made your your own decision accordingly? "Oh, I don't know what to do!" she said out loud. "I want to write you, Percy, but I am ashamed."

That much was true, for whenever she recalled the way things had been between them the night before he left, and the way she had allowed him to ride off that morning, without telling him goodbye, she was deeply shamed.

No, she decided. She could not write him and ask for his help. Not this time; not after the way she had treated him. Without making a conscious effort to do so, she began to look inward, to see herself as she really was.

She did not particularly like what she found.

Why had he stood by her all these years?

Her thoughts began to drift, and she found herself going back to think about that last night they were together. His kiss, both the last night he was here, and the night of the ball, was not the platonic kiss of a friend, but the passionate kiss of a man driven by desire.

Of all the things she had ever done that bothered her, it was her stupid pride in leaving so much unsaid between them, and being so stubborn as to remain silent, when she heard him close the door to his room that morning, and walk slowly down the hall.

She knew then, as she knew now, that if something happened to him, she would never forgive herself.

At the thought of him, a sharp pain settled in her chest. Why? she asked. Why? Why did you watch him ride off like that?

Because you were selfish, a voice inside her said. Because you have always thought of yourself, Maresa, and assumed this was enough to keep Percy's friendship. Dear Percy, who has always been there for you. What, pray tell, have you ever offered him in return?

Nothing.

And the thought of that hurt her far more deeply than any paltry subterfuge of a friend in masked disguise.

She closed her eyes and the days fell away, until she was back to that last night before he left. What was it he said?

A heart rubbed raw with wanting now filled. Between two worlds I hover, like a burned out star.

And then, Serena's words followed, a resounding echo in her mind. *Mama said any fool could see he's in love with you, and a man in love will stoop to desperate measures.*

Maresa listened to the ticking of the marble clock sitting a few inches away, a reminder that her time in Italy was being marked off, as one would cross out the letters on a calendar. Time was passing, and soon it would be too late to make amends to Percy, for she knew that loyal friend though he might be, he was a man, with a man's feelings and pride, and that there would come a point when he would suddenly give up and turn away.

Maresa knew she should write, if for no other reason than to make an apology and ask his forgiveness, but shame prevented her from writing him to say what her heart wanted to declare.

When Nicola called next he was quite the charmer, even more so than before. Although her first instinct was to proceed with caution, she pushed it to the back of her mind and allowed the infatuation of the moment to carry her along. There was also the matter of the letter from her father, reminding her that a marriage to someone she knew was better than one to a stranger chosen by her father.

She closed her eyes and recalled the faces of her father's contemporaries and felt sick. What if he chose someone like Lord Munford... at least sixty, with frizzed red-gray hair (what little there was of it) and a horrible hump, where others had a nose?

Maresa received her next letter from Beatrice on the same day that Nicola proposed.

Dear, Dear Maresa,

I am in receipt of your last letter, and I feel so awful for being the one who always seems to write you of nothing but bad news. However, I find some consolation in knowing that if not I, then who?

I wish, as I always do, that I had something wonderful, or at least clever to tell you, but I fear that shan't be the case, at least not this time.

Last evening, Papa had a visitor, Lord Neville Marwood, who barely made it through the front door, on two wobbly and spindly legs. I vow I have seen better-turned means of support on scaffolding than on his person.

I do not know if you remember who he is, or if you ever had the unfortunate fate to meet him, but he is most assuredly not someone you would be attracted to. In fact, I daresay there is no one I can think of who would find him so.

You would be proud of me, for after Lord Marwood left, I mustered up all the courage I could find, which was a miniscule amount, I must admit, and I proceeded downstairs, reciting the Twenty-third Psalm. I walked into Papa's study to confront him about the absurdity of such matchmaking.

Do you know what he said in his defense? That he was being charitable and kindly disposed toward you by selecting someone who was extremely wealthy, as well as well on in age. "Lord Marwood's ancestral home is finer than Windsor Castle," he said. And I replied, "Lord Marwood might be rich as Solomon, but he is older than the Pantheon and his face resembles a plowed field."

He then had the audacity—did I spell that right—to say it was common knowledge that Lord Marwood had a bad heart, and he probably would not live more than two more years at best, and then you would be a very, very rich widow.

While I was trembling in outrage over

that comment, he then said, once Lord Marwood was gone, you would be free to continue your dalliances and indiscretions in whatever manner you chose.

That he would malign you, his own flesh and blood, in such a manner was completely reprehensive to me, and I am truly ashamed to call him Father, for in truth, he made it sound as though he thought you to be a person with the moral aptitude of Lord Byron.

I am so sorry my words had so little effect upon him, and that when it was all over, you were still in the preliminary stages of being affianced to Lord Marwood. As I went to bed that night, I kept thinking poor Maresa, I cannot imagine her spending the rest of her life seeing such a countenance the first thing each morning when she opened her eyes.

I cannot end this letter to you like I usually do by saying, be happy, for I know there is nothing contained herein that would make you so. Therefore, I can only say, dear sister, to take under consideration all I have told you in truth and in faith that it will enable you to avoid the most horrid of fates that await you, should you choose to return to England in a maiden state.

I am, as always, your loving sister,
Beatrice

Maresa accepted Nicola's offer the next afternoon, in spite of her earlier determination that she was definitely not going to rush hastily into another engagement.

After accepting his proposal, Nicola and Maresa sat in the grand salon discussing their wedding plans.

"I would like a small wedding," she said.

"*Cara,* I want everyone to see you. The wedding will be a big one."

"Oh yes, speaking of the wedding, I do see one slight problem."

"And what is that?"

"I am not Catholic."

"Don't worry, you will be by the time we marry."

"What do you mean by that? I cannot simply become a Catholic."

"Of course you can. It is quite simple, really. I have already spoken to Father Francesco. He will instruct you in the faith, baptize you into the church, and hear your first confession. Then we will be married."

"No, you don't understand. I don't want to become Catholic." When she saw his dark look, she said, "I am sure it is a lovely religion, but I am Church of England, and quite content to continue as such."

"*Cara,* anything worth doing is worth doing right. If you are a Christian, you might as well be Catholic."

"But I—"

He glanced at his pocket watch. "I must be off. I will call on you tomorrow and we can finish making our plans."

Later, Maresa wondered where *our plans* came

into it. So far, all she had seen were Nicola's plans. The next thing she knew, he would be telling her what dress to wear.

And he did, the very next evening.

"My mother wants you to wear her wedding dress, *cara*."

Maresa could not bear to be in the same room with Nicola's mother. How could she possibly spend an entire evening in her dress?

And so, as the days passed, the weight of Nicola's words grew heavier than a quern stone. Maresa must have looked as dejected as she felt, for when she passed the library where Aunt Gisella and Uncle Tito were talking softly, Uncle Tito called to her to join them.

"My dear, your aunt and I are worried about you. You seem to have lost all your luster. Come, come, join us and see if we can bring you good cheer."

Maresa joined them thinking the only good cheer they could bring her would be to say the world had come to an end. Truly, she had never felt so low. Of all the engagements she had ended, and now, she was in one she could not.

"Tell us," Uncle Tito said, "what ails our daughter?"

Maresa felt the burn of tears, and swore to slap herself if she even thought about crying. However, she did allow herself one sniff. "It's nothing, Uncle, only marriage jitters. I'm certain every woman gets them."

"Perhaps, but I know your case must be exceptionally difficult. The Italian male is quite different from the English male, in that they have a strong, and sometimes over-stressed sense of masculinity. This means they often go to great extremes to prove their courage by dominating women."

"What your uncle is trying to say is, Italian men would rather kick the door open than turn the knob. For the English man, courage comes from a levelheaded sort of coolness, the Italian's from a hot head."

Maresa took a seat near the two of them and folded her hands in her lap. Her spirits plunged into despair, with little hope of lifting. She was engaged to marry a man she not only did not love, but one she hardly knew. It was a secret she could not bear to keep any longer. She had to speak of it to someone. Some things simply could not remain quelled forever.

"What is it, child?" Uncle Tito asked.

"I know you will both be terribly disappointed in me, but I don't think I can go through with this marriage. Nicola is nothing like I thought he would be. I was a fool to get myself into this kind of jeopardy again."

"I was certain that was the cause," Aunt Gisella said.

In spite of her need to discuss the gravity of the situation with Nicola, her line of thought kept deviating, until she would find herself thinking, not about Nicola, but Percy. This was something she did not understand. She put her hand to her head, feeling a burst of pressure where her thoughts kept colliding with one another.

Restless, she stood and moved quickly to the

window where she looked out, but saw nothing but her own confused thoughts. "Why does this sort of thing keep reoccurring? How does my life get in such a mess? I seem to go from muddle to muddle."

"Things happen in your life because you arrange them that way," Uncle Tito said. "The problem is you, therefore you are the only one who can answer your questions," he continued. "So, you tell me, how does your life get into such a predicament?"

"I don't think it's all my fault."

"Are you certain? There is one way to find out."

"If you are going to ask my father..."

"I'm not going to ask anyone. You are. You are going to ask yourself one question: Does the problem occur wherever you go?"

She was feeling more and more vexed, and tried to think back over her past, the decisions, the mistakes, the narrow escapes, and all of them were there, vividly clear, but try as she may, she could not find fault with herself.

Blameless though she thought she was, not even Maresa could deny she was having the very same troubles in Italy that she had in England.

"I suppose I would be foolish to deny that there is a great similarity between things here and in England—almost as if I packed them in my trunk and carried them on the ship with me."

She returned to her chair and sat down. It was no use trying to understand herself, or why

259

she followed her heart when she should be listening to her head, or listened to her head when she should be following her heart.

At last, she held herself responsible because she knew she had not been faithful to herself, and that was the direct cause of her present unhappiness. To betray yourself was to believe what you did not believe. In each instance of her engagements, she had professed love where there was none.

In the end, she admitted she had caused her own mistakes by bad decisions. "I feel like I make up my mind more than a bed. I don't know what to do. I wish Percy was here."

"It isn't Percy's decision," Aunt Gisella said.

"Then how will I make the right choice?"

"Who shall decide, when the doctors disagree?" Uncle Tito said. "Will it be Percy?"

"I suppose it will be me."

"Do not be despondent," Aunt Gisella said. "Recognition wins half the battle."

"But that's not the half that I dreaded."

She saw the serene endurance, the patient fortitude in the way they looked at her, and if there was anything she had learned since coming here, it was that the Italians would win any test of patience or endurance. She might as well give up now. "All right. I shall tell Nicola the next time I see him."

The next day, when Nicola came to take her into Florence for tea at the home of his mother,

Maresa decided things had gone too far already. With a great amount of dread, she decided to be painfully honest.

"Nicola, you know I am very fond of you, but I think our engagement was a mistake."

"How do you mean?"

"There are simply too many differences to overcome."

She saw the clenched jaw only seconds before he said, "I am sorry you feel that way, *cara.*"

"I know it is all my fault, just as I know you would not want to marry a woman who does not want to marry you."

"That is where you are wrong. Whether a woman wants to marry a man or not is immaterial in Italy. I proposed. You accepted. It is as simple as that. We will marry in two months time here at Villa Mirandola, and you will be the most beautiful bride in my mother's wedding gown."

By the time Nicola left, Maresa was so angry she was shaking.

"Don't worry, Maresa. He is only strutting like a peacock," Serena said, trying to console her.

"It's not so bad as you have painted it," Angelo said. "A woman will complain about the domination of her husband, but she enjoys submitting to it in bed."

Maresa snatched a feather duster from Anna's cleaning basket and threw it at him. "I don't intend to let it go as far as that!"

He laughed and caught it. "I think your

Italian blood is showing after all. Perhaps that is what you needed, to get angry, and then settle the matter."

"If I don't get a black eye first," she said, recalling all the stories she had heard about the tendency of most Italian husbands to beat their wives—Uncle Tito being the most loving exception.

"I don't blame you for being upset. There must be something we can do," Serena said.

"I hope so, but I don't know what."

When she could think of no way to extricate herself from approaching disaster, Maresa did what she vowed not to do. She turned to Percy for help, and did what she swore she would not do. She wrote him a letter and asked for his help, this one last time, while she vowed to never, ever ask anything of him again.

...If you could find, in that generous heart of yours, enough affection for me and our friendship, however strained it was because of my selfish ways and lack of understanding, I will be eternally grateful if you would, this one last time, come to my aid.

I know I do not deserve it, but then, I have never truly deserved any of the loving kindness you have given me so unselfishly over the years. I know, too, that too much sacrifice can turn even the most charitable heart to stone. Now, I can only think of the words of Juliet, "Too early seen unknown, and known too late." I pray that for me, it is not too late.

Please know that whether you choose to help me or not, I will always remain:

Your most devoted friend,
Maresa

Now, there was nothing to do but pray he would get the letter in time to help her.

"What did you say to him?" Serena asked, when Maresa told her she had written the letter to Percy.

Maresa shrugged. "What else could I tell him? That I was sorry for my lack of understanding and the pain I have caused him."

"And Nicola?"

"I told him the truth about Nicola. I had no other choice than to tell him I had foolishly stepped into another engagement, only this time I could not get out of it. I told him about my father's letter, and Lord Marwood. I said I needed his help desperately, and that if he helped me this time, I would never ask such of him again." Maresa sighed and clasped her hands together in her lap. "Percy has never been angry with me before. I do hope he can forget what happened last time he was here."

"I just hope he comes to help you out, and that he doesn't arrive too late."

Twenty-One

Maid of Athens, ere we part,
Give, oh give me back my heart!
Or, since that has left my breast,
Keep it now, and take the rest!

Lord Byron (1788-1824)
English poet

In the weeks that followed, Maresa tried to remain optimistic. Percy would get the letter, she told herself. He would read it, and then he would weigh all the years they had known each other against that one incident, and in light of that, he would come.

Each time she thought this, and reached the point of telling herself he would come, a voice inside her head would say, "Wouldn't he?" and then she would begin to worry all over again.

Of late, she noticed how Aunt Gisella and Uncle Tito seemed bent upon accepting every invitation they received, when they had not done so in the past. It endeared them to her all the more to think that they were doing so because of her, and their desire to keep her mind occupied on other things.

On the occasions when an invitation did not arrive for a time they had no plans, they would have a party of their own.

Tonight, she dressed for a dinner party her aunt and uncle were giving. Earlier, she had placed her mother's necklace on the table, so she would not forget to wear it.

When she finished her hair, she reached for the necklace, and as she held it in her hand, she wondered if her mother had ever held it and looked at it as she was now doing, with a heart heavy with despair.

She knew she was being morose, but she could not help it. With each day that passed, Maresa felt her morale sinking lower and lower.

There had been no word from Percy and she now feared the worst. She did not fear for his life, but for their friendship, for she knew with Napoleon on Elba, things were relatively safe in the waters of the Mediterranean now.

Six weeks had passed without any kind of confirmation that he had received her letter.

Nothing.

The time when she would have to make a decision was getting closer, although she reminded herself that neither of her choices were really choices. As for Nicola, he was pushing ahead, planning her life for her.

The only good thing she could find out of all of this was, things were as bad as they could possibly get. And that is what she said to Serena. "I mean, when you are lying, face against the floor, you cannot go any lower."

All her hopes unfed, she faced the fact that what she had always sought had been impossible from the beginning. This is the price you pay for such foolishness, she told herself.

She had skated on thin ice for most of her life, and now she had fallen in. It was only a matter of time until she was completely encased.

"Well, at least you won't be able to accept any more engagements," Serena said.

Although having suffered the humiliation of exile on the isle of Elba for ten months, Napoleon was rarely alone. Oddly enough, it was not his French countrymen who came to visit him, but the English, and since his abdication was announced, the English were infatuated with everything Napoleonic, and this included the former emperor himself.

His exile ushered in the revival of the Grand Tour, and he was such an object of curiosity that every shop in Florence sold out of the alabaster busts cast in Napoleon's image.

The Princess of Wales referred to Elba as "irresistible." Chevalier Mariotti, French consul in Livorno, and Talleyrand's agent in the peninsula, was so puzzled by the excessive interest, that he engaged a spy known as the Oil Merchant to observe and report back to him.

By the beginning of August, things had gotten so out of hand, that Colonel Sir Neil Campbell, the British Commissioner on Elba, expressed that he "disapproved most strongly of several instances of voluntary court and unnecessary visits paid by naval officers at Portoferraio," and issued orders to stop these pilgrimages "forthwith."

One of Napoleon's most ardent admirers was Lady Holland, and the habitués of her London salon. It was Lady Holland who supplied Napoleon with the October 19 issue of the *Courier,* which contained an article that first suggested exiling him to St. Helena had been discussed by the allies.

Because of the concern some had for the situation at hand, Percy's ship had been ordered from Malta to Elba as a precaution.

When Percy's ship first sailed into port at Elba he was not prepared for what he saw, for he had been thinking in terms of exile, and punishment. But when he saw the tiny island, Elba's countryside, and high mountain passes, covered in thick Mediterranean vegetation, and numerous creeks flowing into the limpid sea along a rocky coast, his first thought was, no punishment, this.

At first glimpse of the town of Portoferraio, he was amazed that an island of pink granite, pine forests and beautiful beaches could be considered a place of exile, especially in light of knowing Napoleon's repose on Elba was quite pleasant. With a magnificent villa, a full staff of thirty-five who accompanied him to the island, Napoleon had all the trappings of an imperial court.

On two different occasions when Percy was in Portoferraio, he had glimpsed the Little Emperor. And later, when they were introduced, Napoleon had invited him to dinner, along with Lord Ebrington.

During the course of the meal, after Napoleon

had mentioned he might like to go live in America, he asked Lord Ebrington, "Do you think I would be stoned if I came to England?"

Lord Ebrington thought a moment, then replied, "You would be perfectly safe there, as the violent feelings which were excited against you are subsiding, now that we are no longer at war."

After addressing a few words to several other dinner guests, the fallen emperor gave his attention to Lieutenant Bronwell. "I understand you attended a ball in Florence, Lieutenant. Did you find it a pleasant experience?"

"I found it an experience...one that I care not to repeat."

"Why is that, Lieutenant?"

"I am a naval officer, with legs that walk decks, but suffer bouts of awkwardness when attempting to dance."

Napoleon laughed outright, and the other dinner guests joined in.

Percy, never one to laugh at his own jokes, was beginning to see how easily Napoleon charmed those around him, for it was completely natural, and Percy had to admit it was difficult not to like the man.

When the laughter subsided, Napoleon said, "Well now, it would seem that although balls sometimes offer agreeable adventures, they are also apt to cause very awkward ones. In this instance, one was wise to leave with all due haste which, apparently, is what you did."

There was a lengthy pause, in which time Napoleon neither suggested, nor offered, any hint as to the direction of his thoughts.

Percy never knew if Napoleon knew more than he let on, or if it was nothing more than a lucky guess. If he knew the details of Percy's appearance at the marchesa's ball and his encounter with Maresa, he never alluded to it, yet there was something about the subtle smile on Napoleon's face that made Percy think he had many more spies about than the Ministry, or the Royal Navy, suspected.

When Colonel Sir Neil Campbell learned that Napoleon had invited Ebrington and Lieutenant Bronwell to dinner, he took it as a slight, and something to induce him to quit Elba entirely.

This deduction was something Percy knew to be erroneous and not in Napoleon's best interest, simply because Campbell, in Percy's opinion, was admirably inefficient, and he was frequently absent from the island, which afforded Napoleon a dangerous amount of freedom. If Campbell were to be replaced Napoleon would, more than likely, find himself under the watchful eye of someone less prone to turning his head the other way.

No, it was not in Napoleon's best interest to sway Campbell to leave, but although it was common knowledge, no one could convince Campbell of that.

There was little doubt in Percy's mind, that although Campbell had been absent from his post for some time, that he was behind the orders to send him on a diplomatic mission to Florence in February, for no other reason than because he had been a guest of Napoleon's at dinner that night.

It was not until Percy arrived in Florence that he realized the mission's true purpose was not to transport military documents, but to deliver a parcel to Campbell's mistress, Countess Miniacci.

Percy had received Maresa's letter shortly before he left for Florence, but it was the twenty-sixth of February before he finished his mission in Florence with the chatty and flirtatious countess, and rode to the Bartolinis' villa.

Percy was disappointed to learn Maresa had affianced herself to another man, but not surprised—engagements being one of the few areas where she demonstrated any consistency.

As he rode toward Villa Mirandola, he became aware that the closer he came, the heavier the weight of loss hung in his heart. It was the first time he ever went to see her with resignation rather than anticipation, for he had resigned himself to a life without her.

Gradually he had become numb to the reality of unrequited love, and he had closed the door that led to the inner workings of his heart.

Love cost too much, hurt too much, disappointed too much and gave nothing in return.

His last, and fatal, attempt to show her his

true feelings, and to speak to her of the love that he had always carried for her in his heart, had ended quickly and not painlessly. When it came to him, Maresa looked through glass eyes.

When he had seen her that last time, and she had reacted the way she did, it hit him and hard. But the devastation of loss only lasted until he realized something else. She not only showed him that she did not feel the same way he did, but showed him that she would never be his.

The pain of realization was there, but in time it would become nothing more than a dull ache of remembrance. He was ready to give up the responsibility, and in truth, wondered if his always being there, had not given sanction to her flighty nature.

When he reached his ship after riding away from her that cold morning, he knew that he had let go, that he had resigned the care of Maresa to her destiny, or to God, and that he had become truly indifferent as to the outcome.

He would never have Maresa, but he would have peace.

And then the letter came.

While he waited in the receiving room for her to come down to speak with him, he knew this would be the last time he ever saw her, for he had loved her too much, and for too long to remain chastely at her side. He had decided some time ago that the only way to keep her

271

out of his heart was to keep her out of his sight and out of his life.

He was only here now to help her if he could, this one last time, and to tell her that he was no longer a resource upon which she could lean. From this moment on, she was on her own.

He stood, militarily straight, between the fireplace and the window, where he could remain sufficiently warm, yet take in the landscape that lay beyond the walls of the villa.

Italy had always held a certain enchantment for him, although when asked why he never could exactly come up with the reason. Part of it might be because of the debt the present generation owed it; if for nothing else, the Renaissance that had yanked mankind out of the dark drudgery and ignorance of the Middle Ages into a period of enlightenment.

Italy, the world's poor little rich country; a miracle for which there was no understanding.

Perhaps what it was that he loved best was the Italians' irrepressible energy, their determination to make do, their will not to despair, that all flowed freely like the many fountains found in even the smallest village.

He could do well to take a lesson from them.

The painfully familiar staccato of footsteps approached and thoughts of Italy vanished.

When he heard her steps grow closer, he turned ever so slightly, to catch a glimpse of her when she came through the door, for in all their years together, he had never tired of seeing her. While at sea, she was always before him, and reminders of her were everywhere. The blue of her eyes was in the sea, and the sun-warmed hues of sandy beaches were as soft and smooth as her skin. Even at night, there was no escaping, for the darkness would envelop him, as black as Maresa's hair.

Green had always been her best color, not that there was a color that did not suit her. Draped in green velvet that hugged her form, it was easy to see why he had always thought her so lovely, but it was far from the reason why he loved her.

"Dearest Percy, I am ever so glad you are here."

The same old familiar greeting of friendship, and he fell in step with it, as one would do in a military parade. "You look as lovely as I remember," he said, and kissed her cheek.

"Here, let me have your hat." She placed it on the table, next to a bowl of Venetian glass.

"Thank you."

"You don't have to stand at attention. Come and sit, here," she said, patting the sofa beside her as she seated herself.

He wondered if she sensed the change in temperature between them, and if that was what prompted her to say, "I do hope you have found it in your heart to forgive me for the abominable way I behaved when you were here last."

"There is no reason to bring it up."

"But I must! My actions and my words

have grieved me greatly. There were so many times I tried to write you to apologize, but each time, I could not find the words. Then I realized it was because I could not say what I needed to say in a letter. I had to say them to you in person. I don't know what I will do if you cannot bring yourself to say you forgive me."

He wondered what she would say if he told her it was not the first time she had hurt him, only the first time she was conscious of it.

"I don't suppose either of us will lose any sleep over it. It is so much smoke out of the chimney, and each day has enough cares to keep us busy."

She stared at him oddly for a moment, the said, "Yes, well, I suppose so, and I do have so much to tell you."

"You are still engaged?"

A shadow came over her face and she looked down. He had his answer even before she said, "Yes, I fear that I am."

"Have you told him of your feelings?"

"Yes, but he refused to call things off. He said it did not matter if I loved him or not. I was truly astounded to discover how a man as proud as he, could have no pride."

"And your uncle?"

"Uncle Tito has spoken to him as well, but it did nothing more than anger him. So, you see, I desperately need your help."

He shook his head. "Why do you think I could succeed where both you and your uncle have failed? Do you want me to challenge him to a duel?"

"No, of course not."

"Then what would you have me do, Maresa? Tell me, and I will do it, if it is in my power."

"I—I don't know. I suppose I assumed you would have thought of something by the time you arrived."

"Think of the solution, and perform the deed."

He stood and walked the length of the room, and back again, before he turned back to her. "Maresa, it is difficult to say this, but—"

She shot to her feet. "No, Percy! No!"

She rushed toward him. "Don't tell me there is nothing you can do. You are my last hope...my only hope. I have maintained my sanity this long only by thinking that when you arrived, everything would soon be over."

She stepped closer and placed the soft curve of her cheek against his chest. "I know you could think of something...if you only would."

His hand came up to stroke her hair, as he had done ten thousand times in the past, but it stopped short of touching her.

Hurting now, on the inside, he closed his eyes and laid his head back. Love...it required too much, cost too much, hurt too much. He could not risk his heart another time.

He was not born sneering. Love had taught him to be that way. Selfishness, insincerity, and immaturity—they were all a part of love as much as desire and the need to comfort. It takes time to develop a protective callous, not the ideal remedy, of course, but necessary if one wants to look each day in the eye and continue on.

Never again, he told himself. Not ever again.

He was not so foolish as to think he could never love again. Yes, anything was possible, even love...in time, and if that circumambulating aphrodisiac, the moon, was full, and angled just right.

He might.

Perhaps there would be other loves. But always seen in a paler light.

She drew her head back and looked at him, and it wrenched something inside him to see tears on her face.

"Please, Percy, please! I told you I was sorry, and I am. You will never know how sorry I am. Not only for hurting you as I did that day, but also for all the years I so selfishly thought of myself, and thought of you only in terms of existing to soothe and console. It is something I will have to live with for the rest of my life. Don't make me live with the pain of having lost you as well."

He could not help her, not because he refused to do so, but because she was beyond any help he could give her now.

"Just this once. One last time and I'll never ask anything of you again. Please. I am begging you. I will get down on my knees..."

She made a move to do just that, but he stopped her. "I cannot help you, Maresa. Not because I so choose, but because it is impossible."

"It can't be. You cannot imagine what my going through with this would mean. I would rather marry anyone than Nicola!"

"Even me?"

He would die, never knowing why he asked that, or what prompted him to say those exact words, or even where, exactly, the idea had come from.

At first, she seemed disconcerted, and a bit confused, as if she were trying to decide if she had heard him right. He saw the change of expression that told him the moment she decided she had caught correctly his words, and that now she was trying to decide why he had said them. As if he could answer that question for either one of them. God help them both.

It was almost entertaining to watch her, for her face was so open, and he had known her so long that he knew precisely what she felt and knew each nuance of her thoughts. Still, he remained silent. He was waiting for the moment of acceptance that he knew would come. Not that there was any satisfaction in it for him. It would take a rare man who would relish the idea of marrying a woman who did not wish to marry him. No matter how much he loved her. One-sided love was not a shield he cared to carry before him into battle.

He knew when the desperation in her had disappeared, when it had floated out of her, borne on the next breath. Then came shock. Not exactly the reaction he wanted, but then, at least it was not repulsion.

277

Take your blessings where you find them.

He thought about what it would mean if she accepted his offer, and the most important one, he figured, was he would never marry anyone else, but it was a moot point, since he cared little for the idea anyway.

Caution crept into her eyes. "Marry you? Oh, Percy— No, not even someone as selfish as I could ask that sacrifice of you. Someone else, perhaps, but not you."

"Then I cannot help you."

"Don't you understand if you did this, you would be married to me for the rest of your life? How could you do that to yourself?"

"It doesn't matter. I'll probably go down with my ship, anyway. But, since you reject my offer, it is a rather worthless issue. Perhaps you will be fortunate enough to find someone else willing to marry you, someone easier on your conscience, before the date of the wedding."

"Before the wedding? Are you daft? That is two weeks away. It's impossible."

"What about Angelo? He is your friend as well."

"Angelo is... Oh, don't be absurd. To marry Angelo would be like marrying family. Incestuous! It is out of the question."

Past help, past care. Eggs could not be unscrambled. He picked up his hat.

Her gaze traveled down to the tricorn he held in his hand. No, her mind screamed. He could not be leaving her. Not her Percy.

She took in the sight of him, still as tall and slim as he had always been, and the eyes were just as green, but the golden kiss of sunlight in his hair was stronger now, from his time at sea. Oh, yes, she knew the outward appearance of him so very well, but she realized at that moment that even after so many years, she did not know so very much about the man he was on the inside.

Her eyes were wide and startled, like the look in the eyes of deer quietly come upon, while on a walk, just before they run.

"You aren't leaving now, are you?"

"There is no reason for me to stay."

She put her hand over her mouth and turned away.

"Oh, dear God, I don't know what to do." She buried her face in her hands.

This weakening toward her was his own weakness coming out, and something to be overcome. Tomorrow.

He did not know why he did not leave, but he was not surprised. He sighed, knowing he would, more than likely, resent doing it to his dying day. She always had some sort of mystical, magical hold upon him, hadn't she?

"You have two choices, Maresa. You can marry Nicola, or you can marry me." He placed his hat upon his head and made to leave, then checked himself.

He took her in his arms. "Goodbye, my love," he said, and kissed her, pouring out his soul in a way words could never express. Not a kiss of passion, but one born of the suffering of wanting. Always wanting. And at last, came the kiss of goodbye, deep, erotic, almost to the point of pain, a kiss to last, and to be remembered.

And final.

She could live to be an old, old woman, forgetful of even her name, but she would never forget that kiss, for it was not the kiss of a lover, or even a friend, but the kiss of deep and profound loss, a kiss of eternal separation, of lost hope and unfulfilled dreams, a kiss that did what years of longing and a million lines of poetry could not have done.

It made her see him, truly see him as a man and not an extension of herself.

She was so overwhelmed at the discovery that she did not at first realize he had released her and was already out the door, until she heard his footsteps in the hall.

Dear God, he was leaving.

"No! Percy, wait! I'll marry you...of course I will."

She ran after him and threw her arms around him. "I'm so sorry. You deserve more than this, but you won't regret it, I promise. I'll make it up to you, if it takes the rest of my life."

He put his arms around her and she placed her cheek against his chest, as she had done so many times before, listening now, to the steady beat of a resolute heart, knowing he was doing this for her, and knowing, too, that the arms that held her were not the warm, loving arms she remembered, but the cold arms of one resigned to his fate.

Twenty-Two

Love is a tyrant sparing none.

> Pierre Corneille (1606-1684)
> French playwright

A restless man, living in exile far from events, Napoleon kept a close watch on what was happening on the Continent. He knew the Vienna congress considered Elba too close to France, and wanted to banish him to a distant island in the Atlantic.

More than once, Napoleon had accused the Austrians of preventing his wife, Marie Louise, and his son from joining him on Elba. No one had bothered to tell him that she had already taken a lover and had no intention of going into exile with him.

Many of the conditions set aside in the Treaty of Fontainebleau were not being kept. He grew more impatient. When the French government refused to pay his allowance, placing him in danger of being reduced to penury, he decided enough was enough. He made a decision. It was time to take action.

On the twenty-sixth of February, 1814,

Napoleon left the island on a hired frigate, escaped the surveillance of the British fleet at Elba, and sailed toward France.

That same afternoon, Captain John Miles of HMS *Prince of Wales* married Maresa and Percy at Villa Mirandola, with only the members of the family present.

Earlier that morning, Percy had engaged Uncle Tito in deep conversation for over an hour, while he tried to persuade him that an elopement would be the best way, his main concern being the repercussions that were bound to come from the Brancaleones, and their friends who would align with them.

"My niece will be married here, in the home where her mother was born and married, surrounded by those who love her, and if I can't withstand a few hot looks from the Brancaleones and their lot, then I have no right to call myself a man."

That being said and wrapped up neatly, Percy bowed to Uncle Tito's wishes.

Two hours later, Maresa and Percy stood close together with hearts a world apart, as Captain Miles performed the marriage ceremony.

They became man and wife, but it was long after midnight when they became lovers.

Awkwardness hung heavily between them, as they climbed the stairs and went to Maresa's room.

Percy paused outside her chamber door, his hands on her upper arms. His tone was serious, and he looked directly into her eyes. "You understand the marriage must be consummated, otherwise it can be annulled, don't you?"

She looked down at her feet that peeked out from beneath her gown; two curious mice, searching for a way out.

"Yes," she said so softly he barely heard the words, "I understand."

"Come then, the night awaits us," he said, before he swept her into his arms and carried her into the room.

He lowered her to her feet beside the fire, and although he had held her in his arms for only a moment, he could feel the chill on her flesh. "Warm yourself for a moment, while I light a lamp."

When the mellow glow of light cast out the last shadow, he said, "I will leave now, while you prepare for bed."

She shook her head. "There is no need. I will change in my dressing room."

He considered her for a moment, as an artist about to put her image on canvas and bring it to life. He noticed the look of expectation on her face, before allowing his gaze to drop lower.

This was his wedding day and she was his bride, and he tried to etch in his memory the image of her standing in the firelight in a shimmer of green and gold.

He watched her walk toward her dressing room with silent dignity. When she was almost beside him, she caught her foot on the carpet.

If he had not reacted quickly, she would have

fallen. But he caught her, finding it odd that for the first twenty years of his life he had done everything to get her here, and now that he was no longer resolved to look upon her in that way, his arms were where she always seemed to end up.

He took in the sight of her startled face looking up at his own. Unable to tame the need within, he drew her to him with a powerful hold and said, "Perhaps it is better this way."

He breathed the words into her startled mouth a second before he opened his own and placed it over hers. He tasted her now, as a lover would, slowly, sensuously, and with deliberation.

Her head was tilted back, her throat slim and flowing down to where the flesh grew softer and round, with only the tips of her breasts left unexposed by the low-cut gown. He slowly slid his mouth over her skin, where the emerald necklace flashed brightly enough to show a candelabrum a thing or two about giving light.

Fingers moving undirected traveled down her spine to leave a trail of buttons open. His hand slipped inside.

A lifetime of loving, wanting and waiting; always waiting to have what he now had the right to take. But it was different than he had imagined, or hoped, for he could feel the difference deep down, to the center of his bones, the difference between making love to a woman who allowed it out of gratitude, rather than to one who gave it out of love.

But there comes a point when the intensity

of desire flares into intense hunger, and reason, like second thoughts, smolder like embers of a dying fire.

The dress fell away from her body, and he set himself the task of freeing so much loveliness from the torturous confines that lay between them.

He had never seen a woman's body who needed the discipline of a corset less.

She was smaller than he thought she would be, her breasts fuller, and her skin pure and white—Shakespeare's queen of curds and cream.

He buried his face in her hair and the scent of her filled him with a godforsaken longing, until his own clothes lay atop hers, and he took her hand to lead her to the bed.

Her step slowed. "No, not there. Here, by the fire."

He took a step back from her. "By the fire? On the floor? Are you sure?"

Her gaze traveled over him, tiller to stern, with a slow, methodical survey he would have thought her too shy to perform.

"Yes, I am sure."

"To see you naked burns me," he said, and took her in all her beautiful nudity, chaste, willing and warm, down with him to lie upon a blanket hastily cast over the carpet.

"You must tell me what to do."

"Love requires no teacher."

He scattered kisses along her neck and over her breasts, kissing her and touching, until he knew that she wanted him. He positioned himself above her, knowing as he did that she was waiting, anticipating, but knowing, too, that anticipation was worth the wait, he prolonged it, because he knew he would only have her this once.

He heard the change in tempo of her breath, could feel the restlessness mounting inside her body.

"The room is cold, yet I am so hot. Is this part of it, this feeling of subduing warmth? Do you feel it?"

"I feel it," he whispered, cutting off the rest of the words he wanted to say, words that would have told her how, for years now, his body filled with warmth, pure, liquid warmth whenever she came into his line of vision.

When the moment arrived and he knew she wanted him with the same passion he held in check for her, he moved inside her, slowly, easefully, giving her time to adjust. "Am I hurting you?"

"In a good way. Is it supposed to be like this?"

"Oh, yes," he said, and thought it was supposed to be like this, but rarely was.

When it was over, he rolled off her, and pulled her to him until she settled herself in the crook of his arm, her head upon his shoulder.

He knew the warmth of the fire, the tension of the last few days gripped her, when she said sleepily, "I am glad it was you, Percy," and floated into the place of sleep, while Percy only dozed off for a few minutes.

When he awoke, he carried to her to her bed, and joined her there.

She slept soundly, curled up against him, while he remained awake, long into the night, and fought the demons of lust that pressed him to take her again, as was his right.

But love interfered, and he knew the old feelings for her were not gone, and he realized a lifetime of torture would never shake them loose, for the fire in him had yet to turn to ashes.

But he would keep the secret of it within himself, and give to her a heart, both cold and numb.

Twenty-Three

The most happy marriage I can picture
or imagine to myself would be
the union of a deaf man to a blind woman.

Samuel Taylor Coleridge (1772-1834)
British poet

When morning was nothing more than a shimmer of pearl upon the dark horizon, Percy stirred, and dreamed he heard a knock at the door.

The second time he heard it, he knew it was no dream.

He climbed out of bed quietly, and took up the blanket from the floor in front of the fireplace to wrap around himself.

287

When he opened the door, Tito was standing there.

"Excuse the intrusion. There is a Lieutenant John Murray waiting downstairs to speak with you."

"Did he say what he wanted?"

"No, he said it was urgent, that's all."

"I'll be down as soon as I get some clothes on."

Percy pulled on his pants and left the room with his shirt in his hand, which he finished buttoning a moment before he walked into the receiving room, where Lieutenant Murray stood talking to Tito.

Lieutenant Murray said, "Sorry to disturb you, but Napoleon escaped yesterday. You are to return to Elba immediately."

Percy cursed silently under his breath. Of all the stupid blunders! If he did not know better, he would have sworn Sir Neil to be under Napoleon's employ instead of England's.

Only yesterday, he had learned in Florence that Countess Miniacci was possibly an agent of Napoleon's. Worse, Campbell was away from the island almost as much as he was there.

There was no doubt that much of the blame for Napoleon's escape was due to Campbell's blundering.

"I would be happy to accompany you back, if that is all right with you."

"I would be glad for the company. If you would give me enough time to finish dressing and time to say goodbye to my wife, I will rejoin you shortly."

"Could you have someone saddle my horse?" Percy asked Tito, only moments before he quit the room.

Tito nodded. "Right away."

When he entered their room, Percy saw that Maresa had slept through the disastrous news. He dressed swiftly and paused a moment beside the bed where she lay sleeping. He started to kiss her goodbye, but decided against it.

No need to wake her.

He would write a note to her downstairs and leave it with Tito. A moment later, he was going down the stairs.

After he penned the note to Maresa, he handed it to Tito.

"Give her this when she awakes. I don't know how long it will be before I return. The situation is grave at best."

"This means the war will resume, I suppose," Tito said.

"Only if Napoleon can raise enough troops to fight again."

"That is a given," Tito said.

"Yes, I fear it is."

Lieutenant Murray was already mounted and holding the reins to Percy's horse when Percy went outside.

Soon they were riding at a fast clip down the lane that led to the main road. Percy's thoughts were on Maresa, when he should have been focused on Napoleon.

In the aftermath of lovemaking last night, he thought her an enchantress and for a moment was so rash as to imagine it could be a love match.

Today he saw it for what it truly was, a way to save her from a disastrous marriage.

Nothing more. Nothing less.

He was not sure if these sobering thoughts were due to the coming of morning, or to the news of Napoleon, or was it because he and Maresa were so long acquainted, that he knew all her ways?

Ahead of them, the sun was beginning to present itself, rising over the Tuscan hills, a fiery red brilliance that illuminated the sky with pink and golden hues, giving light, but no warmth, to the frozen stillness.

He found a personal resonance in the calm of winter when the world, and the heart within him, lay dormant and asleep.

When Percy and Lieutenant Murray arrived in Livorno, they learned that Sir Neil had left Elba several days before Napoleon's escape, despite the urgings of Lord Burghersh, who had urged him to return to the island on December 24.

It was, unquestionably, a dereliction of duty, but Percy doubted anything would ever come of it.

With Lieutenant Murray at his side, the two of them sailed to Elba, where the uncertain future waited.

When Maresa awoke and saw Percy was no longer there, she placed her hand upon the smooth linen sheet where he had slept, expecting the warmth of his body that still lingered there to tell her how long he had been gone.

She was shocked to find the sheet stone cold.

She could not help wondering why he had arisen so early and, if last night had not been so wonderful, she might have given in to a bit of petulance at the thought of his leaving her so soon after their lovemaking.

Awash in new feelings, she continued to lie abed, stretching, smiling and feeling undeniably beautiful, loved and content, unable to believe she could be so much in love with Percy. She tried to understand how it was that she never knew before, and decided she must be one of those sorts who must be hit over the head with a fact before they can absorb even the slightest amount of truth. She was also the kind of woman that held on to that truth when she finally came around to realizing it.

She closed her eyes and allowed her thoughts to drift to that place where memories of last night resided, and immediately felt a penetrating warmth spread slowly through her, touching her as he had touched her, in the most private places that now belonged to him. She could not imagine it was possible that there had ever been a time when she did not love him, for it was too perfect, and too complete to be new.

Surely she had always loved him. She must be a woman too sightless to capture the obvious, as looking into the light often blinds one so they cannot see. And so, overly concerned with the trivial pursuit of a husband, she was unable to grasp the idea that the perfect man for her had always been there, right beside her. She had never realized, until this moment, that none of the men in her past could measure up to all that Percy was.

All this time, she thought, I have pursued one goal and now I find it was the wrong one.

Never had she felt so deservedly stupid, and she pounded the pillow in frustration. "Maresa, what a fool you've been. Faith! If they were to examine your head, they would find nothing there."

She could not blame Percy if he never forgave her.

She dressed, unable to deny she still felt a little put out that Percy had left her in the room, without awakening her, but on the other hand, she knew she could not be angry with him.

Not after last night.

The house was quiet as she descended the stairs, and she wondered if Percy and Uncle Tito had gone hunting for wild boar, or had they opted for an early-morning ride? She walked past the library and saw she had been at least half wrong, for there sat Uncle Tito with a paper which Percy had brought to him when he rode over from Florence.

"Good morning, Uncle. Is Percy about?"

Uncle Tito dropped his paper. "Come,

dear, join me here by the fire. There is still a chill in the air."

She smiled and stepped into the room.

"Percy was called away early this morning. He left this for you."

He pushed a folded piece of paper toward her and stood. "I think I'll find someone to bring in more firewood. Read your letter while I'm gone."

My dearest Maresa,

This is not the parting I would have chosen, but perhaps quick and unannounced is the best way after all.

By now, Tito has probably told you that Napoleon escaped yesterday and I have been called back to Elba.

I am thankful I was able to help you this one last time before Napoleon came between us. I do not know what your plans are now, but I would advise remaining in Tuscany, at least until we know if this is a peaceful escape, or if he is, at this moment, trying to muster troops to resume the war.

I will keep in touch, only to let you know my whereabouts. Although I realize this marriage was not a love match, you are legally my wife, and I will honor my role as provider and protector. Once things are improved, if you so choose to return to London, my town house is at your disposal.

I will dispatch a letter to Mr. Townsend,

my barrister, informing him that you are to be given access to a living allowance, as well as advising him to begin the preliminaries of drafting my will.

In any case, rest assured you will be provided for, albeit humbly, as the wife of a naval officer. I pray I have done the right thing, for in saving you from one marriage, I have prevented you from ever having another. I say this, not to make you unhappy, or to censure. Neither of us is more to blame than the other. We are in this together, as the saying goes.

If you should have need of me, I have left information on how to contact me with your uncle Tito.

In time, the pain of all this will lessen. In time I will forget your kiss, as you have already forgotten mine.

Be happy, Maresa,
Percy

A tear splashed on the paper.

Then another and another, until the world beyond her eyes grew too dim and blurred to see. She could not bear the thought of anyone seeing her like this, so she quietly quit the library and returned to her room.

There was no fire in the grate and the coals had burned to ash. Maresa sat in a chair near the fireplace. She felt no warmth, no cheerfulness, no satisfying ease. There was no comfort, either in her thoughts or in any part of her chilled body.

Winter settled about her, no warmth, no sunshine, no birds chirping, no buzzing of bees.

Sadness and guilt consumed her, for she understood the price he had paid for her foolishness.

She tried to shy away from the things he said. She did not want to deal with the scars they left. There would be time enough to deal with them in the long months ahead, now that he was gone, and the threat of being in war once again loomed overhead, dark and threatening.

If she was honest, she would have to admit his was a difficult task. If he spoke the truth, she could not bear to hear it. If he tried to soften it with tender words, she would have rejected it as pity.

Had she always been so difficult?

Please, she thought, please give me another chance. Don't let it be too late.

Once Napoleon had evaded the British blockade in the rented frigate, accompanied by 125 men including his Elba bodyguard, they landed on the coast of France at Cannes.

From there, he marched his troops toward Grenoble, then to Laffray where he encountered a battalion of the Fifth Regiment of the Line.

The troops had been given orders to open fire, but they hesitated at the sight of him standing so brazenly before them. Napoleon threw open his coat and shouted, "Let him that has the heart, kill his Emperor!"

The soldiers threw down their arms and cried *"Vive l'Empereur!"* They joined the ranks and marched toward Paris with Napoleon, picking up more troops and many of his trusted commanders along the way.

On March 20, Napoleon rode into Paris, mounted on his white horse, but the Bourbon king, Louis XVIII had already fled France and gone to Belgium.

Immediately, Napoleon proclaimed himself Emperor of the French and offered peace to the crowned heads of Europe.

The allies were not favorably disposed toward trusting Napoleon a second time, and his offer was rejected.

Austria, England, Prussia and Russia allied themselves against Napoleon, and began to raise an army, led by the Duke of Wellington.

Percy was still on the island of Elba, and he and Lieutenant John Murray were assigned to the *Ajax* and sent to Sicily. Since Sicily and Sardinia had never been under the rule of the French, they continued to be ruled by the Bourbons, so the islands remained friendly to the allies and under the protection of the Royal Navy.

The *Ajax* was the senior ship of a squadron off Sardinia and Corsica. They were under orders to secure and maintain the blockade of the French ports and the Mediterranean.

In the early morning fog, they engaged two ships of the French fleet, the *Resolue* and the *Pomone*. The *Ajax* overtook the *Resolue*, a corvette with only twenty eight-pounders and two brass sixes, but before they could fire a shot the *Mignon*, a French brig, sailed out of the fog and caught the *Ajax* in a vulnerable position.

The *Mignon* fired her cannonade, and opened her broadside a few minutes later.

Percy reported the damage to the captain. "We've lost the slings of the brig's gaff, Captain. When the gaff fell away, the boom-mainsail covered the quarterdeck guns on the side engaged."

The brig's main mast fell by the board, and she was rendered unmanageable and unable to return fire with the wreck lying upon some of her guns. Unable to do anything but drift, they were taking on water, completely at the mercy of the French. They were expecting another broadside, when suddenly the three French ships made sail before the wind.

Wondering why the French turned tail, Percy took up his glass and sighted four British brigs headed their way. They signaled the closest brig, the *Castilian*, that they were sinking, and the *Castilian* sailed closer and managed to fire one round of her lee guns before the French were out of range.

The *Castilian* hoisted out her boats and saved the crew of the *Ajax*, shortly before she went down.

"That was the closest one yet," Lieutenant Murray said when Percy followed him aboard the *Castilian*.

"Close enough that I don't care to repeat it," Percy replied, even though he had a strong feeling that something far worse lay ahead.

Twenty-Four

The thorns which I have reap'd are of the
tree
I planted; they have torn me, and I bleed.
I should have known what fruit would
spring from such a seed.

Lord Byron (1788-1824)
English poet

"Papa is going to Florence this morning to see the British Minister, Lord Burghersh. Mama thought we might all go, and spend a little time in Florence. We'll have most of the day there," Serena said. "Say you'll come, Maresa. Mama said you've been too mopey of late. She thinks the outing will be good for you. The weather is most cooperative today, so even the ride over should be delightful."

"You are coming," Angelo said. "We won't give you a choice."

Maresa did not feel she would be good company and told them so.

"We will be the judge of that," Angelo said.

"If you don't come, we won't have a good time, because we will all be worried about you," Serena said.

No matter what they said, it did not make the prospect of going to Florence for the day more attractive, but sometimes giving in is less trouble than fighting with the wishes of others.

"I know you are worried about Percy, but

you must have more faith. He will return to you. I am certain of it," Angelo said.

"He may return, but it will be out of a sense of duty."

"Married in Lent, and you'll live to repent," Serena said.

Angelo and Maresa both glared at her.

"What? I didn't make that up. It's an old saying," she said in defense.

Angelo shook his head. "It isn't what you said, it's the appropriateness and the timing of it. What is in your head, Serena? Tomato sauce?"

"Perhaps." Then, smiling encouragement like a ham-handed dentist she said, "Well, I don't understand it. If love and marriage is such a natural occurrence, then why is getting there so complicated?"

No one had an answer for that.

After Serena and Angelo departed, Maresa returned to her room to write a letter to Percy, which she found impossible to do, because of the numerous thoughts that kept darting in and out of her consciousness like a school of minnows.

Never would she forgive herself for not speaking what was in her heart the last night they were together. Why, she wondered, did she have to fall asleep?

She thought about the sacrifice he made, and recalled something he said—that he would probably go down with his ship anyway.

Cynicism had never been a part of Percy's character. It both frightened and grieved her sorely to think she was the catalyst for this change. It also made her worry more about his safety, for she could not help wondering if his comment was only the cynical remark of a wounded heart, or was it a premonition of that which was to come?

She could feel the change taking place within her, for she was slowly starting to see she was becoming more mindful of someone else's feelings than she was of her own. The old fear that she would never find the right man to marry was gone, but a new one had taken its place: What if something happened to him?

It was an epiphany of sorts, for it was at that point that she knew she had to do something—and she prayed she would be given the opportunity to do anything to prove herself and make her worthy of his love—for she could not ever bear to see a look in his eyes that said he was sorry he married her.

Almost immediately, she decided she wanted to go to Florence with the family, so she dressed quickly and hurried downstairs to find her uncle.

If there was any way to find Percy, and go to him, she wanted to find out for herself. And a visit to the British Minister's office in Florence was the best way to do it.

Uncle Tito was delighted she would join them for the outing to Florence, but he would not allow Maresa to go with him to the office of the British Minister. "I will find out all I can about Percy. You go enjoy yourself in town."

"Uncle, I am curious about something," Maresa said. "Now that Napoleon has escaped, do you think Italy will be under his control again?"

"Who knows? Anything is possible, but there are more who would resist French rule now than there were before. I was born in Florence, a city with a long history of distraction by domestic squabbles which, for years, killed off the most promising youth of the population in senseless wars. Most Florentines, like myself, have a distinct hatred for war, just as we have a grand passion for art, and that does make us susceptible to being conquered."

Maresa never grew tired of seeing Florence, as it came into view when they reached the top of the last hill before the road led down into the city. Today, the weather was clear and sunny, and the winding Arno sparkled jewellike as it wound its way through the huddled roofs of the city, but it was the view of the duomo, and Brunelleschi's dome in particular, that she found as humbling as she did breathtaking.

After the carriage crossed the Arno, Uncle Tito kissed Aunt Gisella and stepped into the street. "I will meet you at the coffee house near the Piazza della Signoria when I am finished."

As he started off, he turned back to Maresa, and said, "Don't worry, I will do as I promised and find out what I can about where Percy is, but I don't think they will be able to tell me much today."

They traveled along the Arno for a few

more blocks, and then Maresa, Angelo, Serena and Aunt Gisella left the carriage at the Ponte Vecchio, the old bridge covered with the shops of jewelers and goldsmiths.

Maresa decided she wanted to buy something for Percy, so they joined the other shoppers and visited several shops before she found the perfect gift—a small, gold sailing ship.

"What do you think?" she asked the others. "Do you think he will like it?"

They all looked at Angelo. "Of course he will like it. It's from you, and it's the appropriate sort of thing one would give for a wedding gift, for it will last, and the subject is perfect for a naval officer."

As she often was, Maresa was astounded by his reply, for Angelo was the type who often came across as too carefree to ever have a serious thought in his head.

"I will take it," she said. The shopkeeper, in the Florentine tradition, took great care with the manner in which he wrapped the package, using the loveliest paper, painted with scenes of the Renaissance, and tying it up neatly with a bit of colored string.

She tucked the package safely in her reticule, and they shopped their way back along the bridge. By the time they left the shops, Maresa had purchased a replica of the leaning tower of Pisa carved from Carrera marble, a small fish of Venetian glass and two exquisite combs for her hair.

After leaving the shops, they turned up Piazzale degli Uffizi, which Maresa found less crowded than it had been the last time she was here. Just beyond one of the statues that lined the open area in front of the Galleria degli Uffizi, Maresa saw two young lovers steal a kiss.

She looked away from the painful reminder of all the opportunities for such she could have had with Percy—missed opportunities she had foolishly turned away.

Aunt Gisella was full of conversation today, and took it upon herself to point out the names of each statue as they passed, and gave a brief history of each one.

When they reached the center of old Florence, the Piazza della Signoria, they passed the *loggia* and the statue of David, to cut across the piazza in front of the Palazzo Vecchio, with its overhanging battlements and great, lion-topped tower.

Delicious aromas lingered in the streets as they passed a *trattoria,* and farther down, the place where street vendors sold spaghetti from wooden vats over charcoal fires, and the patrons ate it with their hands.

The smell of food did cause Maresa's stomach to growl, but she was always so captivated by the sights and the recollections of history each time she came here, that thoughts of food tended to fall down the ladder of importance.

"Mmm, that smells good," Serena declared. "Is anyone else hungry?"

"Angelo," Maresa said.

"How do you know?" Angelo asked.

"Because you are always hungry."

"And yet, look at his legs," Serena said. "They are not much bigger than spaghetti."

"Do not say a word," Aunt Gisella said to Angelo, when he opened his mouth to say something back to Serena. "This is going to be a pleasant excursion, and I intend to see that is accomplished without the two of you casting barbs about."

When they reached the coffee house, Aunt Gisella insisted Maresa should have a bit of biscuit with her coffee.

"Thank you, but I'm not hungry."

"Angelo, bring her a biscuit anyway," Aunt Gisella said, and was kind enough not to notice when Maresa ate it all.

A few doors back, they had passed a shop with a beautiful *torta di Marzapan* in the window, and Aunt Gisella had paused a moment to look at it. Unable to forget how delicious a Marzipan cake would be about now, she sent Angelo back to buy it.

Serena decided to go with him.

"Be nice," Aunt Gisella said as Serena started off in the direction Angelo had taken.

"Aren't I always, Mama?" Serena said over her shoulder and hurried to catch up with Angelo.

Aunt Gisella gave her attention to Maresa. "Don't worry so much. God has not brought you this far to abandon you."

"I wish I could be as certain as you."

"There is something I want to show you, something I think you need about now, but we must wait until Angelo and Serena return," she said, and the two of them fell into conversation about several subjects before Serena and Angelo returned.

They heard them first, and by the time they could see them, Serena was literally hanging on Angelo's arm, weak from laughter.

"Your *Torta detta Marzapane*," Angelo said, offering it to Aunt Gisella with a bow.

"You hold it for a moment," Aunt Gisella said. "I want you to wait here for Tito. Maresa and I will be back soon."

"Where are you going?" Serena asked.

"To Dante's church," Aunt Gisella answered.

The two of them set off, and after several blocks of walking they turned up a narrow street to a tiny church off Via Dante Alighieri.

"This is the church where Dante worshipped. His house is across the street. It is a simple church, but then our Lord is a simple man," Aunt Gisella said.

They stepped into the dark interior of a church that was remarkably plain and small, but Maresa forgot about the size of it when she kneeled at one of the pews and unleashed a storm of prayer.

She prayed for her family, both here and in England, and she prayed for herself, and for an end to the war, but mostly she prayed earnestly for Percy, and a miracle, for that is what she felt it would take to set things right between them.

When she finished, they stepped outside again into the meager sunlight and saw Uncle Tito coming toward them, followed by Angelo and Serena, who were almost running to keep up, the Marzipan cake swinging from Angelo's arm.

"Did you have any luck finding what you were after?" Aunt Gisella asked.

"Not as much as I hoped, but I did get more information on Napoleon's escape. He slipped through the English blockade quite easily. Some say it was the rumors of his removal to St. Helena that prompted it, but it is well-known that he never expected to stay in exile long. He is headed for Paris."

"Paris! Dear God, he seeks to be Emperor again," Aunt Gisella said, crossing herself.

"Was there ever any doubt?" Uncle Tito said.

"Any word of Percy?" Maresa asked.

"There was talk of his being sent to meet Wellington who is on his way back from Vienna, but then I was told that was incorrect. Last report he was under the command of the Mediterranean blockade in Sicily. The important thing is, he is still in the Mediterranean, and not on his way to fight in America."

With the news of Napoleon and Percy's exact whereabouts uncertain, Maresa knew she would be forced to postpone going to him. She had no choice but to wait for his next letter, whenever that might be.

The ride home was a quiet one, with everyone lost in private thoughts.

Even Serena and Angelo, who were always able to find something cheerful, humorous, or uplifting to say, remained relatively quiet.

And the threat of the war continuing marred an otherwise lovely day.

It is said that life sometimes repeats itself, and a few weeks later, Maresa learned that was the truth.

Early that morning, Serena and Aunt Gisella went to Florence with Angelo. Maresa was captivated by Ann Radcliffe's Gothic romance, *The Italian,* and preferred to remain at home, so she could finish reading it.

It was almost dark by the time they returned, for Anna, the maid, had come by only a short while before their carriage arrived, to light the lamp on the table next to Maresa.

Their timing was perfect, for Maresa had finished reading only a few minutes before, and was still seated with the book on her lap, when she heard them come into the house.

"Oh Maresa, it's all over Florence," Serena said. "I heard people talking about it everywhere."

"Talking about what?"

"You know the stories that circulated about you in England?"

"Yes, I remember all too well," she said, remembering the horrible rumors that she came to Italy to have a child.

"Well, now they are saying it here."

"What?"

"I know it's absurd, but the story is going around that Nicola discovered your state, and called off the wedding, and your friend married you in name only to give the child a name."

"That doesn't make sense. Whose child do they say it is?"

"Percy's."

"That's absurd. Percy has hardly been here."

"You don't have to prove it to me."

Maresa was surprised at the calm feeling that enveloped her, especially when she remembered how angry she had been when the rumors in England reached her ears.

This was not the time for hotheadedness, she decided. The best way to get even would be to prove them wrong. She had created the image of flirtatious insincerity, and the idea that she was a woman who played with hearts until she broke them was the perfect setup to give merit to such a story.

Maresa knew there was little she could do but wait, and give time the opportunity to prove the rumor false. In the meantime, she was not going to hide away. She would confront the gossip, head-on.

It was later in the week, when Signora Bellini paid the ladies at Villa Mirandola a call, and during the course of their conversation confirmed that she, too, had heard the rumors about Maresa.

"Time is on our side," Aunt Gisella said, and gave Maresa a look of encouragement, "for time will prove it to be nothing but lies. I simply cannot understand why anyone would maliciously say such things about Maresa."

Signora Bellini glanced at Maresa. "I hope I am not upsetting you, my dear."

"I have heard the rumor already," Maresa said, although she did feel somewhat subdued by having to hear it again.

"I find the whole idea of it upsetting," Serena said. "One would think the news of Napoleon and the war would give them something else to talk about."

"You should consider the source and try not to let it bother you."

"The source?" Aunt Gisella said. "Do you mean you know who started all of this?"

"Of course! You don't mean to tell me you don't know."

"No, none of us have heard anything about how the rumor got started," Aunt Gisella said.

"I am truly astonished someone has not told you that it was none other than Signora Brancaleone who began to spread the story about."

"You are right, of course," said Aunt Gisella. "I should have realized that she would have the most to gain by saying such."

"I am certain most people see it for what it is—a mother's desperate attempt to hide the truth, and draw attention away from the fact that someone would choose not to marry her son," Signora Bellini said, while giving Maresa a sympathetic look.

Aunt Gisella nodded. "Yes, that should be obvious."

"Oh, that awful woman," Serena said. "Maresa, I am so glad you did not marry Nicola. Can you imagine having to live with his mother meddling in your affairs for the rest of her life?"

"Have you seen or spoken to the Brancaleones since Maresa's marriage?" asked Signora Bellini.

Aunt Gisella glanced at Maresa. "Tito paid Nicola a call after Maresa was married. He was visibly upset of course, but he did not give the impression he was after blood."

Maresa was surprised to hear this, for she had not known about Uncle Tito's visit to Nicola. It made sense that someone had to inform him as to what had taken place, but she had been so carried away with the event of her marriage, and Percy's leaving, that she had not considered it until now.

She understood the Brancaleones would have seen it as a humiliating situation and, in all fairness, could not think of Signora Brancaleone as too insufferable for wanting to defend her son, even if she did choose a rather underhanded method of doing it.

This was another first for her, when she took the time to think about how her marriage affected someone other than her, Percy and her immediate family. She had been so wrapped up in what was happening in her own life that she had not thought about all the repercussions it was bound to have upon others.

After Signora Bellini's departure, Maresa was left to her own thoughts and speculations on the subject, which seemed to linger in the front of her mind for several days.

As time went on, she discovered a rather interesting fact about herself and that was, she had a tremendous capacity for remorse. Before long, she began to understand that a person's spirit also has, by a predetermined set of parameters, the capacity to heal itself.

Time, spent alone in silent contemplation, taught her to face the past, deal with it, and see it as a lifelong companion who taught her much about herself, and that included the knowledge that it was a natural part of life not only to be right, but also to be wrong.

During the course of her reflection, she did comment to Aunt Gisella that she admired her ability to deal rationally with whatever she was confronted with.

"I was not always this way," she said, glancing at Tito. "When we first married, I had an abominable temper, but as time passed, I learned to be amused rather than angry or shocked."

"It's all about maturing," Uncle Tito said, "which is a nice way to say you are growing older, or becoming an adult. Do not worry over-much, Maresa. You are like fine Chianti. You will improve with age."

At that point, Maresa learned families are so much more than the people you are related to, and that there were other ways of dealing with failure and disappointment besides running away from it.

Now, a new, more subdued Maresa began to emerge, and in the place of the young girl, was a woman of resolute character, who was no longer frightened by the struggle with her own troubles.

Because of this, her newfound maturity made her more striking and more beautiful in her new, elegant married state, than she ever was as the darling of the masquerade ball.

Aware now, that one's behavior is a lot like their past, always ready to come back and haunt you, she was determined to be seen as a changed woman, and a married one at that. For this reason, she was always very careful never to be seen in public alone, not even with Angelo.

She was guilty of hurting Percy in the past, of using his friendship to her own gain, but that was all behind her.

New insight. A change of course.

Now, she wanted nothing more than to win his love, his respect and admiration. It would not be easy, but it would be right.

Twenty-Five

I am ashes where once I was fire.

Lord Byron (1788-1824)
English poet

Because of the many instances of valor on Lieutenant Bronwell's part, talk of Percy's heroism began to spread, until he received a letter from the Admiralty, informing him of his promotion to Captain.

A few days later, he received another letter addressed to Captain P. Bronwell, R.N.

He tore the envelope open and read the following:

Mediterranean Fleet

Sir Hammond S. Eden, Commander in Chief of His Majesty's Ships and Vessels employed, and to be employed in the Mediterranean, Tyrrehenian and Ligurian Seas, along the Eastern coast of Italy and the islands of Corsica, Sardinia, and Sicily.

You are hereby required and directed to proceed on board the *Invincible* and take upon you the Charge and Command of Commander of her...

He skimmed over the next two paragraphs, which were basic navy jargon pertaining to the *Invincible* and the fact that she was docked at Palermo, a fact he already knew, since he passed where the *Invincible* was docked, almost daily.

He paused at the end of the letter.

"To Captain Percival L. Bronwell, Hereby appointed Commander of His Majesty's Sloop *Invincible*, by command of the Admiral Sir Geoffrey Crane."

His gaze lingered a moment longer on Admiral Crane's signature, while slow realization began to sink in.

And then he started to grin. He had his own ship! And a sloop of war at that! A sloop, lately launched, with twenty 32-pounder can-

313

nonades and two long 18-pounders on its carriage, and she was a beauty!

Since he was already in Palermo when he received his orders to report to the *Invincible,* he left ship shortly after reading such, to make the short trip to the office of the commandant of the Port of Palermo.

The sun was shining bright, which left half the street shaded by the buildings across the way. Percy chose the side in the sun.

He already knew Palermo was not an easy city to learn one's way around, because it was cut right down the middle, from the foot of the mountains, to the sea, by a street several miles long, which was in turn bisected by another street. Anything located on one of these two streets was easily found. Anything that was not was a different story.

Thankfully, the commandant was available to speak with Percy shortly after he arrived, and while he was being briefed, he learned only two members of the crew left the *Invincible,* to continue to serve the previous commander, Captain Slagle, who assumed command of the *Neptune* in Gibraltar.

He also learned one of those two hands would be replaced before he sailed the next day, but there was no replacement for the other one, a Lieutenant Patterson.

Percy made a request to have Lieutenant John Murray transferred to his command, and was informed the commandant would take it under advisement.

Their talk did not last long, and when they

finished the commandant said, "Your orders will be delivered to you tomorrow morning aboard the *Invincible*. In the meantime, I recommend you have your belongings transferred, while you stop by the tailor to have the necessary adjustments made to your uniform."

As he left the commandant's office, Percy was feeling like a fool.

That he would need the uniform of a captain had not occurred to him. It was embarrassing to be caught off guard like that, but there was nothing to be done about it now, save to go in double time to the tailor, as Captain Conley advised.

His orders arrived the next morning.

He was to be employed on a confidential mission to the Kingdom of Naples, to take possession of certain intercepted documents that Joachim Murat, the King of Naples had dispatched in secret, to Napoleon.

While there, he was to verify if Marchese Angelo Catanelli had indeed come to Naples to meet with King Joachim to negotiate on behalf of King Ferdinando, who was trying to regain his throne, while hiding in Sicily.

If Catanelli was there, and he was being held prisoner, then Percy was to ascertain the situation, and rescue Catanelli, if at all possible.

On the night of the fifteenth of May, the *Invincible* was moored outside the mole head at Naples.

315

Percy and Lieutenant John Murray were rowed ashore.

Near a signal tower, Lieutenant Murray stashed two bags of explosives in the bushes. From there, they made their way to the Botanic Gardens on Via Foria, and there they were given some dispatches of importance from a woman in a carriage, who also verified Marchese Catanelli was in Naples.

"He is under detention in a small building next to an old aviary that borders the woods behind the king's palace."

That was all the information they were to receive, for the woman dropped the shade over the carriage window and instructed her driver to drive on.

Percy and Lieutenant Murray made their way to Murat's palace, Palazzo di Capodimonte, which was not too far away.

They found the marchese and freed him easily, after overpowering the two guards, but then their luck ran out when one of them managed to get off a shot, which alerted the palace guards.

The marchese was free, and he ran with them at a fast pace until the shouts of the palace guards came from far away. Breathing heavily, they slowed their pace as they retraced their steps and headed back the way they had come, toward the bay.

They stopped near a large signal tower, which was occupied by several members of the Queen's Neapolitan troops.

Lieutenant Murray waited with the marchese,

while Percy climbed a ladder to a loophole in the tower and crammed in the two bags of gunpowder they had stashed earlier. He lit the canvas fuse, shimmied down the ladder and took off in a dead run.

When the explosion ripped through the tower, Percy was behind Murray and the marchese, as the three of them ran toward the shore and their boat.

By the time sparks from the explosion reached the magazine and set off a second explosion, the three men were being rowed back to the *Invincible* which was still stationed off the mole.

They boarded, and immediately set sail for their point of rendezvous with the brig *Constantine*, two miles offshore, where they handed the marchese over to Admiral Harrington, and the *Constantine* readied to set sail for Port Mahon.

All went well until Lieutenant Murray and Percy were back aboard the *Invincible*, and then, almost immediately after they boarded her, a seventy-four-gun ship, the *Joachim* sailed out to attack them, accompanied by a frigate and several twenty-two-gun corvettes.

Outmanned and outgunned, the *Invincible* was fast enough to escape, but Percy knew the *Constantine* was big and slow, and needed time to gather speed if she was going to escape.

If she decided to join the *Invincible* and fight, then she needed time to come around.

It was a dilemma no commander wanted to face.

317

If the *Invincible* ran, it left the *Constantine* vulnerable. If they chose to fight, they could be blown out of the water before the *Constantine* came around in order to deliver a broadside, and come to their aid.

There was no choice but to have the *Invincible* take on the approaching convoy, to buy time for the commander of the *Constantine* to decide if he wanted to make a run for it, or turn and fight.

With the *Constantine* in front of her, the Italian coast on one side, and the convoy on the other, the *Invincible* maneuvered to turn and face the enemy, but before she could complete the turn, the *Joachim* got abaft the beam of the *Invincible*, tacked and shortened sail.

The *Invincible* received the broadside from the *Joachim*, as the latter kept away with the wind on the larboard beam. The *Invincible's* rigging and sails were cut away. After a continued discharge of star and bar shot, she caught fire.

Shortly after the fire erupted, a secondary explosion ripped through the ship and turned it into a burning inferno.

When the smoke began to clear, Percy found himself in the water with Midshipman Garrett, who was badly wounded.

There was a blinding pain in his leg, but Percy managed to get one arm around Garrett and hold his head out of the water long enough to see that at least one of the boats from his ship was in the water.

He continued to tread water and to hold Garrett's head up long enough for the boat, manned by five or six seamen who survived the explosion, to come close by. The swells were rough, and the men exhausted, which made it difficult, but after several attempts, they managed to grab enough of Garrett's uniform, to haul him over the side and into the boat.

Before Percy could climb over the side of the boat after Garrett, it began to drift away from him, driven by the wind. The crew paddled furiously, in an effort to come around again, but being rescued was not Percy's fate.

For about that time, one of the crew spotted a fast-approaching corvette flying the French flag.

"Go on! Get out of here!" he called to them, but the men were still trying to reach him.

"Leave me!" he said, "and that is an order!"

After he ordered their retreat, he watched the boat move farther away. He hoped that with any luck, the corvette would not spot him, and he could make it to shore, if he did not pass out from the pain in his leg first.

Afloat in the water, Percy watched the rowboat move away from him, until it was nothing more than a small dot in the horizon.

His luck ran out after that.

He was fished out of the water and taken on board the *Celeste*.

"Welcome aboard, *Capitaine*. You are now the prisoner of Capitaine Jean Louis Reynier."

Percy swayed, and Captain Reynier glanced at his bleeding leg, where the fabric of his uniform had been torn away. "We shall have the ship's surgeon look at that."

"And then?" Percy asked.

Captain Reynier smiled, "And then, *mon capitaine,* you will be taken to Corsica as a prisoner of war."

"Your prisoner?"

Reynier dipped his head. "Most assuredly."

"And here I was under the distinct impression that Napoleon had surrendered once. Surely he does not think he can win what he has already lost."

Reynier's short frame stiffened, and a cold, mirthless smile stretched his lips back over his teeth. "Surely you know that surrender is not the same thing as defeated, *Capitaine.* Surely you know that."

The only thing Percy knew was his leg hurt like bloody hell and he was losing blood by the cupful. He needed that surgeon or he wouldn't be conscious much longer, or alive, either.

He never took his eyes off the little French captain, struck by the way the color of Reynier's black hair reminded him of Maresa, and he thought, wouldn't it be ironic if she became a widow now?

The French captain's face blurred, and his words came from far away.

Percy had a vague recollection of being carted off to a dark, windowless cell belowdeck.

He was wondering how long he would be incarcerated at Corsica, when he remembered the feel of Maresa's dark hair dropping over him like a cool shroud, and he was consious of nothing save the dull, aching pain in his leg.

He tried to keep his thoughts focused on her, but the pain in his leg grew worse.

And he was so very, very tired.

Twenty-Six

There are some feelings time cannot
  benumb,
Nor torture shake, or mine would now be
  cold and dumb.

> Lord Byron (1788-1824)
> English poet

Maresa did not receive a letter from Percy, but she did receive one from her father.

It was a letter she did not understand.

Dear Maresa,

I am at this moment, in receipt of your letter informing me of your marriage to Bronwell, which I can neither bless nor condone.

Since your year in Italy was almost up, and you had not managed to find yourself in a married state, I began preparations to arrange a marriage for you myself, as I had already informed you.

Lord Neville Marwood, the Duke of

Mayerling, and I reached an agreement and had the marriage contract drawn up. To say I was furious to read of your marriage to the youngest son of a man with no title, who stands to inherit nothing, would be an understatement.

You continue to be a disappointment to me, as you have always been. I realize most of the fault is mine, for allowing you to your unchaperoned ways in Yorkshire, and that the time for such shows of independence you tend to exhibit has come to a close. It is, therefore, my intention to have this marriage annulled, and if that is not possible, then I shall persuade you to seek a divorce.

Do not think you can thwart me in this, Maresa. Lord Marwood is most upset over this, as am I. If you do not acquiesce quietly to my requests, rest assured that Lord Marwood and myself are influential and powerful enough to see that Bronwell's military career and any hope for a life in the Royal Navy is ruined.

Need I tell you where this could lead?

You are not capable of understanding at your young age, that this is the best thing for you, for your consequent marriage to Lord Marwood will secure your future.

I expect you to make immediate arrangements to return to London. I have written a letter to your uncle, in regard to this. Once you are here, we will proceed with the annulment or divorce, whichever is the most expedient.

You may be angry now, but in time, you will thank me for my concern for your welfare and my devotion in planning for your future.

Your father,
George Marcus Willingham,
The Marquess of Strathmore

Maresa realized she was biting her lip in order to keep herself from crying. Her first thought was to burn his letter and ignore everything he said. She wasn't the same foolish young girl who sailed to Italy a year ago.

She would hold on to Percy, and to her marriage, and her father be damned.

With her next breath, came the reminder of her father's threat, and she asked herself, what about Percy and the life he has made for himself in the Royal Navy?

There was no doubt that her father was wealthy enough and powerful enough to do exactly as he threatened.

And Lord Marwood, well educated, well-born, and well informed, was a cousin to Lord Castlereagh, the British Foreign Secretary, who was highly unpopular. Maresa knew the unpopular Castlereagh would not blink twice over ruining the life of a young naval captain in order to secure the support of two of England's wealthiest and most influential members of the House of Lords.

Maresa wished she were the crying type, for

it would be such an easy solution to lose herself and her sorrows in a good cry, but she could not. Instead, she continued to sit at her writing table, with her father's letter in her hand, while she imagined what would happen if she did not obey her father again, and what would happen if she did.

In the end, she decided whatever happened, she could not do anything to damage Percy. This had all happened because of her own foolish behavior, and she was determined that Percy, being wholly innocent, was not to pay the price for her in this.

There was nothing to do, except concede to her father's wishes and return to England, thereby placing herself and her future in the hands of a man who had badly bungled everything he had ever done for her, starting with her birth.

Later, when she had composed herself, she went downstairs and found Uncle Tito. When she inquired as to whether he had received the letter from her father, he informed her that he had not.

She explained by giving him the letter she had received.

When he finished reading it, he said, "Take up your cloak, Maresa, and you and I will take a walk through the vineyard."

The vineyard, besides being Uncle Tito's favorite, was also a beloved place to Maresa, and she had spent many long hours walking its rocky slopes.

The vineyard was the first thing she saw each

morning when she threw back the shutters in her room, only then, in the early-morning hours, a mist pointed the way out of the valley to curl around the mountains, where only the turrets of medieval castles were visible.

Later in the day, she could see the vineyards clearly, and if it was a particularly clear day, farther over, the meadows where sheep grazed, guarded by a big yellow dog.

In the courtyard directly below her window, just beyond the terra-cotta pots planted with lemon trees, was the path they now walked down, that led to the vineyards.

Even now, as they walked along in silence on their way to the vineyard, she could hear the sounds of life going on around her—wood being chopped, cows being turned out to graze, chickens clucking as they scratched and pecked the hard-packed earth, and just ahead, she heard the meow of a cat, and looked up in time to see the tip of its tail disappear behind the twisted trunk of an olive tree, planted back when Galileo's grandfather was just a boy.

Whenever she walked here, the world seemed a smaller place, and the peace of this spot of ground always managed to drop into her fragmented spirit and leave her feeling whole.

After almost an hour's walk, Uncle Tito said, "It seems then, that we are in agreement that your first concern should be for your husband and his future."

"Yes, in perfect agreement."

"Write your father and tell him you are

returning. In the meantime, I will contact friends in London and ask them to look into the matter. I do not think it will be as easy as your father thinks to have your marriage annulled or to force you to divorce. England is at war, and your husband has an excellent record of service. According to the British Minister in Florence, he is considered to be quite a hero. But right now, we need time, and your returning to England will buy us that. In the meantime, all we can do is pray."

That night, while Maresa lay in bed thinking about returning to England, she could not help praying that something would happen to change her father's mind, or at least prevent him from following through with his threat. She ended her prayer with a simple plea, "Please God, let my father see the light."

After a grueling journey, where bouts of seasickness kept her belowdecks for most of the trip, Maresa arrived in London.

The ship docked not far from the wharves where dozens of merchant ships unloaded and embarked at the ramshackle port of the Pool of London.

She immediately hired a hackney and was relieved that the driver, although not friendly, was civil and obliging enough to help her with her luggage. As she stepped inside, she took note of the coach number painted on a tin plate, affixed to the door. Number eleven, although she did not know the exact significance of that.

" 'Tis the law which governs hackney coaches," the driver responded to her inquiry. "Against the law, it is, to remove it."

The floor of the hackney was covered with straw, due to the rain. She brushed a bit of straw from her skirt, and sat in silence as the hackney passed along the wharves and warehouses, where nothing existed but industrial buildings and the squalid housing of those working in maritime commerce.

The cab crossed the Thames, and brought her into a different world where beautiful buildings lined up to greet her without a feeling of welcome or home.

The streets were busy, but then London's streets were always busy, and so crowded that if one foot passenger stopped to look at something, fifty people behind him had to stop.

There was so much to catch her wandering eye, and she occupied herself for a minute or two, reading the signs carried by men to inform the passersby of the best eating houses, or the latest medicine to cure everything from bunions to idiocy.

She caught a glimpse of a clock out of the corner of her eye, and imagined her father would be sitting down to the breakfast table about now, always a cheerful sight, with elegant porcelain and a kettle of boiling water singing from an urn of Etruscan shape, ready just about now she supposed, to pour into a fine silver pot.

He will not take cream or sugar, and will order his bitter bread, "thin sliced with butter and marmalade," she thought, and it seemed so real, she could almost hear the viscount's voice saying it.

The hackney pulled to a stop and Maresa looked out to see the front door of her father's town house. But the scene that greeted her was not what she expected.

A black wreath hung on the door.

She waited for the driver to help her alight, then turned up the walk and climbed three steps. She paused a moment to study the black wreath, unable to grasp what it could possibly mean. That someone had died was obvious, but what puzzled her was who could it be.

She knocked, then opened the door and stepped inside, to find herself greeted only by the ticking of the clock in the hall.

She directed the driver to deposit her luggage inside the door, then she pressed the coins for her fare into his outstretched palm.

He looked at the money in his hand, then at Maresa.

She put two more coins in his palm, and he tipped his hat and departed.

Maresa closed the door and left her luggage where it had been deposited, while she went to find where everyone was.

After quite a lengthy search, she found Beatrice upstairs in her room.

Bea was sitting on a stool in front of a looking glass, dressing her hair. Maresa glanced at the bed, where a black gown lay spread over the coverlet. She glanced down at her own gown of pale-yellow and felt even more out of place in her father's house than she did before.

She cleared her throat, and Bea jumped. The hairbrush clattered to the floor. "Maresa!"

"Bea, what has happened? I saw the wreath...."

"Oh, Maresa, Papa is dead."

The words hit Maresa with a jolt and she walked to the window seat, removed her cape and bonnet and placed them there, too stunned to think much beyond that.

"I cannot believe it," she said, "but it has been a long journey and the seas quite rough, and only an hour ago my stomach began to feel as if it might accept a cup of something hot. Let us go down for a bit of tea. Afterward, I want you to tell me everything."

Beatrice rang for tea, and followed Maresa into the sitting room.

"You are looking well, in spite of your sickness from travel," Bea said. "I am glad you are home."

Maresa looked at Bea's sweet face and could not bring herself to say this was not home, nor was she happy to be here. "I am happy to see you as well, although now that I am here, I don't know what to say," Maresa said. "His last letter did not indicate that he had been ill."

"It was an accident, Maresa. He was in Yorkshire, at Hampton Manor. He had decided to sell it, and had gone there to take inventory.

He was out riding when a storm came up. Apparently, he took shelter beneath a tree."

"Take your time," Maresa said, when she saw the way Bea was wringing her hands nervously, as if she suspected their father might walk into the room at any moment.

"They said it was a frightful storm."

"Yes, they are usually so, especially in the spring and early summer."

"Mrs. Brampton said there was a great deal of thunder and lightning, and the tree papa was under was struck. It was the lightning that killed him."

"How awful."

"When he did not return home that afternoon, they went in search of him. I was told they found his horse first, with a badly injured leg, and then they found Papa, not very far away."

"When is the funeral?"

"It was three days ago. I only returned home last evening. The other members of the family and the staff are due back tomorrow."

"Returned home? From where? Where was he buried?"

"In Yorkshire. His will stated he wanted to be buried beside our mother."

Maresa found that curiously odd, for all these years she had the distinct impression that he wanted nothing to do with even the memory of her mother, and now he wanted to spend eternity buried beside her?

"You know Papa has always been terribly afraid of lightning."

"Yes, I think I do remember hearing that, but I suppose I'd forgotten, until you mentioned it."

"Do you suppose, I mean, I wonder if that is why... No, do you think..."

Bea was obviously agitated, so Maresa said again, "Take your time. You've been through a great deal. Have some of your tea."

Maresa realized she was beginning to sound like Uncle Tito, for she recalled how many times he had said the same thing to her—"Take your time, Maresa."

Maresa picked up her own cup of tea as Bea drank hers.

After a few sips, Bea returned the cup to the saucer. "Do you think he might have always had a premonition that he would die this way? Perhaps that is why he was so afraid of lightning and thunderstorms."

"Oh, I don't know, Bea. I am still so shocked over the news of his death. I do not know if we will ever know the answer to that," she replied, unable to stop thinking that if she had known God was going to answer her prayer, she wouldn't have prayed for something he could answer so literally.

She could not deny that along with the feeling of sadness that came from knowing that things would never be mended between her father and herself now, there was also exhilaration—not over her father's death, but from the extreme relief that Lord Marwood was out of her future, and Percy's prospects in the navy were as promising as they had ever been.

It was her intention, after she heard the news of her father's death, to spend a night or two in London, but she had decided to return to Tuscany as soon as she could arrange passage. She had only one thing she wanted to do while she was still in London. She wanted to go to the Admiralty office to see if she could learn some news of Percy's whereabouts.

It occurred to her that if Percy was in Sicily, or even Elba, it would be no hardship to go there on her way back to Tuscany.

She had not realized that because she was one of the viscount's daughters she would be asked to remain in London until all the matters of her father's estate were settled.

This forced Maresa to see her other sisters, but on a superficial basis, for aside from Beatrice, she was generally ignored, until they were all informed one afternoon by their father's barrister, that Hampton Manor and everything it entailed, had been left to Maresa.

Maresa learned the estate had been purchased by money from their mother's dowry. "But, I thought our father went to Yorkshire to prepare to sell Hampton Manor," Maresa said.

"Apparently he had a change of heart, and decided to sell it instead of leaving it to you, but he was killed before he made the necessary changes to his will."

"Well, I simply do not understand why he would leave it solely to Maresa," Fanny huffed.

"Perhaps he wanted to make amends for the fact that Maresa grew up without a mother," Jane said.

In spite of what Jane said, Maresa could not ever have imagined that her father would even mention her name in his will, and certainly not to leave her the sole ownership of such a valuable piece of property. But then she was reminded that it was his intention to sell it, and that he had been killed while making preparations, which made her wonder if his change of heart had been prompted by her marriage to Percy.

"I suppose you will sell it," Jane said.

"I haven't had much time to accustom myself to the idea that it is mine, and certainly no thoughts of whether or not I plan to keep it. However, since you ask, I think my answer will be no, I do not wish to sell it. Why would you suppose that I would?"

"Well, you have removed yourself to Italy, and I feel certain you will be returning there."

"It is a decision based upon the fact that it is the most logical place for me to be, given that Percy is in the Mediterranean. Once the war is over, I shall go where my husband goes."

Maresa did not have much time to deal with the issue of her father's estate, or what it would all mean to her, for she had been in London no more than a fortnight, when she read in the *Daily Courant* that a ship called the *Invincible* had been sunk by the French off the coast of Italy.

All hands, including Captain Percival L. Bronwell went down with the ship.

Maresa sprang to her feet and put her hand on her forehead unable to decide, for a moment, which direction she wanted to take. "This cannot be happening to me," she said to Bea, but was unable to say more, for the tears were beginning to come. "Excuse me," she said, and ran out of the room.

Upstairs, in her room, she cried until the pain in her temples was so intense she curled up into a tight ball and fell asleep.

It was dark when she awoke, and the pain in her head was now a dull throb.

Percy...

Don't think about him right now.

Percy...

You can remember all of your moments together later.

Percy...

Right now, you must get control of yourself, Maresa.

Think...

She tried to think, but sadness has a way of overriding the thought processes, and before long she was crying again.

It was raining the next morning when she awoke, and she decided to remain in her room. From time to time, she heard someone knock at her door, or call out her name, but she said, "Go away," and they did.

On the third day, she knew this could not go on. After having had nothing but water since coming to her room, she got out of bed, rang for a bath and a glass of milk.

After she drank the milk, she bathed and washed her hair, then dressed herself and went downstairs.

She found Bea in the sitting room.

"Good morning, Bea," she said, and felt as dead inside as a piece of wood.

"You look ghastly," she said, "Would you like breakfast?"

"No." Truly, Maresa did not feel hungry, and saw no way she should bother herself with food, while heartbreak clouded everything, including her thoughts.

It was a very strange sensation to wake up one morning and feel you are quite alone in the world, cut adrift from every connection, every anchoring thought, every person you felt at one time, some link to.

She thought of this time as a journey, and she was uncertain whether the destination she had in mind would ever be reached, and yet the place she had left was not one she could return to.

Percy was gone, and she had to move on and make a life for herself without him.

There was no pride now in the thinking that this was some new sort of adventure, as one of life's challenges that she had to best, as one would climb a mountain and feel better when one reached the top.

In this there would be no pinnacle, no point she could reach and look back and find herself a better person because of it. The better part of her was gone. And lurking in the shadows was the fear she might not survive the journey at all.

Bea, after Maresa did not say anything for some time, took the initiative. "You must eat something," she said, and rang for tea and biscuits.

Maresa did not realize how hungry she was until the tray was placed before her, and the aroma did a bit of enticing.

Bea regarded her silently while she ate and finished her tea, and then she asked, "What are you going to do, Maresa? Will you return to Italy? I do hope you decide to stay here, though."

Maresa opened her mouth to say she did not know what to do, when she glanced down at her pale, trembling hands and thought, What am I doing to myself? How have you managed to turn yourself into such a weakling? What would Percy think if he saw you now?

She recalled the article in the paper, and how it referred to Captain Bronwell of the *Invincible*. She found that strange, for the last time she saw him, Percy was still a lieutenant, and his ship was the *Ajax*. Of course, it was certainly possible that he had been promoted to captain, and even given his own ship. Still, it did make her wonder if there could possibly be another Percy Bronwell.

She realized that she did not know anything save what she read in the paper, and recalling how many different versions of Napoleon's escape she read, and how many different tales of Percy's whereabouts she heard after he left Villa Mirandola, there was always another possibility, and that was that the newspaper report was not wholly accurate. At least she owed herself to find out.

"I don't know if I will return to Italy. It is too early to tell, but I can tell you that I shall go to the Admiralty office at Whitehall."

"The Admiralty office? What for?"

"Although I read a report of Percy's death in the paper, the Royal Navy has not notified me it. I have read no more reports of it in the newspaper. I think I owe it to myself, and to Percy, to at least make an effort to find out what happened, and if the reports are true."

"Very well," Bea said, rising to her feet. "And I shall go with you."

Twenty-Seven

Who so loves believes the impossible.
Elizabeth Barrett Browning (1806-1861)
English poet

It was a not a long carriage ride from their house in Mayfair to Westminster and the discreet, but imposing set of buildings at the eastern end of The Mall, between St. James's Park and Whitehall, that housed the offices of the Royal Navy.

After alighting from the carriage, Maresa instructed the driver to wait. "I do not know how long we will be gone, so do make yourself comfortable," she said to the driver.

Since this was her first visit to the Admiralty office, and the building was quite large, Maresa and Bea spent the better part of the next hour asking for help and being sent to the wrong place.

After many questions and receiving directions to several different offices, none of which proved to be the place they needed, Maresa was at last headed for the office of Admiral Reginald Winston.

When they arrived at the admiral's office, Bea took a seat and said, "I will wait for you here."

Maresa nodded and went to speak with a lieutenant sitting at a desk across the room. "I would like to see Admiral Winston."

"With regard to what?"

"With regard to the fact that I read of my husband's death in the newspaper, and I would like to verify it."

"The admiral is quite busy."

"As was my husband when he went off to fight this war, and I do not think the women of this country should be expected to sacrifice their husbands and sons, without so much as a word from the Admiralty as to whether they are in fact dead, and some explanation as to how it happened."

"I understand. Well, if you will wait here for a moment, I will try to find out if Admiral Winston will see you, but I doubt it will be possible."

Maresa was about to sit down when she saw the door next to the desk was partially ajar, and that there was a man sitting behind a desk inside.

Without really making an outright decision to do so, she rushed around the young man's desk and walked brazenly into the office, while she pushed the door open farther as she passed through it.

"I apologize for my boldness in coming here, Admiral, but I must find out what happened to my husband."

"You cannot go in there," the young lieutenant said as he hurried toward her.

Maresa turned and held her umbrella out like a weapon. "I am already in here."

"You may go now, Lieutenant Beasley. I will call you if I need you."

They waited until the lieutenant had gone, then Admiral Winston said, "I suppose there is a reason for your barging into my office like this, and for your sake, I hope it is a good one."

"My name is Maresa Bronwell. My husband, Percival Bronwell was a lieutenant in the Royal Navy, and although I was not aware of either his promotion or his being transferred to a different ship, I did read in the newspaper that he was captain of the *Invincible* in the Mediterranean."

"The *Invincible*. Ah yes, she's been sunk, I believe."

"You believe? You are not certain?"

"Madam, we are fighting two wars at the present, and there are many ships, many captains and many casualties. I will have to check on that."

"Please, if you would be so kind. I really must know, Admiral, if it is true that my husband is dead. I am sure you understand how difficult this is for me."

"Of course. Excuse me for a moment, will you?"

He stepped from the room, said something to the lieutenant outside, and then she heard the sound of his footsteps as he departed.

He was gone ten or fifteen minutes before he returned. He began speaking the moment he came through the door.

"Forgive me for taking so long, but due to the nature of the matter at hand, I wanted to be certain before I gave you any information. I have learned that it is true that *Invincible* sank. I am sorry to say there were no survivors, all hands being lost including your husband, Captain Bronwell. Several bodies were recovered however, and were transported to Sicily for burial. I do not have much more information than that at this time. In a few days, we should know more."

Pain gripped her, spreading outward from her stomach to her throat. Memories of their last night together pierced her heart. "I see."

"I am very sorry." Admiral Winston stood and walked around the desk. "Will you be all right? Shall I call someone to escort you home?"

"My sister awaits me outside your office. She will walk with me to the carriage. Thank you, Admiral, for your time."

When she and Bea stepped out onto the street, Maresa found the sun too brilliant and her eyes too clouded with tears to see well.

"Here, take my arm, Maresa," Bea said, and drew Maresa's hand through the crook in her elbow. "I see the carriage. It is waiting just over there."

Once they were inside the carriage Bea said, "I am so sorry. I wish there was something I could say or do. Perhaps we should take a trip...to Bath perhaps, or Brighton."

"I'm going to Sicily."

"What? Why are you going to Sicily? You cannot mean that, not with the war, and the ships being sunk. You cannot go now. Think of the risk. It is far too dangerous."

"I don't care. I have to go."

"Why, Maresa? Tell me why?"

"I don't know why, Bea. I only know I must go. I need to know what happened. I need to know if he is buried there."

"And if he is, then what?"

"I don't want to leave him there, on that island, in a foreign country, too far from home and the people who loved him. If he is buried there, I want to have his body brought back here, so it can be buried at Danegeld Hall. I know his family would want that."

"And you? Shall you go to Danegeld Hall as well?"

"Only until I have settled the matter to my

satisfaction, and feel I have done all I could do for a man to whom I owe so much."

"No one expects that of you. Not now."

"I expect it!" she almost shouted.

"I'm sorry."

Maresa sighed deeply. "No, I am sorry for taking it out on you. Forgive me," she said, and hugged her sister.

"There is nothing to forgive. I am sure I would do the same in your situation."

"Bea, why don't you come to Sicily with me? Once this is settled, we can go to Italy together. You would love Uncle Tito and Aunt Augusta. You would love Italy."

"Oh, I couldn't!"

"Why not?"

"I—I—I have too much to do here."

"What?"

"I must sort through father's belongings. What our sisters do not want, I will give to charity. Then I want to change a few things about the town house."

"And once that is done? Will you promise me you will join me in Tuscany?"

"I promise."

Percy's memory floated into Maresa's consciousness and her heart ached.

"Don't be sad, Maresa."

"You cannot imagine what it is like to carry inside you the burden of knowing there was something you could have said, should have said, to someone you loved, but you foolishly kept it inside you when it would have made all the difference to them, and now that you have the words burning in your heart and on your lips, it is too late."

"Nothing ever seems to turn out the way we plan, does it?"

"No, and the frustrating part is, we so rarely have a second chance." Maresa began to rub the tiredness from her eyes. Temporarily bewildered, she was not sure of anything at this point, except anguish. "I am so torn, Bea. I feel my Italian roots pulling me back to Tuscany, yet I am also English, and this has always been home."

"Perhaps you should decide before you go to Sicily, for if you choose to return to Tuscany, do you not think you would want to bury him there?"

She knew she had neither sound judgment nor the spirit to make such a decision right now, for her pain overshadowed all other thought. "My heart is too heavy to think right now."

Maresa closed her eyes and lay her head back against the seat. Percy was dead, and she would have to deal with it alone.

She was thankful to him for many things, the most important of these being that he had pushed her toward self-reliance. Now, it seemed he got his wish, for his death assured it.

In the distance, Sicily appeared like an enormous sculpture polished by the sirocco wind that blew across the Mediterranean from Africa. Against the dazzling blue of the sea, the lizardlike slopes of the mountains and a blue plume of smoke rising straight up into the stratosphere from Mount Etna in the distance, the port of Palermo came into view.

Maresa alighted from the ship and walked down the plank, and felt the intensity of the overhead sun beating down upon the black dress and veil she wore, although the air was soft and warm, instead of hot.

She hired a carriage to take her to a hotel near the office of the Naval Commander, where she arranged for a room and had her luggage carried up ahead of her.

From the hotel she went directly to the office of the Naval Commander in the center of the oldest part of the city, near the cathedral, Palazzo Reale and the Cappella Palatina.

Palermo was beautiful, with mulberry trees in full leaf, oleanders in bloom and lemon hedges that lined the avenue. The public gardens were filled with an abundance of flower beds and dotted with anemones and ranunculus. The air was fragrant and fresh as the sea it crossed to reach the island, yet Maresa's heart was too broken to do more than stare as she passed by.

The offices of the Naval Commander were located in a lovely villa with obvious Arabic influence. After stepping from the carriage, she paused to study the coat of arms above the double-arched windows, and then stepped inside.

She had better luck here than she had at the Admiralty office in London, for when she stopped to ask directions as to where she should go, she was sent to the office of Commander Miles Sperry.

When she arrived at Commander Sperry's office, there was no one sitting outside. She paused in the doorway, hesitant for a moment to interrupt the commander, who was particularly devoted to something he was writing in a ledger.

Papers, maps and nautical memorabilia were scattered everywhere.

Still, she knew to remain in the doorway would not get the answers she needed, so she stepped into the room.

He was a middle-aged man, tall and quite slim, with brown wavy hair, worn a bit longer than was fashionable. An air of efficiency seemed to pervade the room, like a perfume given off by a flower.

"Pardon the intrusion, Commander. My name is Maresa Bronwell. I apologize for my boldness in coming here, but I need your help."

His face bore an expression of irritation when he glanced up, but he must have taken note of her mourning clothes, for his expression softened. "What kind of help do you need?"

"I was told you might be able to help me gather some information about my husband."

"We get many requests of that sort. Unfortunately, we do not have the time or the staff to conduct such a search. The Mediterranean fleet is quite large."

He must have realized how close to tears she was, for he pushed the papers away from him and said, "I did not mean to be harsh."

"It's not you, it's just that..."

"Please, sit down." He indicated a chair opposite his desk.

She noticed, as she sat down, that he glanced at his watch, and she felt there was an air of polite preoccupation about him, that made her think he was doing this as a courtesy to her, when he was due to be someplace else.

"I am not keeping you from some previous engagement, or commitment, am I?"

"Nothing to worry about," he said, in a genuine manner that put her somewhat at ease.

"Now, tell me, what you would like me to do?"

She collected herself for a moment. "I have been informed that my husband is dead. I was also told there were several bodies recovered and they were buried here. I want to know if his body was one of those they found."

"Wait a moment. I think we need to fill in a few details at the beginning of this story before we get around to burials. Your husband is with the Mediterranean fleet, on one of our ships?"

She nodded. "Yes. I'm sorry. I don't suppose I am making much sense."

"That is understandable, given the circumstances. Please, take all the time you need."

"I was told my husband's ship was sunk and there were no survivors. I later learned a few

346

bodies were recovered and brought here for burial."

"No survivors, and only a few bodies recovered," he said, repeating what she told him.

"Yes. That is when I decided to come here. I wanted to see if my husband was one of those...if he was buried here. If he is, well..." She paused. Her throat tightened.

"I know this is difficult for you."

Five seconds. Fifteen.

She took a deep breath. "If he is buried here, I would like to make arrangements to take his body back to England."

"Well, let's not bury him until we are certain he is dead. Awfully shocking, when that happens. Where did you first learn of this tragedy?"

Maresa felt her heart take a tiny leap from grief to guarded hope at his words. "Why, I first read of it in the London paper. Afterward I paid a visit to the Admiralty office at Whitehall, for verification."

"And the Admiralty office confirmed it?"

She nodded. "Yes. I spoke to Admiral Winston."

He smiled. "Old Reggie. He's been there almost as long as Whitehall."

A wan smile, then she said, "Yes, I did notice some similarity between the two."

He returned the smile briefly. "Who is your husband and what ship?"

"Captain Percival Bronwell, of the sloop *Invincible.*"

"Good Lord! I know Percy Bronwell. And yes, the *Invincible* was lost, but..."

She was aware of a slight tremor of hope, when Captain Sperry did not come right out and confirm anything.

An expression of deep thought appeared on his face for a few seconds before he said, "If you would excuse me for a moment. There are a few things I need to verify before I raise your hopes any further."

He wasn't gone long, and when he returned, he carried several documents, which he proceeded to shuffle through after he returned to his chair. After some time, she heard a grunt of satisfaction that she took as an indication he was finished. He then sat back in his chair and made eye contact with her.

"I have both bad news and good news."

She was not aware she had been holding her breath until she released it with an audible sigh. "Oh, thank you..."

"Well, don't go overboard thanking me yet," he said, with a twinkle of promise in his eye. "Let me tell you what I do know for certain. Captain Bronwell's ship was employed on a confidential mission to the Kingdom of Naples. On the night of the fifteenth of May, the *Invincible* was moored outside the mole head at Naples. Shortly after five o'clock in the morning, Captain Bronwell and Lieutenant John Murray, having completed their mission, returned to their ship. She set sail immediately. A few miles out, she was under heavy attack by French frigates and caught fire. She was adrift in the wind, which by this time was blowing quite strongly. She was driven through the water, enveloped in flames. She exploded, and sank."

"Exploded?"

He nodded. "She carried quite a few barrels of gunpowder."

She tilted her head back and closed her eyes. "Dear God. Such a terrible way to die."

"Yes, it is, but your husband was not among those unfortunate ones."

"He's alive?"

"There were some eight survivors, two in the water, six who managed to get into one of the boats from the *Invincible*. Your husband was in the water, holding on to a wounded midshipman. He managed to get the midshipman into the boat with the other members of the crew, but due to the rough winds there was some difficulty maneuvering the boat back to where your husband was. At that point, two or three French ships were spotted a short distance away. Your husband ordered his men to leave him and save themselves."

"And Percy? What happened to him?"

"He was picked up by one of the French frigates."

"And the men in the boat?"

"They were rescued by a British warship. Evidently the frigates saw the *Manchester* approaching, and decided to make do with one prisoner."

"Where is he now?"

"Two days ago, we learned he was in Corsica."

"Corsica?" She sat back in her chair. "But why would they take him to Corsica?"

"It is the only island nearby that is under French control."

"What use would he be to them?"

"That is probably why they took him to Corsica. They will interrogate him, and then decide the best way to use him. You must understand Napoleon and his backers are desperate. They know if they fail this time, it is over. Consequently, they will not overlook any opportunity to gain anything that might be useful to them."

But Maresa was barely listening. Percy was alive. "He's alive," she said, needing to say it to believe it.

"Alive, but not out of danger."

"What will become of him?"

"The possibilities are endless. Perhaps they will keep him a hostage there until they have need of him. Or, they might decide to send him to France for safekeeping. Then again, they might hold him for ransom. They might even lose him to a band of Italian sympathizers."

"What do you mean?"

"There are many Corsicans who have never given up hope of becoming part of Italy again, and throwing off the yoke of French rule. It would not be out of line for them to decide they could use the ransom money for their cause and take him from the French."

"Unless the French decided to kill him," she said softly.

"Unfortunately, that is also a possibility. Please understand, we will do everything in our power to secure your husband's release."

Captain Sperry came to his feet, studied her for a moment before he walked around the desk. "I am very sorry the news could not have been better. Rest assured that I shall keep you informed of any new developments. Will you be staying here in Sicily, or will you return to London?"

"I only made plans to stay overnight. I naturally assumed I might be returning to England to bury my husband. But in view of the situation, I think I might go to my relatives in Tuscany, since it is closer."

"On your way out, if you wouldn't mind leaving information about how we can contact you with the clerk downstairs, it will make it easier for me to stay in touch."

"Of course," she said.

Maresa stood and offered him her hand. "Thank you, Captain. You have given me the greatest gift imaginable."

"I only regret it was not more. Please, allow me to walk you back to your carriage."

"Oh no, you have been far too kind already. Thank you again, for your time."

The bells of a nearby cathedral were ringing for Vespers when she stepped outside. She walked back to find her carriage, bathed in the warm Sicilian sun.

Maresa stood in the sun for a moment. Although not well acquainted with the workings of the Royal Navy and the degree of punctuality and devotion they would employy to rescue Percy, she had noticed the tendency, both at the Admiralty office in London, and again here in Sicily, that information was slow to come, and when it did arrive, the volume of such meant there were delays, which often led to inaction. She knew, too, that while Percy's safety and rescue was of the utmost importance to her, the Royal Navy would see other wartime affairs as more consequential and of greater magnitude. Good men were sacrificed to the cause on a daily basis, and more the fool she, if she thought Percy to be the exception.

Although not an astute politician, she was well aware that Napoleon's cause was one of desperation, a last chance to regain the crown of France and the control of Europe, and his followers were like drowning men grasping at water; more interested in the end result than who or what they had to sacrifice to get there.

Weren't desperados born out of desperation?

By this time, her fears were tightly coiled, an end product of her mental anguish, for her reasons for wanting to save her husband were twofold: because she loved him, and because she had to tell him so.

There would be no rest, no long nights of peaceful sleep until Percy was restored to her, but that was not the direction of her current thoughts; rather, what she could do to help him.

She was resolved to risk all to save him, but knew that this noble thought was featherlight, and bore no weight whatsoever, for she possessed no power, no influence and had no financial resources of her own.

Truth was, she realized as she began to walk down the street, that all she possessed was a strong desire to rescue him, and a good dose of mother wit.

She could not defer to tomorrow. She must act now.

She quickened her steps and soon arrived back at the carriage. It was during the ride back to the hotel, that she took a small miniature out of her bag, and studied her mother's face, as she asked herself this question: What would you have done, Mother?

She looked at her mother's young face, the dark hair, and the emerald necklace around her neck, and suddenly Maresa had an idea.

When it came to Percy, she could not sit at home with her knitting and wait to see if the British rescued him, or bungled it. Then she recalled something Captain Sperry said.

"Perhaps they will keep him there as a hostage. Or, they might decide to send him to France. Then again, they might hold him for ransom."

It was the last sentence that intrigued her.

Hold him for ransom...

Maresa remembered the other option she mentioned that Captain Sperry chose not to offer. Death. For she knew all too well that the French could decide to kill him at any time.

Hold him for ransom. Her mind kept coming back to this one. She looked at her mother's picture with thoughts and heart uplifted.

"Thank you, Mother," she said, for at that moment, she knew exactly what she had to do.

Her mind was made up. She would not wait to see if they decided to offer Percy for ransom. She would do the reverse, and offer a ransom for Percy.

Even failure was better than doing nothing.

She knew there were those who would say she was completely mad for going to Corsica alone, but she was convinced this was something she had to do. She refused to involve anyone else. She had spent the better part of her life involving others and seeking their advice, relying upon their solutions. It felt suddenly good to know that the girl she had been was gone, and in her place stood a woman of more resolute fiber. Saving Percy was a challenge, and one she was more than willing to accept.

Later that evening, she sat on the balcony of her room, her heart relieved of many fears, and conscious of new ones, for she knew that to attempt Percy's rescue and fail, might very well be the signature on his death warrant.

With great calmness, she watched the fading tints of the sunset, and later the rising of the moon, and wondered if Percy might be watching that same yellow orb climb across the sky.

Twenty-Eight

We that are true lovers run into strange
capers.

> William Shakespeare (1564-1616)
> English poet and playwright

The next morning, Maresa moved forward into battle, armed with little more than one woman's wit and the wisdom of all the mothers who came before her.

She took a carriage down to the harbor, hardly noticing she was passing the same rows of ilex trees and shrubs of myrtle that she had passed by the day before.

Once at the harbor, she asked the driver to wait with her luggage. She walked up and down the quayside to ask this boat captain, and that one, if they knew of someone who would take her to Corsica and who was familiar with the island. After several inquiries she was given the name of Pierre Francesco Balmain, who had a boat by the name of the *Moor's Head.*

"He is familiar with the island?" she asked again.

"*Sì, sì, Senora,* Captain Balmain is from Corsica. He was born in Ajaccio, where Napoleon was born."

She noticed he spat when he said Napoleon's name, a wordless way of expressing his sentiments, and quite effective. "Where might I find Captain Balmain?"

"Along the waterfront."

Maresa returned to the carriage and asked the driver what he knew about Corsica, since she decided it would not hurt to know as much about the island as she could.

They drove along the waterfront searching for a boat named the *Moor's Head,* while she listened to the driver tell her what a shame it was that Corsica, which had always been Italian and under the rule of Genoa, came under French rule the year before Napoleon was born.

That would explain why Napoleon, although born of an Italian family, was educated in France. Of her own accord, Maresa vaguely remembered hearing that Corsica had been under British control for a year or two, during the early period of the Napoleonic wars, and found herself wishing it had remained so.

"The *Moor's Head,*" the driver said, and pulled to a stop.

Once again, she asked the driver to wait while she went to the boat and found the captain, Pierre Francesco Balmain, whose name reflected Corsica's history, but the dialect he spoke to the crew was neither French nor Italian, but hovered somewhere in between.

She was curious as to where his sympathies lay. Was he a French patriot, or did his loyalty lie with Italy? She decided that since his first and last names were French that perhaps his sympathies lay in that direction.

"Excuse me, Captain Balmain, but I have a matter of the utmost confidence to speak with you about."

He grinned and showed her his small, gray teeth, while his gaze took a leisurely stroll over her. "You are a widow, no?"

Well, he was no Leonardo da Vinci, considering she was dressed in a widow's black clothing. "A very recent widow," she said.

"Then tell me what you need to speak to me about, for I am anxious to hear what could be troubling such a young widow with no husband to protect her."

She decided the truth would serve her in this, and she told him why she had come. "I want to arrange for the release of my husband, who was captured and taken to Corsica."

"I thought you were a widow?"

"I thought I was until an hour ago, when I learned differently. I have not had time to change. However, that really has no bearing on my purpose for being here."

"You think your husband is being held on Corsica?"

"I am sure of it. Could you give me any idea of where I should go, or who I should speak with to find out where he is, or a name perhaps, of someone I could speak with to arrange his release?"

"You think to go in and rescue him all by your little self, eh?"

"No, I have come to buy his freedom."

Captain Balmain looked around cautiously and lowered his voice as he brought his face close to hers. He smelled of fish and tobacco.

"You have money with you now, on this boat? That is very dangerous, you know."

Maresa took a step back. "Of course I do not. I may be young and a woman, but please, Captain, I am far from stupid. I know how much my life would be worth if I were foolish enough to do such. I assure you the funds are quite safe."

"I will give it some thought."

"Thank you, and now, I would like to buy passage to Corsica, if that is where you are going."

Captain Balmain had two rather frightening men bring her luggage aboard, and Maresa wondered if she would ever see it again.

It was something she could not worry about. If she was fortunate, they would only search through her things, and find nothing but disappointment, for she had hidden the necklace in a small pouch that she tied around her waist.

She remained on deck for the entire journey, having decided she felt safer there, and less likely to become seasick. Thankfully, she had only a few twinges of nausea, due to a relatively calm sea, where only a warm mistral wind blew, gentle as a breeze, yet it managed to shorten somewhat the already short trip to Bonafacio.

When she caught her first glimpse of a dazzling white town against the blue of the Mediterranean, she pressed against the boat's railing, anxious to put her feet on dry land and begin her search. Anticipation, she learned, only makes the docking process drag with impossible slowness, and by the time the planks were secured and the passengers had begun to leave the ship, she had to practice the greatest self-control not to push her way to the front so she could be the first one to go.

When it came time to disembark at last, Maresa guessed Captain Balmain was still thinking, for she had heard nothing from him. She took a short stroll around the deck, but he was nowhere in sight. I cannot waste any more time looking for him, she told herself, and decided she would simply have to find someone on shore to help her.

Once off the ship, she looked for a carriage. She had to settle for a donkey cart, whose last passenger had obviously been a load of mushrooms, and there was one squished against the seat where she would sit. While she waited for her luggage to load, she noticed Captain Balmain had surfaced and was now headed in her direction.

"Where are you going?" he asked as he drew near. "I thought you wanted my help."

"I looked for you before leaving the ship. When I could not find you I assumed you had nothing to tell me, Captain."

He looked around and took a piece of paper out of his pocket. "Here is an address for you. When you arrive at your hotel send a message to Antoine, at that address. Tell him where he may contact you."

She took the paper and tucked it away in her reticule.

"Thank you, Captain."

He nodded and disappeared into the crowd along the street.

Maresa took a kerchief from her bag and wiped the mushroom from the seat, then helped herself into the donkey cart. She held on when the cart started up with a lurch, and then began to wind its way through dairy-women pulling their donkeys, water merchants with kegs wrapped in ferns and fountains where small children played.

As they entered one of the old alleys and began to climb upward, between the cliffs, she understood why there were no carriages. Only a sure-footed donkey could maneuver such steep streets. At the top, she looked out over the sea and saw Sardinia in the distance.

Immediately on arriving at the *locanda,* she sent the message as instructed by Captain Balmain.

An old woman owned the *locanda,* and at first Maresa thought the place had seen better days. After she was shown to her room, she decided there had never been better days for such a hovel.

The room was miserable at best, located on the ground floor, not far from the kitchen, where the smell of food lingered on into the night.

Her room, she learned later, was next to the storage room, which explained the pervading odor of mold and old onions.

When she went down to dinner, she wondered what they did with the onions, for their only fare was a plate of not-so-warm macaroni, and a pannikin of watered-down wine.

When she returned to her room and threw back the covers on the bed, she took one look at what was beneath it and covered it back up. The bed was dirty, and more than likely still retained the crawling companions of its previous occupant, so Maresa made a bed by artfully arranging herself upon two wooden chairs she pushed together, covering herself with her cloak. It was the most miserable attempt to sleep she had ever experienced, and by the time she awoke the next morning, her hands were asleep, her feet numb and everything in between ached like the blazes. It was worse when she stood up, but things began to work a little better by the time she went into the main room to inquire as to whether she had received a message and was handed a small envelope.

The message was short, and to the point, for it said she was to be at the church at three o'clock that afternoon, to discuss a matter of mutual interest.

Ask for Father Fabrizio. Do not be late.

Maresa left the hotel, only to realize she did not know where the church was, so she stopped a woman on the street.

"Where is the church?"

"Down the hill."

She went down the hill, and walked up and down the street, but did not find the church. She stopped a young man, and asked him, "Where is the church?"

"Up the hill."

Back she went. It took some time, but she

found the small, white church, but there was no one inside, save an old man sweeping the floor.

"Do you know where I can find Father Fabrizio?"

"He is not here."

Disappointed, she walked back outside and met an old woman coming up the steps. She asked her, "Do you know where Father Fabrizio is?"

"He is in the church."

Maresa went back inside, and wandered around until she found Father Fabrizio, wondering how anyone ever found anything in this town. She explained Antoine had sent her.

"Ah, yes, he asked me to tell you to meet him at the butcher shop near the fountain."

"Where is that?"

"Down the street, across from the bakery."

After more walking, she found the butcher shop and went inside. There was a man behind a table unloading dead chickens. The room smelled like wet feathers. Maresa put her hand over her nose.

"I would like to see Antoine."

"Antoine only works here on Saturday."

By this point, her exasperation was reaching a high level. "Father Fabrizio told me to meet him here!" she said.

"Oh, then he will be here shortly," he said, and slapped another chicken on top of the pile.

Maresa looked at the vacant, staring eyes of the chicken and said, "I will wait outside."

It was almost three o'clock when Maresa

seated herself on a small bench near a fountain.

At three-thirty, Antoine appeared.

Maresa was more than a little put out by his tardiness. "I thought you said not to be late."

"*Oui, madame,* I did say that you were not to be late. I did not say the same for me."

She narrowed her eyes. "You don't sound French."

"I confess that I am not."

"You sound Italian."

"Perhaps that is because I consider myself such."

"I was told your name was Antoine."

"It is Antoine when it serves me, and Antonio when it does not."

"You have information about my husband, Captain Bronwell?"

"What information are you seeking?"

"I want to know where he is, so I might arrange for his freedom."

"You wish to buy his release?"

"Yes."

"For how much."

"I have told you all I will tell you, until you give me some information."

"Your husband is safe, *signora.* Now, for the amount..."

"I do not have money."

"Then I shall hold you here for ransom as well. You will write a letter to your family...."

"You don't understand."

"And we will enclose one of your lovely ears as proof that we are not to be trifled with."

"If you would stop trying to frighten me, I am trying to tell you—"

"Perhaps we should add your tongue as well."

"Will you stop threatening me, and give me time to speak?"

"*Per Dio!* With such a temper, your family will probably pay me ten *baiocchi* to keep you."

She decided not to offer any more explanations, but to cut directly to the point. "I have an emerald necklace, with extremely large stones and many diamonds. It is worth a fortune."

"May I see it?"

"You may see a picture of it," she said, and removed the miniature of her mother from her bag. "This is a picture of my mother wearing the necklace."

He studied the tiny portrait. "The necklace... it is in your possession?"

"The necklace belongs to me. I inherited it when my mother died. It is in my possession, but of course, it is not here."

"How long would it be before you could get it here?"

"I am not so foolish as that. I will bring the necklace. You bring my husband. When you are satisfied the necklace is as priceless as I say it is, and I am satisfied my husband is alive, we will exchange them."

"And where will this exchange take place?"

Stupidly, she had not thought about that, so she quickly grabbed the name of the first small Italian port that came to mind. "On the coast of Tuscany, at Marina di Pisa. Are you familiar with it?"

"I know where it is, yes."

"You will meet me there?"

He nodded. "I will meet you there just before sundown, four days from now. Build a small campfire on the beach. We will look for the smoke. Come alone."

"I will bring my two cousins with me."

When he looked uncomfortable with that, she said, "Surely you cannot expect me to travel alone with so valuable a necklace. Do you plan to sail to Marina di Pisa alone?"

"You make a man want to bite his own arm, *signora*."

"Please refrain from doing so in my presence."

"What assurance do I have that you will meet us there?"

She thought for a moment. "You have my husband. Isn't that enough?"

"I would like something else. Something valuable."

She shook her head. Idiot! Did he not think her husband was valuable? She opened her bag and removed the miniature. "You may keep this until the exchange, but bring it with you, for it is more priceless to me than the necklace."

He took the miniature and tucked it away in his pocket. "You drive a hard bargain, *signora,* but I would hate myself if I did not do all that I could to help someone so young and lovely."

She did not believe that for a second, and found herself wondering why he thought she would. She knew it was none of her business, but she could not seem to shake her curiosity. At last she said, "Why are you holding my husband? Are you trying to help Napoleon?"

He turned his head and spit. "That is what I think of Napoleon, for turning his back on the land where he was born."

"You are not a member of the French military?"

He spit again. "I fight for the liberation of Corsica from the French," he said, and pulled a small, dirty flag out of his pocket. The emblem on the flag was a Moor's Head turned toward the left with a blindfold on the forehead, tied behind the nape of the neck, and a necklace with two or three beads.

"But the French pulled my husband from the water after they sank his ship. How did he end up in your possession?"

"The French made one mistake."

"Which was?"

"They trusted us."

Well, that was a great thing to say to her at a time like this, she thought, but she did not tell him that. Instead she said, "We all have our causes, don't we?"

"*Sì, sì, Signora.* We all have our causes." He bowed. "*Grazie,* Signora Bronwell. I will see you in four days."

She dipped her head. "Yes, in four days, in Marina di Pisa," she repeated, in case he had forgotten. "Thank you, Signore Antoine Antonio."

He laughed and Maresa turned away.

Soon she was making her way back through the crowded street, dodging the donkeys and the water carriers yelling, *"Acqua, acqua fresca!"*

With all the spitting these Corsicans did, it was little wonder why the water vendors were so popular.

Twenty-Nine

In war as in love, to bring matters to a
    close,
you must get close together.

> Napoleon Bonaparte (1769-1821)
> French Emperor

Maresa caught the next boat to Liverno, happy that it was such a short trip, she did not have time to get seasick. Maybe she was becoming a sailor after all.

When she arrived back at Villa Mirandola she did not tell Aunt Gisella or Uncle Tito about Percy, for she knew if she did, they would insist on involving themselves.

She did tell Serena and Angelo, however.

"How are we going to leave here without Mama and Papa asking where we are going?" Serena asked.

"Lord Pelligrew and his wife are in Lucca. Before I left London, they invited me to pay them a visit, and asked that I bring my family. I shall tell Uncle Tito and Aunt Gisella we are going to Lucca as their houseguests for a few days."

"*Santa Maria!* I shall be the second person burned in the center of the Piazza della Signoria if Papa finds out," Serena said, and hastily crossed herself.

"It is nothing I haven't done before," Angelo said.

Maresa and Serena exchanged believing glances.

"Well, it isn't," Angelo said.

"Angelo," Maresa said, "that is one of the few things you've said that I do believe."

Angelo pinched her cheeks. "You better be nice to me, *bella*. I might come in handy."

"When there is anything secret, dishonest or cunning, you are always handy, but I hope we do not encounter anything where your extraordinary talents will be needed."

The journey to Marina di Pisa was uneventful, with Serena talking most of the way.

"I cannot believe Mama and Papa accepted your story about visiting friends in Lucca so readily. I have the feeling if it had been me trying to convince them, we would all be sitting at home right now."

She looked at Angelo who had just stretched out his legs and rested them on the seat next to her. "Really, Angelo, you shouldn't put your feet on the seat like that. This isn't a hired carriage, you know."

"I know, and that's why I'm making myself comfortable, because it's as much my carriage as anyone's."

"Only one fourth of it is yours." She glanced at Maresa. "I mean one fifth."

Maresa was relieved the two of them were having such sport with each other, for it helped to reduce her inner stress. It was one of the things she enjoyed so much about being around the two of them. One simply could not maintain any frame of mind other than cheerful or amused.

It was late afternoon when they crossed the Arno near Pisa. The Pisan coast was now close enough that she could smell the salty air coming from the sea.

The sun was beginning to drop lower in the sky when they came to a stretch of Mediterranean pine forest, where they left the warm sunlight, to enter the cool shade.

It had rained recently, and the air in the coach became cooler and fragrant with the scent of pine and the sea. Overhead, they could hear the sound of *Libeccio,* the southwest wind that frequently blew along the Pisan coast, as it ruffled across the tops of the tallest pines.

Maresa closed her eyes for a moment, absorbing the sound and scents of this restful place, only seconds before the coach plunged into the light and they were greeted with the crash of land meeting the waves of the Tyrrehenian Sea.

The coach stopped.

"We are here," Angelo said. "Wait inside while I tell the driver to take the coach back into the trees so it will be out of sight."

Angelo returned a few minutes later and helped the two of them alight.

"It feels wonderful to stretch," Maresa said.

"Take a short walk if you like, while I gather some wood for the fire."

Maresa and Serena walked along the beach, sometimes coming too close to the water, and not moving in time to prevent their skirts from getting wet.

"Where is the necklace?"

Maresa patted her pocket.

"I'm sorry you have to lose it."

"It is for a good cause."

"I know Papa would have given you the money, if you had only told him what you were doing."

"I know, but this is something I have to do by myself."

Serena stopped and looked toward Angelo. "He is a clever thief, but he cannot build a fire. I shall have to go help him. Do you see anything that looks like a boat?"

"No, nothing." Maresa took one last look out over the water, toward the Tuscan archipelago, but saw nothing but water. "I will walk back with you."

Angelo had the wood gathered, and by the time they rejoined him, it was stacked neatly, needing only a spark to bring it to life.

Or so they thought.

The wood did not cooperate, however, for Angelo tried several times to coax a spark of life from the damp wood, but got nothing.

Maresa was becoming quite agitated, for the sun was dropping rapidly. It would be dark soon, and if there was no fire... She turned her head away and tried to think of something they could do.

"We need dry kindling," Angelo said at last, after he came to his feet, and accepted that it was fruitless to continue to try to light wet wood.

"This cannot be happening," Maresa said. "If there is not fire, they will not know where we are."

"We will have a fire," Angelo said, "if I have to burn the carriage."

"Where could we go to get dry kindling?" Serena asked.

"We don't have time to go anywhere!" Maresa said, and suddenly she had an idea.

A moment later, she hiked her skirts and dropped her petticoat. When she stepped out of it Angelo said, "Well, this is a fine time to arouse my interest."

Maresa tossed him her petticoat. "I am giving you dry kindling, which should arouse your interest in building a fire."

They not only had the fire going in a short

while, but the cotton petticoat smoked abominably, which gave a signal even the worst seaman could not miss.

Angelo tossed a handful of pine needles into the fire. They burst into flame with a crackling hiss and more billows of smoke rose upward. "They should see us now," he said.

"Perhaps I should wait in the coach," Serena said.

"We are in this together," Angelo said. "There is safety in numbers."

"Yes, but our numbers are quite small." Serena scooted closer to Maresa. "Are you nervous?"

"No," Maresa said. "You are nervous enough for both of us."

"I don't know why you are so jumpy," Angelo said. "It is still daylight, and there isn't a soul in sight."

"There will be," Serena answered, "because a boat is coming."

Maresa stood on her toes and spotted a small fishing boat coming toward them, but she could not make out the shapes of people. It was still too far away. Her heart began to pound. Her mouth was dry. What if something went wrong? What if they did not bring Percy? What if they only intended to take the necklace?

For a moment, Maresa felt faint, but she caught herself with the reminder that she had to be strong, for Percy, for herself, for the safety of them all.

When she saw Angelo looking toward the boat

she asked, "Can you tell how many are in it?"

Angelo stood on a pine log, so to have a better vantage point. "Not from this distance," he said, "it could be as few as four or as many as six or eight."

"Five," he said a few minutes later. "I see five figures."

It was not long until the boat bounced across the waves and two men jumped out and pulled it toward the beach.

Antonio was the first one out of the boat.

He approached them, walking slowly. He came alone, while the others waited with the boat.

Maresa saw Percy immediately and her heart gave a leap. He had the Moor's Head flag tied over his eyes.

Serena leaned close and whispered, "Don't forget to have the necklace ready."

"It's in my pocket. Why would you say something silly like that?"

"Because they don't look like they will give you much time to find it."

"Don't worry. We're safe. We have what they want."

Serena gulped loudly. "I know...that's what I'm afraid of."

At that moment, Antonio called out, "I see you are a woman of your word, Signora Bronwell."

"The same can be said about you, for I see you brought my husband. And the miniature of my mother?"

Antonio smiled. "Just like a woman...they never forget their possessions."

"Which is something you men should be grateful for," Serena said, obviously overcoming her earlier fear.

Antonio put his hand in his pocket and pulled out the small, oval miniature of her mother. He handed it to Maresa.

"Thank you." When she dropped it in her pocket he said, "And the necklace? You have it, no?"

"Yes, I have it," she said, and withdrew from her pocket the pouch that contained the necklace.

She pulled the rawhide string and opened it enough for the necklace to slide into her hand, where it lay cold, brilliant and beautiful.

"*Magnifico*," Antonio said. "A jewel fit for a queen."

"It belonged to one," Maresa replied.

Antonio reached for the necklace. Maresa dropped it back into the pouch. "I want to see my husband first, with all his fingers and toes, if you please."

Antonio smiled slyly, then turned toward the boat and called out to his compatriots. A moment later two of the men hauled Percy from the boat, and led him, still blindfolded, toward the fire.

Maresa noticed the limp immediately, and she wanted to cry. He looked tired, and thinner. She had never been so happy to see anyone. It was all she could do to keep from running to him, but she knew she could not show any emotion. Not now. She needed her wits about her until the exchange was made and the Corsicans were back in their boat. Only then, would Percy be safe.

"Are you certain it is Percy, and not an imposter?" Serena asked.

"Oh, yes," Maresa said.

"He is limping," Serena noticed.

"Yes, I saw," Maresa said, "but at least he is alive and walking. I thank God for that."

"If you are satisfied that your husband is well, might we conclude our business, *Signora*?"

Maresa quickly turned toward Antonio, as she reached deep into her pocket and withdrew the pouch. She handed the necklace to Antonio, who quickly dropped it into his pocket. He nodded at one of the men who removed Percy's blindfold.

"Maresa! What are you doing here?" He obviously had not been told about his rescue, for the shock upon his face was too great.

"I came for you," she said, and forgot her determination to remain steadfast. She went to him and after looking him over, raised herself on her toes and embraced him with a kiss. "I had so many things I wanted to say, and now I cannot think of anything. I have never been happier to see your face than I am at this moment." And then she remembered his leg. "You are wounded."

"I'm on the mend. Seeing you has made me forget all about it," he said, with a glance toward Antonio.

"Our deal is concluded," Antonio said,

"for you have your husband and I have the necklace."

Percy looked at Maresa with an astonished expression, which quickly turned to anger. "You used your mother's necklace?"

He did not get a chance to say another word, and neither did Maresa, for at that moment, Angelo was suddenly so overcome with emotion that he grabbed Antonio and kissed him with much exuberance on both cheeks. *"Grazie, Signore! Grazie! Grazie! Grazie!"*

He then burst into a round of jubilant Italian, talking, singing and waving his arms as he sang about his joy in seeing his dear, beloved friend Percy, in that wonderfully physically animated way that only Italians seemed to have conquered.

Maresa was about to throw herself into Percy's arms again, but Angelo got there first. *"Grazie a Dio!* My dearest friend, you are safe!" He kissed Percy on each cheek, and then started on each of the men who accompanied Antonio, babbling like the idiot he was, then bursting into song again.

The Corsicans shook their heads, mentioning something about an *idiota,* then turned away and walked back toward their boat, but Angelo was still too excited to let this meeting die so abruptly.

Still chanting his eternal gratitude, and claiming to love the little band of Corsican's until his dying day, he ran after them, stumbling over two of the men before he reached

Antonio and grabbed him again, pouring himself over him like so much tomato sauce over linguini.

He kissed him three times on the cheek, in the same adoringly flagrant manner that he had done before.

"Enough!" Antonio said, trying to back up and finding it difficult in the soft sand.

Angelo lunged to give him another hug, tripped, and they both fell to the sand.

Antonio was on his feet in a second. "Let us be away from this place of lunatics," he said to the others, and the three of them ran toward their boat.

Angelo was on his feet now, and took off after them, babbling once again. *"Grazie! Grazie molto! Gli uomini dovrebbero aiutarsi nei momenti difficili! Si vogliono molto bene! Ed giusto che stiano insieme! Si conoscono da quando erano bambini molto tempo prima che i gioielli venissero rubati! Ma a chi importa? Loro sono insieme adesso! Dio vi benedica! Arriverderci!"*

Maresa was so distracted by the nearness of Percy, that she did not hear everything Angelo said.

When the Corsicans reached their boat, Antonio dived into it, while the other two began to push it into the waves.

Angelo followed them to the water's edge, then he bowed and blew them kisses, as he waved energetically, a huge grin on his face. *"Arriverderci! Arriverderci!"*

Percy stood next to Maresa, with his arm around her waist. He was laughing so hard she could feel the vibrations through two layers of clothes.

"Did anyone understand all of that?" Maresa asked.

"I doubt Angelo understood all of it," Percy said.

Between the three of them, they translated it as the foolish gibberish of an overly emotional Italian:

"Men should help one another in bad times, no? They love each other very much. They have known each other since they were children, long before the jewels were stolen! But who cares? They are together now! God bless you! Goodbye! Goodbye!"

"If he wanted to come across as a simpleton, that was an excellent way," Maresa said with her arm around Percy's waist. "But, what I do not understand is why he wanted to lower himself to play the buffoon?"

"He didn't have to lower himself very far," Serena said. "Still, it has always been a mystery to me—what goes on in Angelo's head—if he has one."

While Angelo walked back to join them, Percy inquired about their transportation, and upon learning they had left it behind them, in the trees, he limped in that direction.

By the time Angelo rejoined them, Percy was back with the coach.

After Angelo and Serena were seated inside, Percy took Maresa's arm to detain her a moment. "Why, Maresa? Why your mother's necklace? I know how much that meant to you. My life is not worth a hundred *scudi* to anyone."

"To me, it's priceless." She put her foot on the bottom step, paused, and turned halfway to face him, with her face level with his. She put her hand on his shoulder and leaned forward with a kiss.

"You are my past, my present, my future. You are my life." When she pulled away, she could feel her pulse pounding in her throat. "I am so sorry it took me so long to realize how much you mean to me. I did not know how much I loved you until it was too late."

He started to speak, but a gust of wind came along about that same time, swirling sand and debris around them in a whirlwind.

"Hurry! Inside with you, before you get sand in your hair. We can talk later." He must have seen the disappointment, the uncertainty she felt, for he kissed her quickly and said, "Don't worry, my little guardian angel. It would take years to undo a lifetime of loving you. In with you, now," he said, and gave her a push.

Buoyed by joy, she stepped into the coach, followed by Percy who sat down beside her. When he put his arm around her shoulders, she lay her head against him, thinking how much she adored this man, and vowing she would never, ever be so foolish as to overlook that fact again.

Thirty

The memories of long love gather like
    drifting snow,
poignant as the mandarin ducks who
    float side by side in sleep.

                Murasaki Shikibu

They arrived back at Villa Mirandola early the next morning, tired, hungry and in the finest of spirits.

The first thing that greeted Maresa was a letter from Bea lying on the table nearest the door. She read it immediately, and happily announced, "My sister, Beatrice, is on her way here!"

"How old is she?" Angelo asked.

"About your age," Maresa replied.

"Is she as beautiful as you, *bella?*"

"She isn't coming here to marry you, Angelo, so what difference does it make?" Serena asked.

"A man must know these things, in order to be prepared."

"You are always prepared, Angelo," Maresa said, unable to stop thinking about Angelo and Beatrice together. No, she told herself. It would never work. Angelo will frighten Bea to death. I should have warned her, poor dear.

Maresa did not think further upon it, for Aunt Gisella came rushing toward them. "My darlings, you are back early!" When she saw Percy, she drew up short, and gave them all a look that said she was beginning to suspect something wasn't right here.

During the next hour or so they explained, in detail, everything that had happened since Maresa had left for England, and just how it was that the three of them had ended up in Marina di Pisa, instead of Lucca, and returning with Percy, but not the necklace.

Aunt Gisella accepted everything without a second thought, but it took a little cajoling and explaining before Uncle Tito arrived at a point of forgiveness for their duplicity.

Maresa was never certain if this was because he was truly angry over what they had done and the deception involved, or if it was simply because he felt the occasion called for him to play the authoritative Italian male.

She had a suspicion though, that it was the latter.

Aunt Gisella declared it was a day of celebration, and sent the four of them out of the room. "I want all of you to rest. No objections from anyone. Especially you," she said, before she kissed Uncle Tito and said something in Italian about him being part *lupo* and part *agnello*—wolf and lamb. Maresa could have sworn it caused his chest to swell.

Aunt Gisella then announced she was off to the kitchen, where, with the help of Maria and Bettina, she would plan the perfect dinner for such a happy occasion.

Percy stopped her with a detaining hand on her arm, as Maresa started up the stairs. She paused and asked, "You don't want to rest?"

He slipped his hand beneath her elbow as he spoke softly, "Walk with me, first."

They walked among the olive trees, where this year's crop of olives were starting to show among the silver-gray leaves, tiny and insignificant, but not for long. Soon, they would grow large and heavy, until Uncle Tito would instruct the helpers to prop the weighted branches, so they would not break, just as their ancestors had done, back in the days before the Caesars.

She stopped and pulled one of the hard little olives, no bigger than a cherry stone. "Uncle Tito said when Angelo was younger, he liked to pull these and shoot them through reeds. He thought he was going to go broke before Angelo grew up."

He came up behind her, put his hands on her shoulders, and placed a dozen small kisses, where her neck met the collar of her dress. "You were impossible to forget."

"As were you."

"Why did you come?"

"For a lot of reasons."

"Name a few."

"Is it important?"

"Very."

"I came..." She paused and thought this

might be the most important declaration she ever made, and that it could very well impact her life and her future happiness, and yet she knew that what she replied could only come from the heart, and so it was with her heart that she spoke. "I came because I could not imagine a world without you any more than I could bear to live in it if you were gone. I came because I am completely and wholly selfish when it comes to you, and even when you were in danger, I could not trust anyone else with something as dear to me as you are. I feared I was too weak to go on without you, afraid that your absence in my life would leave too big a void. Not because I did not think I would survive, for I know I would. I came because I could not help it, for in saving you, I saved myself. The moment I knew you were alive, nothing in this world was as important as finding you. You are part of me...you have been part of me for so long that I know I took your constancy as something that was per-manent, no matter what I said or did. I did not understand what it meant to love someone until I realized I loved you. After you were gone, I felt trapped in silence, destined to go through life repeating the same mistakes again and again, living a life I had already lived, everything in reverse, as my present surged softly back-ward."

"And the cause?"

"You, always you," she said, turning to clasp his hand in hers, and bringing it up to her lips to place a kiss there. "Because you were always there, Percy, and I had an infinite capacity for taking you for granted."

She looked down at the hand in hers, larger, rougher and infinitely dearer. "To think that I would never again know the magic of these hands." She was crying now. "I cannot think of anything to say, except I love you. But, is it enough? I feel both desperate and terrified inside. I love you. I have always loved you, even when I did not know it, and I will never reach a point when I do not. And if you don't love me in return, I do not know what I shall do."

One step and she was in his arms, and pressing her head to the place on his chest she had always considered hers. "Tell me it isn't too late. Tell me you love me in spite of my foolishness, and all the pain I've caused you."

"I adore you...every inch you, and if you don't come up to your room with me right this minute so I can show you what I mean..."

She grabbed his hand and laughing, ran with him back to the villa.

Uncle Tito was standing in the doorway speaking with Aunt Gisella, prior to taking his customary walk outside.

He saw them coming and took a step back, and watched them pass, without stopping, but continuing on, to rush up the stairs.

"God in his infinite mercy was kind to allow that sort of passion to ease in time. Can you imagine, my angel, what we would be like if we had kept that intensity much longer than we did? We would both be afflicted with a palsied heart, I swear."

Gisella came to stand beside him and entwined her arm in his. "We still have it, my love, but not so constantly. It is passion tempered to an ebb and flow."

"Yes, we do," he said, and kissed her. "Hmmm. I was, only a moment ago, going to take myself for a walk, but after giving the matter absolutely no thought, I feel my ebb is ebbing away. Shall we go see if we can discover what they were in such a rush about?"

"See how perfectly matched we are, Tito, for I was thinking the same thing."

And as Percy and Maresa had done only a moment ago, the two of them went up the stairs, arm in arm, but at a pace one could only call slow.

Dinner was two hours late.

"Saint Leonardo!" Serena said. "I cannot ever remember dinner being this late. Where is everyone? What are they doing? I am starved."

"Apparently, you aren't the only one," Angelo said, and downed the last of his glass of wine.

Serena opened her mouth, as if to question his meaning, when his meaning obviously became quite clear. She snapped it shut. "Well, I'm not starving, starving."

"I am," he said, "but it will have to wait until later—as long as it is not too much later."

Serena thought a moment. "Are we talking about the same thing?" She narrowed her eyes. "Are you going out tonight?"

"Alas, I cannot say that I am not."

"You cannot go out tonight! It's a celebration!"

"And one I would not miss, even for the loving arms of the Countess of Castiglioni."

She sucked in her breath. "The Countess of Castiglioni! She is lovely, but Angelo, she is ten years older than you, at least!"

He saluted her with his glass. "And twice that in experience."

She put her hand to her head. "I do not know what is going on around here. Everyone is speaking in riddles and acting quite strangely."

She joined Angelo on the sofa for a drink.

Maresa went down to dinner on Percy's arm.

In honor of her mother, she wore her green silk gown.

When everyone was seated, Uncle Tito lifted his glass. "To the glow of love that I see gathered around this table. The love of family, and that of friends. To honor, and dignity and knowing the time to do what is right. To kinship and friendship, may they never cease to grow. To Maresa and Percy. Welcome into the bond of this family, and into the blessing of the circle of love. May your love be strong, your days long and your decisions always right...and no, Serena, you may not go out with Angelo tonight."

Maresa could only call the expression on Serena's face as, well, it was priceless.

"I know your mother would be very proud

of this moment," Aunt Gisella said and held her glass aloft, "just as I am very proud of you."

"And I," Percy said, lifting his glass. "To my wife, for her devotion, her sacrifice, and most of all, for her love...slow arriving, though it was."

"Ah, here comes dinner at last," Uncle Tito said.

The servants entered the room, carrying trays of food, led by Maria who carried one large silver-domed tray. She placed it before Uncle Tito, who picked up the carving knife and fork, just as the lid was removed.

Everyone gasped.

For there, lying on a bed of parsley, lay the emerald necklace.

"How?"

"Who?"

"When?"

At that moment, and in perfect unison, every head turned to stare at Angelo.

"What?" he asked.

Maresa's hand came up to her breast. "Angelo! I cannot believe it! You stole it from the Corsicans? Are you mad? You could have gotten us all killed! What were you thinking?"

Angelo shrugged. *"Il fine giustifica I mezzi,"* he said. "The end justifies the means. Do you want me to give it back?"

As if bewitched, everyone was suddenly consumed with the gift of laughter.

And that is when Maresa began to understand: happiness is a laughing matter; it is always better to count your blessings instead of airing your complaints; wisdom doesn't come cheap; nothing is impossible to a willing heart; and love is never afraid of giving too much.

She thought of Percy and knew she was truly blessed to have such a good man who was both husband and friend.

That is when she made a promise to herself to welcome every morning by remembering five things:

Each day is a gift. Friends are presents. Families are everything. Laugh often and love a lot.